A MAYFIELD FAMILY ROMANCE

Rakes AND *Roses*

PROPER ROMANCE

JOSI S. KILPACK

SHADOW
MOUNTAIN

Visit us at shadowmountain.com

Library of Congress Cataloging-in-Publication Data

Names: Kilpack, Josi S., author. | Kilpack, Josi S. Mayfield family ; bk. 3.
Title: Rakes and roses / Josi S. Kilpack.
Other titles: Proper romance.
Description: [Salt Lake City] : Shadow Mountain, [2020] | Series: Mayfield family series ; book 3 |
Summary: "When Harry Stillman finds himself deep in debt after a losing streak at the gambling tables, he turns to Lord Damion, a generous nobleman whose agrees to pay off Harry's debt, provided Harry turns his life around. Unbeknownst to Harry, Lord Damion is actually Lady Sabrina in disguise. Keeping her secret identity hidden from Harry proves difficult when she starts to lose her heart to the handsome rake"—Provided by publisher.
Identifiers: LCCN 2019054433 | ISBN 9781629727356 (trade paperback)
Subjects: LCSH: Nobility—England—Fiction. | Nineteenth century, setting. | England, setting. | LCGFT: Romance fiction. | Novels.
Classification: LCC PS3611.I45276 R35 2020 | DDC 813/.6—dc23
LC record available at https://lccn.loc.gov/2019054433

Printed in the United States of America
Lake Book Manufacturing, Inc., Melrose Park, IL

10 9 8 7 6 5 4 3 2 1

The Rose

When given as a gift, different colors of roses represent different feelings. For example, yellow is for friendship, white is for purity, and pink is for joy. Known for both their thorns and longevity, rosebushes are also one of the only flowering shrubs that produce fruit; the rose hip is edible and used in décor, perfumes, teas, and medicines. The red rose was created in the early 1800s when roses from China were bred with European roses, resulting in the first true red rose, which has come to symbolize passionate love.

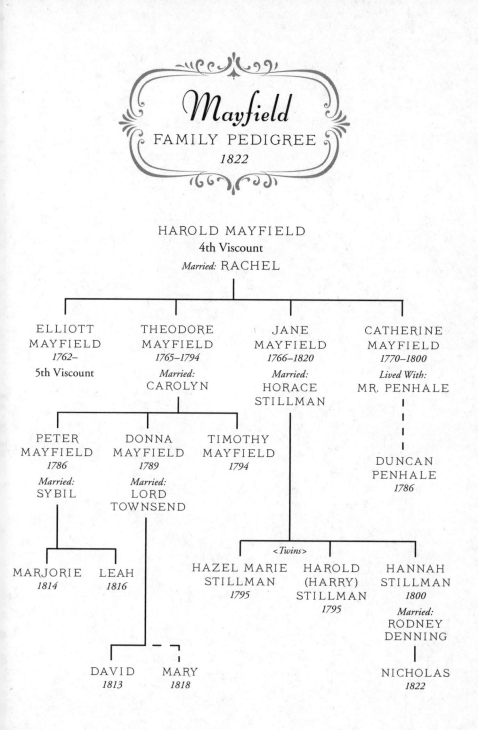

Prologue

*H*alfway through the harpist's performance, Sabrina Carlisle slipped through the French doors of the Gilmores' music room, her eyes fixed on the six-foot rose arbor near the back of the garden. It would afford her the privacy she desperately needed. Her breath came in quick gasps, and she put a hand to her heaving chest. This extreme reaction had happened before: a physical attack of such fear and panic that she could not breathe, could not think, and most certainly could not recover herself in that room full of people.

She moved beneath the arbor woven with climbing roses and pressed her back into the thorny branches of the hedgerow that spread out on either side of the archway. The needle-pricks helped ground her in time and place, and the yellow roses of the climbing vine helped remind her of better days. Whatever happened tonight, she needed to keep her wits about her, which meant she had to calm her mind.

Breathe, she commanded herself silently the way Therese, her housekeeper, had coached her on similar occasions. *Think of nothing but your next breath.*

She forced her mind away from any other thought.

Breathe in.

Hold.

Breathe out.

Hold.

She began to breathe the heady scent of the roses in through her nose and out through her mouth in audible release, focusing on the vibrations of the air moving in her chest and throat and mouth. Picturing Hortencia's rose garden in Wimbledon helped her remember the peace she often felt there. Richard never came to the rose garden his mother had designed, and Sabrina was careful not to let on how much she liked it so that he would not somehow take it away from her.

A minute passed.

Then two.

Finally, the grinding sensation in her brain subsided, and her thoughts began to clear. Not clear like a stream racing over rocks, but clear like the still pond located in the center of Hortencia's garden. How she wished she were in that garden now instead of this one that was not her own.

She patted at the sweat on her forehead with the back of her gloved hand, careful not to disrupt the curls around her face, and then moved her hand to her belly, only barely rounded beneath her high-waisted dress.

Richard won't hurt his own child, she told herself. *Which means he won't hurt me.*

The affirmation had proved true for three months now, ever since she'd told him she was finally going to have a child. That he'd not hurt her since that day almost convinced her that he would never raise his hand to her again.

Almost.

Perhaps that security was why she'd been lulled into foolishly commenting on his poor luck at the racetrack. Why had she said such a thing? And in company too. She knew better than to embarrass him. And she knew the look that had flashed over his face when he'd turned sharply toward her.

When he'd announced to the same company that they would not be staying in London for the weekend as previously planned, the old but not forgotten panic had begun to build. Richard was careful in London, where there were morning callers and daily social events she was expected to attend, but at Rose Haven, the Wimbledon estate some seven miles from the city, no one would call on her. No one would know what happened once the doors had closed them in. She had learned to defend herself over the years even though it infuriated Richard into greater brutality, but the baby . . . She didn't dare do anything that would increase the violence.

How is this my life? What would I give for a second chance to make a different future?

Sabrina pressed on her belly to remind herself it was real. She had reached the halfway point in the pregnancy and had only another four and a half months to go. Therese had impressed upon Richard the delicate nature of Sabrina's condition, and he'd respected that, refraining from exerting his dominance over her.

She'd had a growing hope that this child could change everything. Remedy his rage. Soften his heart. Give them a place to build from so they could have the kind of marriage God intended. She did not expect to be cherished by such a man as Richard, but as the mother of his child, she'd have some security. She could no longer be so easily replaced, and therefore, he would not handle her so roughly.

Right?

Could she still believe that?

She *had* to believe it. She would be a mother, and for the first time since Mama's death, she would have someone to love her. What would that feel like? What would it mean to hold her own child in her arms? A part of her. A part of Mama. A future.

Four and a half more months.

A giggle from the other side of the hedge froze the air in her lungs. A male laugh, low and seductive, closely followed, and Sabrina closed her eyes as though that could hide her. There had been several numbers left in the program when she'd slipped into the garden, and she'd thought she'd have time to compose herself before returning in time for the final performance. How would she explain herself, hiding behind a wall of roses, alone in the dark?

Tears of frustration and anticipated embarrassment pricked the backs of her eyes. She nearly gave into them, except then she would rejoin the party with puffy eyes that would give away her distress.

She looked around for better cover when a man suddenly came into view. He was walking backward through the archway, leading a woman by her gloved hand toward the dark corner where Sabrina had sought her own refuge. He stepped back far enough that he faced Sabrina—her back against the foliage that blocked her from the view of his companion. He stumbled a step before coming to a stop. The man pulled his eyebrows together in confusion.

Please, she prayed, widening her eyes and shaking her head slightly to emphasize how much she needed his help to remain unseen. *Please.*

"I think there must be a better corner," the man said. He held Sabrina's eyes another moment before shifting his gaze to the woman he'd kept, literally, at arm's length. He stepped back toward the house, and their laughter moved away with their voices until Sabrina was alone again.

Sabrina took a shaky breath, sending a grateful prayer to the heavens for the stranger having spared her. If only she could orchestrate a means to be spared from Richard.

Perhaps if she were particularly attentive and complimentary for the rest of the evening, his anger would cool by the time they returned home. She could praise his hunting last week—he'd brought home three pheasants in only one morning. Maybe if he drank enough he would forget his anger. The baby's movement had become stronger this week; if *he* could feel it, perhaps both she and their child would become more human to him. More real. Maybe he would see both of them as worthy of his protection.

As confidently as she could, she stepped away from the wall of roses and looked around the empty garden. The notes of a flute carried from the back doors of the music room as she brushed down her dress and straightened her spine. She had taken only a few steps toward the house when a man stepped into her path.

She put a hand to her mouth to keep from screaming, then lowered it as she recognized him as the one whose tryst she'd interrupted. He put his hand on her arm and steered her back behind the roses. Her heart was in her throat. If Richard learned she was in the garden with a man . . .

"Are you all right, madam?"

She blinked at him. "What?"

"Are you all right? When I came upon you a bit ago, you looked . . . Well, you looked terrified."

The man's honest concern brought tears to her eyes, and she tried to swallow the lump in her throat so she could assure him she was fine. Except she wasn't fine. Her plans to deflect Richard's anger might not work. They might return to Wimbledon this very night.

"May I help you?" he pressed when she did not answer.

Sabrina blinked. "Help me?"

He smiled sheepishly, as though embarrassed for having assumed himself capable of the assistance he offered. "I am hardly the heroic type, madam, but if I can assist you in some way, I will do what I can. My name is Harold Stillman."

She'd never heard his name before, and her wariness increased even as hope fluttered in her chest. "You are new to London," she surmised. She was tapped into the best gossip networks of the *ton*, and she'd have heard of a man like him if he'd been in Town for any length of time.

He was handsome—golden-haired, blue-eyed, tall and lean—and he carried himself with the arrogant confidence of youth and freedom. There was a roughness to him too, however, a sense that he didn't quite belong. It made her wonder where he'd come from.

She had struggled to find her place in the Polite World too. Being the illegitimate daughter of the duke of Anglesey had its privilege; for instance, she had always been called Lady Sabrina, even though she did not technically deserve the address, but the privileges could not overcome the scandal of her birth completely. She'd married Richard because of the security he offered. His grandfather had been an earl, and his family was both wealthy and well-respected. He gave her a legitimacy she'd never had before. However, she'd paid too dear a price for that security. She thought of the child she carried, and she wondered if she were not bringing in someone else to pay too high a price alongside her.

"I *am* new to Town," Mr. Stillman said. He looked past her

toward the light of the house. "And out of place and eager and all those things us young bucks are when we arrive in such a place as this." He rolled his eyes and waved his free hand in the air. "Lady Gilmore is my friend's aunt, so I don't know many of the other guests, but is there someone I can fetch for you? Your husband, perhaps?"

"Not him," she said quickly, then felt heat in her cheeks when he lifted his eyebrows. Luckily, her anxiety led to a quick solution this time—perhaps the perfect solution. "But there is someone else you could alert for me, if you are sincere in your offer."

"Of course," he said with a nod, a glimmer of eagerness in his blue eyes.

"There is a woman inside the music hall," Sabrina said. "Her name is Lady Townsend. She is wearing a green ostrich feather in her dark hair and an emerald pendant." Sabrina touched her throat to indicate its placement.

His expression was intent as he focused on her words.

"Could you tell her that I am ill, and direct her this way? I shall move closer to the house once you leave so she will find me easily enough."

"Certainly. Is that all?"

"Yes," Sabrina said, her optimism of this newest idea growing.

Lady Gloria Townsend was Sabrina's dearest friend in London, and had been from their very first introduction during Sabrina's Season. She had not held Sabrina's birth against her and championed her in the social circles Sabrina could now take for granted.

Sabrina had not announced the pregnancy because it was not yet obvious, and the *ton* was oddly uncomfortable with pregnant women. Once word was out, invitations would slow, and Sabrina would be expected to remove to Rose Haven in anticipation of her confinement.

Gloria would understand all of that once Sabrina revealed the secret, and she would insist on a visit tomorrow morning to discuss the particulars. Richard would not be able to take Sabrina from London until the other women of her acquaintance had all come to get their share of the news. Sabrina had been hoping for a child for five long years, and to finally be on the brink of motherhood was reason to celebrate with her friends. As long as she remained in London, she—and the baby—would be safe.

Sabrina being ill from the pregnancy would also explain her leaving the music room in the first place, furthering the protection she needed should Richard have noticed her disappearance.

"Having you pass my message to Lady Townsend would be a great help to me, Mr. Stillman."

Mr. Stillman looked toward the house, then back at her. "*Are* you ill? Is that why you are here?"

She could tell by his expression that he suspected something else. Something more. Something that better explained the terror he'd noted on her face when he'd first come across her. It was unfair to lie to him when he'd come to her rescue, and yet she could not tell him the truth. "If you could fetch Lady Townsend for me, I would be forever in your debt."

A smile suddenly lit the young man's face, so bright in the darkness that she had to blink against it. The face she'd already deemed handsome was suddenly breathtaking. "I am all about having beautiful woman in my debt."

He winked, and she made a sound that was part gasp and part laughter. Such boldness would do him no favors in such high circles as that of Lord and Lady Gilmore, and yet that same boldness might just save her tonight.

"I shall fetch Lady Townsend. Who shall I say has asked for her?"

"Sabrina," she said, then hurried to clarify. "Lady Sabrina."

Mr. Stillman raised his eyebrows, then nodded. "I shall do as you ask, Lady Sabrina." He took her hand and raised it to his lips, keeping his eyes on hers. "And I hope that one day we might meet again under better circumstances."

Sabrina was appropriately offended by his suggestion—she was a married woman, soon to be a mother—and yet she felt a rush of validation. This man thought she was beautiful. This man was kind, even if he was obviously a rake. This man treated her with gentleness. They held each other's eyes until she remembered to speak.

"Lady Townsend," she whispered, needing him to leave, needing to begin the process that would take her safely back to the party.

Mr. Stillman lowered her hand and nodded. "Lady Townsend."

Chapter One

Six Years Later

*H*arry Stillman swirled the set of dice within the cup and would have prayed if he were that sort of man. Instead, he rubbed the pad of his left thumb against the tip of his ring finger for luck, held his breath, and flung the dice, tracking them with his eyes as they tumbled across the brown velvet of the gaming table.

The dice settled, both showing five dots—a total of ten.

"Chance!" the men positioned around the table yelled.

Harry sighed in relief as the setter gathered the dice and dropped them back in Harry's cup.

Harry moved his hand in a circle so the dice swirled and tumbled inside. Eight times counterclockwise, then six times clockwise because six was the number he'd called out for this round—the main. On his first roll, he had wanted to roll the main. Now that he was in the chance round, however, a six would lose everything he'd won back tonight, which was almost enough to hold Malcolm off another week.

He finished his sixth clockwise circle, rubbed his thumb against his ring finger again, held his breath, and threw the dice.

The crowd cheered, Harry could breathe again, and the setter added eighty pounds to the growing pile of winnings—enough for Malcolm's payment plus nearly enough to catch up rent for Harry's rooms. His landlord had threatened to lock him out if he did not settle his debt soon.

The thin line of the setter's mouth added to Harry's triumph. The unhappier the house, the better things were for Harry.

"Way to show the rest of us up, Stillman," Ward said as he fell into the seat next to Harry, knocking him with his shoulder.

Harry did not take his eyes off the setter.

Ward placed a glass of warm scotch in front of Harry, who slung it back in one swallow. He wiped his mouth with the sleeve of his shirt.

Ten hours of going from one gaming hell to another in search of the right luck had left Harry's once snowy-white shirt stained with ale down the front and soaked with sweat through the collar and under the arms. He had no idea where his cravat was.

There had been a time when he cared about his presentation, but he could not remember how long ago that was. Probably back when he gambled for the thrill instead of to save his skin and drank for the looseness of it instead of to stave off the shakes or the disgust he felt at what he'd made of himself these last years. Life had become a day-to-day existence with the day's quality defined by the winning or losing he'd done within that twenty-four-hour period.

"You're not even going to thank me for the drink?" Ward teased, though there was no mirth in his tone.

"Thank you," Harry said dryly, his eyes fixed on the dice as the setter picked them up again. It was bad luck to take your eyes off the dice. Harry held out his dice cup as his stomach growled. There was no time for something so irrelevant as food.

He won the next round, and the next. Each win drew more people to the table in the dimly lit corner of the club. Harry never looked up, and his pile of winnings grew. Success should have lessened his anxiety, but it didn't. Malcolm expected payment by noon tomorrow—or, rather, noon today. If Harry's luck held and he could pay a double payment, he'd buy himself a full month to sell the western parcel that would pay off the principal of Malcolm's loan.

Another round started as Ward returned with another drink. Harry ignored this one, his stomach burning and his head pounding. The smoke in the room was thick enough to choke on.

"Can we call it a night, Stillman? It's nearly three o'clock in the morning."

"Not yet."

Ward leaned in and lowered his voice. "Every round is a new risk. You're farther ahead than you've been in months."

"Bad luck!" Harry turned to scowl at his friend. One never talked about losing when at the tables. It was almost as bad as having a woman stand on your left side. Thankfully, the light-skirts who ran pretty fingers down a man's arm and laughed at jokes that were not funny thinned out considerably after one o'clock in the morning. However, women had not served as a distraction for him for months now.

Harry ran a hand through his hair, which felt as grimy as his skin, willing his heart to slow. He began to swirl the cup—his main was nine this round, so he needed to swirl the cup eight times counterclockwise—eight was his universally lucky number—and nine times clockwise.

". . . Stillman's got a fortune waiting if he'd just find himself a wife."

"Shut your mouth!" Harry yelled, snapping his head toward

Ward, who sat backward in his chair, elbows propped on the table.

Ward raised his eyebrows. "I was just telling these blokes that I don't know why you spend so much time here when you've a fortune just waiting to be—"

"Stop!" Harry barked as his heart sped up even more. It had been a mistake to tell Ward about Uncle Elliott's *gracious* offer— an inheritance if Harry married a genteel bride—but Harry had been too drunk to be wise the night it had come out. Harry was too drunk to be wise most nights. He was not too drunk tonight, however, to keep Ward from revealing private information.

"Why should I not tell your *friends?*" Ward challenged, his eyes bleary with drink but also anger. He wanted to leave.

If only Harry could.

"Afraid the rest of us will be jealous of your opportunity?" Ward pressed. He was trying to pick a fight, likely thinking it would force Harry out of the hall, but he did not understand that Harry *needed* to stay. Ward was as much a gambler as Harry was, but he had better income and more understanding parents. Harry's parents were dead, Uncle Elliott had cut him off more than a year ago, and he'd burned through his quarterly profits— such as they were—within weeks of the last payment.

"I shall ask you to keep my business private, Mr. Ward," Harry said through his teeth.

Harry tried to focus his attention on the game, but his thoughts had been jumbled by Ward's reminder of the world outside this club. There was no doubt in Harry's mind that Uncle Elliott's "bribe" that he settled upon his nieces and nephews when they made a good marriage had mostly been directed at Harry— Uncle Elliott had never liked Harry very much. Two of Harry's cousins—Peter and Timothy—had already saddled themselves with wives, but Harry had no plans to do the same.

Harry had inherited his father's estate, which meant he *could* make his own way. However, Uncle Elliott was no longer paying Harry's debts now that he'd presented an opportunity that he believed would turn Harry into a respectable gentleman.

Harry had seen his uncle only once since his explanation and presentation of the "marriage inheritance" plan almost a year ago. Harry had lost nearly five hundred pounds the night before and had been in the depths of misery, so many of the details had been lost on him.

He'd been able to sell fifty acres of his land soon after meeting with Uncle Elliott, however, which paid off his debts and allowed him to live well through the fall and winter off the remaining profits and improved luck at the tables.

In January, he'd received his profits for the last quarter of the previous year and been surprised at the decreased revenue. The fields had not produced well, his solicitor had explained, and there were concerns about the old steward's ability to manage. Two tenants had moved to a neighboring estate due to unfinished repairs Harry had neglected for three years. The solicitor had suggested Harry spend some time at the estate setting things right and improving profitability, but Harry had been sure that the faster way to make up for the lost profits was at the tables.

Not long after that meeting, however, his good luck had begun to change. Instead of the slow increases between losses, he began leaving the clubs with lighter pockets than he'd entered with. His anxiety about that led to more drinking, which reduced his luck even more. He took greater risks, which led to bigger wins for a while, but bigger losses in the end.

He'd taken his first loan from Malcolm in March, and the

principal had steadily built through the spring until he'd had to sell another forty acres in order to pay Malcolm in full. He had been determined not to borrow again but somehow, he had.

He'd written to Uncle Elliott two weeks ago, desperate, but received a brief response—Uncle Elliott was sorry for the difficulty but had already laid open a course of success for Harry, which was all the assistance he would give.

Having a rich and titled uncle had bought Harry a great deal of latitude with lenders in the past, and if it got out that Lord Howardsford was no longer a resource for securing Harry's debts, he might find doors closed to him.

Ward cleared his throat and coughed twice—a signal the old friends had developed for when one recognized the need to get out of a poor situation. But Harry was on a roll, quite literally.

He'd already begun the process to sell a full hundred acres of his land in order to pay off Malcolm for good. The sale would put his estate in serious jeopardy of being able to support itself, let alone support him living in London, but he'd promised himself that after all was settled, he would spend a year addressing the needs of his estate. Harry was not so far gone that he did not recognize he had a problem with gaming and drink. They ran him like a mill, and he would be crushed if he did not find a way off the wheel.

He just needed one big win—either at the tables or through this newest sale of land—and he could get himself out of debt and out of London.

"Your roll," the setter said, drawing Harry's attention back to the game.

Harry stared at the cup, which was still but for some tremor in his hand. He couldn't remember where in his count he'd stopped swirling. He swallowed the burst of panic that rose in his throat. To not execute the precise routine would be bad luck, but he couldn't turn out the dice to start over because the dice touching the table would count as his roll.

"Come on, man," Ward whined. "Can we please bring this night to an end?"

"Your roll, Mr. Stillman," the setter said again, drumming his fingers on the other side of the table.

Harry had bet his entire winnings on the last three rolls and was nearly to fifteen hundred pounds. If he won this round and doubled his winnings, he could pay almost every debt he'd accrued and get out of London by the end of the month. Escape. Redemption. Freedom.

Everyone was watching him, convincing Harry that he must have finished the counterclockwise rolls. He began the clockwise rolls, but his breathing was short and his vision tunneled. This was all wrong. Harry touched his thumb and ring finger together before holding his breath and throwing the dice. All sound disappeared as though he were underwater.

The dice seemed to roll longer than usual, one of them hitting the side of the sunken table before stopping. A five—and a . . . six.

A wave of sound returned, a mix of gasps and groans that roared like a thunderstorm in his ears.

Eleven?

That can't be right, Harry thought. He stared. He recounted. He couldn't breathe.

The setter used his stick to pull the enormous pile of money from Harry's side of the table.

Harry jumped to his feet and reached across the table to pull the stick from the man's hand. "No!"

He threw the stick to the side and lunged for the pile of coin and paper claims. He needed three hundred pounds to make the week's payment and secure his rooms for the rest of the month. He had to get out with at least that much.

The setter lunged forward, but Harry knelt on the table and elbowed the man in the face, sending him to the floor. Harry desperately grabbed handfuls of coin, intending to stuff them into his boots, if necessary.

Someone grabbed Harry from behind, pulling him from the table. The money scattered from his fingers, the tinkling of coins sounding like discordant chords on a pianoforte as Harry landed hard on the floor.

The setter's booming voice overpowered the din. "All patrons will stand where they are and raise their hands overhead or have your skulls caved in by the protectors of this club!"

The crack of a club against a man's skull reverberated through the room a moment before the man fell unconscious to the floor, his limp hands releasing the coins he'd been fisting. Every other man froze, rose to their feet, and lifted their hands over their heads as commanded.

Except Harry.

Already on the floor, he rolled to his stomach and reached for a scattering of coin an arm's-length away. A man kicked his arm out of the way, and the hall's protectors grabbed him under each arm and dragged him toward the door before he could make another attempt.

Harry fought like a man drowning. "That is my money!" he roared, kicking and twisting in an attempt to escape the restraining hands of men twice his size. He cursed and screamed and threatened until he was thrown head over end into the alley behind the discreetly marked door of the club. The air was knocked from his lungs, and he groaned in pain and frustration, his face pressed to the wet and dirty cobbles.

"No entry for sixty days, Stillman!"

The door banged shut as Harry rolled onto his side, his entire body throbbing. After catching his breath, he tried to stand, but the arm that the guard had kicked buckled when he put weight on it, and his feet slipped in the oily refuse of the alley. He fell onto his back, unable to muster the energy to make another attempt. He pressed his hands against his aching side as an unexpected wave of emotion gripped him.

What am I going to do? He choked down a sob. If he didn't pay today's interest payment, he would default on his loan to Malcolm, which would require the principal be paid in full, plus a penalty, within two weeks. The western portion of his land could not sell that quickly, or for enough to cover the debt, which would continue to rise by ten pounds every day.

Dear God, he wailed in his mind but could not finish. Why would God hear the desperate pleas of a pathetic man like him?

Chapter Two

"Is that all, Lady Sabrina?"

Sabrina smiled at her lady's maid's reflection in the mirror of her dressing table. "Yes, thank you, Molly. I am sorry for having been so late tonight."

"Not at all," Molly said. "You remember that I'm spending the day with my mother tomorrow?"

"Clara confirmed she would be available, should I need assistance." Clara was the girl of all work for the three apartments in the building. She was not as skilled as Molly, but Molly's mother was failing in health almost by the week now.

"Thank you, ma'am."

"Of course, and do take your mother some of the coal from the bucket when you go."

"That is very generous of you, ma'am."

Sabrina nodded, keeping to herself that helping Molly in small ways helped assuage Sabrina's guilt at the disparity of their circumstances. Molly was the illegitimate daughter of a nobleman just as Sabrina was; their mothers had both been mistresses, an arrangement that was as unjust as it was immoral.

Molly and her mother had been discarded and sent to a different part of the country where they had no family or prospects. Her mother had gone into service, and when Molly was thirteen, she had done the same.

Sabrina and her mother, on the other hand, had been financially supported by the Old Duke from the start, though the intimate relationship between Sabrina's parents had ended when the duke had married a year following Sabrina's birth.

Sabrina and her mother had lived in a comfortable house in London, had servants and dresses and even a tutor for Sabrina when she outgrew the governess. When Mama had died near Sabrina's tenth birthday, Sabrina had been publicly recognized as the Old Duke's natural daughter and brought into the household.

Only a duke could get away with such a thing, and though there were plenty of whispers about how "that ought not to be done," Sabrina was eventually accepted. Never as one of the Old Duke's legitimate children, but above what most children born on the wrong side of the blanket would ever know.

Molly served as a continual reminder to Sabrina of how much grace she'd been given—grace, followed by a miracle Sabrina reminded herself of each time she was tempted to feel sorry for herself.

The miracle was that Richard had died—just like that. One minute he was cheering on a horse at Epsom Downs, and the next minute, he'd fallen against the rail. She'd been told he was dead by the time he hit the ground, his heart having given way.

She'd lost the baby a month earlier, and so Richard had died without an heir or entailments. Sabrina had therefore inherited all of the Carlisle holdings. She now lived an absolutely independent life, free from control of any man. There were very few women who would ever know the freedom she had been given, and she

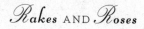

tried every day to live up to her privileges and share her good fortune in ways that gave others the sort of second chance she'd been given.

The door clicked closed behind Molly, and Sabrina moved to the window. It was a quarter moon tonight, the crisp sharpness of the outline making the night look like black ink against bright white paper. Sabrina was grateful for her life, her freedom, and her opportunities, and yet was she happy?

"'With how sad steps, O moon, thou climb'st the skies,'" she whispered, loneliness seeping into her bones now that she did not have to laugh and smile and put on a show.

The year following Richard's death, Nathan—Sabrina's half brother and the Old Duke's heir—had asked her to serve as his hostess when he was in London. The loss of her child had pulled her into blackness, but with the responsibility and connection Nathan afforded her with his invitation, Sabrina slowly found her way back to the light.

She had flourished in society again and was acknowledged as a woman of poise and quality in her own right. She would continue to play hostess until Nathan married, and likely be called upon to help now and again after that, but her position in Nathan's life would end eventually. Perhaps sooner than she was ready—he had his eyes on a young woman who would make an excellent duchess.

As that possibility came closer, Sabrina found herself more and more at a loss as to what to do with the rest of her life. No husband. No children. And soon, no brother to need her encouragement and encourage her in return—at least not like he did now. She was thirty-two years old, and her future sometimes felt like an empty, dusty road stretching ahead of her.

Nathan's solution, when she'd confessed her growing

melancholy some weeks ago, was that she marry again. He did not understand how horrible her first marriage had been or what she would be signing over to a new husband. She wanted her friends and her causes to be enough purpose to make her life meaningful, but was it?

She closed her eyes, remembering the invitations she'd been given to conduct discreet affairs so common among young, beautiful widows such as herself. It was how many others like her—determinedly single—countered the loneliness.

The human, lonely part of her wanted such things sometimes. But the wiser, God-fearing, and stronger part knew that such an arrangement would never satisfy what she truly longed for and would eventually leave her emptier than she was now. If she believed there was a man she could trust with her body, soul, and wealth, she would consider joining her life to his, but she had never had the privilege of believing in fairy tales. Not for girls like her. Not in a world like this.

Instead, she spent the London Season flirting and dancing and laughing and attending to her duties as a hostess, then traveled for the fall and winter months—Germany, Scotland, even Southern France last year.

This year—in just seven weeks' time, in fact—she would sail to Naples where Meg, a friend from Sabrina's school days, now lived with her vineyard-owning husband and their three children. It would be a lovely distraction from the life Sabrina did not have in England. Traveling had been what she'd lived for these last years, yet even her upcoming voyage did not seem like enough this year, which made her feel spoiled and ungrateful.

She leaned her head against the glass of the window, relishing the coolness and hoping it would cool her thoughts. But for the grace of God she would be Molly, she reminded herself. But for the miracle of Richard's death, she might very well be dead. Instead, she had received a second chance very few people ever had. She wanted for nothing money could buy, she was surrounded by people who genuinely cared for her, and she would sail to Naples before the leaves began to change.

Be grateful, she chided herself as she often did when life felt heavy. *Live worthy of your blessings.*

But, oh, how she wished the joy she felt at the end of a party or tea or ball or luncheon would follow her home and stay. How she wished that, though she was looking forward to sailing to Naples, she wasn't already dreading that she would have to come back.

Chapter Three

A hand touched Harry's shoulder where he lay in the proverbial and literal gutter, and he flailed his arms to defend himself against certain attack.

Ward stumbled back and stared down at Harry with wide eyes. "Good grief, Stillman. It is only me."

Relieved, Harry pushed himself up with his good arm and climbed to his feet. Wet had soaked through his shirt, and the right knee of his breeches was torn, blood dripping from a cut he couldn't yet feel. He cradled his injured arm against his chest like a broken wing.

"I managed to save your jacket," Ward said, holding out the blue coat Harry had taken off hours ago. The coat—along with two shirts—had cost Harry nearly one hundred pounds, though that bill was still outstanding with the tailor. Harry had managed to sweet-talk the tailor's wife to make him the clothes, but when the articles had been delivered to Harry's rooms in St. James, there had been a note from the tailor proclaiming that there would be no more orders accepted until the bill was paid in full—and that Harry was never to speak to the man's wife again.

Harry straightened his posture in an attempt to regain his dignity even as he recognized the smell on his clothes. Alleyways in this part of London were little more than public toilets, and there had been no rain to wash the refuse away for a few days. He would have put on the jacket to cover the disgraceful state of himself except he could not afford to have the coat cleaned. He'd brought his last twenty-two pounds to the club tonight, increased it to nearly ten times its value, and then lost every penny in a matter of seconds. A drum beat in his head.

Lost it all. Lost it all. Lost it all.

"I need to beg for a chance to win it back," he said, stepping toward the door. He had to convince the men to let him in. Maybe he could use his uncle's name. He just needed a loan of twenty more pounds. In a couple of hours, he could be up again.

Ward grabbed Harry's arm. "You have been *banned*, Stillman. Trying to enter will earn you a black eye and a fat lip."

Harry shook out of Ward's grasp, his body trembling from the rush of adrenaline. "But they can't *do* that. They can't take every farthing I have left and refuse me the chance to recover my losses!"

"You attacked the setter and tried to steal from the establishment. They tend to frown upon such things."

"Steal? It is *my* money!" He hit his palm against his chest.

Ward rolled his eyes. "Of course it is. You started with, what, twenty pounds tonight, yet you believe that entire pot was your due?"

"I earned it!"

"You *gambled* for it. Winnings are not wages!"

Ward turned and began walking out of the alley. Harry followed because he did not know what else to do. He shivered for the first time, his physical senses returning. The irony of holding a coat he could not wear against the chill held no humor. What time was it? He looked up into the night sky, but he could barely see the stars for the soot in this part of the city.

"Ward," Harry said after a few steps, reality weighing down his feet.

Ward kept walking toward the street.

"Ward," Harry said more loudly, coming to a stop before they emerged from the passageway. Brick walls rose up a few dozen feet on either side, offering a semblance of privacy. Glass crunched beneath his shoes. A woman's laughter floated down from one of the levels above him. Laughter was as foreign as sobriety these days. He flexed the hand of his injured arm, turning it this way and that. Nothing was broken, though it ached like the devil.

Ward, his closest friend—perhaps the only friend he had left—stopped and turned to face him. There were fleshy bags under his eyes, and he needed a shave. Harry surely looked just as poorly but smelled worse.

"I am ruined," Harry said softly. "I've *nothing* left and no income for at least another month. It would not be near enough even if I were to receive it tomorrow."

Ward looked irritated rather than sympathetic. Someone shouted from a street over, reminding Harry that they were not in a genteel part of the city. But he had nothing for thieves to steal, and he looked and smelled like an urchin, save for his coat, which he held over his injured arm and away from his soiled clothes.

"I told you to leave," Ward said tightly as he pointed toward the door of the gaming hell behind them. "I did everything I could to get you away from the tables in time."

Harry raked his hand through his hair, belatedly remembering the filth on his fingers. Would his landlord allow him a bath even though he was behind on his rent?

"I am ruined, Ward," Harry said again. Did his friend understand what that meant? Did he know how low Harry truly was? "I've nothing to sustain me until the parcel is sold, which could take weeks."

Suddenly Ward was striding toward him, anger adding power to each step. Harry shrank back as though Ward were going to strike him.

"What do you want me to say, Stillman?" Ward snapped, leaning toward him. "Do you want me to pat you on the head and tell you all will be well? Shall I convince you that one more night will change your circumstances?" He shook his head and pulled himself up to his full height, a few inches taller than Harry. "I am near my limit with this . . . dissipation. There is no fun in it anymore, and each night is a bigger disaster than the night before."

"What can I do?" Harry pleaded. "I've no money to pay my expenses, and I can't get credit with even a blacksmith anymore. I do not have the ten percent necessary to keep Malcolm at bay for another week." He swallowed against the dryness in this throat. He had mere hours to come up with two hundred and seventy pounds. "Help me, Ward. I cannot think straight enough to come up with a solution. Malcolm knows where I lodge. He'll come for me, and I have nothing to offer him." He'd once been so good at clever answers to the scrapes he found himself in. Now it was just that beating drum.

Lost it all. Lost it all. Lost it all.

Ward took a breath, forcing calm as though he were the parent and Harry the disobedient child. "My parents have returned to Sussex, leaving the London house empty. We could stay there for a time. I don't know where you'll get funds, though."

"Can I . . . Can I borrow enough from you to hold off Malcolm for one more week?"

Ward's eyebrows came together, and his jaw clenched.

"You shall be the first person I pay back when I sell the parcel," Harry said desperately. "And if I could borrow an extra fifty, I could triple it by the end of next week."

Ward's face went dark, and he turned to leave again.

"Ward, hear me out," Harry said, hurrying to catch up.

It was the only solution, and Harry *could* make good on the loan. Not at this club, of course, but there were others he had not been barred from where he could win back all that he owed and more. Tonight was the perfect example of how lucky Harry could be. If he'd just left when he was ahead, or if Ward had not interrupted his luck routines, then things would have turned out very differently.

I need to get out of London, he told himself, a whiff of his former decision passing through his thoughts. But he couldn't. Not now. Only in London could he win enough money to pay off his debts.

Ward turned to Harry, his nostrils flared, but then his eyes focused on something past Harry's shoulder, and his expression went slack.

Harry belatedly heard footsteps on the cobbles and turned to see three men coming toward them from the shadowy end of the alley. His first thought was that they were the protectors from the club, but as they drew closer, he realized the man in the middle was familiar. Harry noted the scar that ran from beneath the man's left eye to his jawline. Pocked skin and eyes as black as night confirmed the man's identity.

"M-Malcolm," Harry said under his breath, every part of his body going cold. The moneylender did not make it a habit to come after his debtors himself, and the fact that he was here now triggered Harry's stuttering, left over from his childhood when fear and anxiety had made his tongue thick in his mouth.

"A little bird told me you didn't come out ahead tonight," Malcolm said with a tone of superiority. "I thought I better see to you before you thought about skipping out on your debt."

The thick man to Malcolm's right withdrew a short black club from beneath his coat, swinging it casually enough to emphasize that the movement was not casual at all. Harry remembered the man sent to the floor of the gaming hell with a single hit from a similar weapon.

The man on Malcolm's left made no expression at all.

"W-what are you doing here?" Harry said, keeping his focus on Malcolm.

"Shoring up my bet. Desperate men sometimes attempt desperate measures, Mr. Stillman, and you strike me as the type to run out on me if you could. You owe me a great deal of money. Have you my payment?"

"I w-w-will have it by n-noon."

Malcolm gave a punchy laugh. "How?"

"M-my friend is going to give m-me a loan." Harry gestured to Ward but kept his eyes on Malcolm. The taps of the bully stick made clear Malcolm's purpose in coming tonight. A man who could not walk could not run away from his debt. Harry had heard of it happening to others, but never imagined he would be fool enough to land himself in such a situation.

Malcolm turned to Ward, who stood frozen a few feet behind Harry, reminding him that Ward could very well pay for Harry's sins even though it was Harry who had chosen this path over and over again, even when the pleasure was gone. Even when he'd burned through his estate's profits and started to sell off his land in pieces.

"You have this money on your person, *friend*?" Malcolm asked Ward, lifting his eyebrows.

Ward blinked, then licked his lips. "No, sir."

"But you are going to loan two hundred and seventy pounds to this waste of human flesh?" He waved toward Harry, who was trying to draw a full breath.

Harry stared at the club swinging from the bigger man's hand. Uncle Elliott's words from more than a year ago echoed in Harry's mind: "I am attempting to save you from yourself before it is too late."

Was this what "too late" looked like? Felt like? Had Harry reached the bottom of the barrel that had once seemed to have no end?

"I have until noon," Harry said again. "And I'll have p-payment by then, I p-promise."

Malcolm looked at him again. "And what is your promise to me?"

The big man tapped the club against his thigh, the sound matching the new drumbeat in Harry's throbbing head.

Get away. Get away. Get away.

Harry thought of the open end of the alley behind him. He might not be able to get the money in time, but he could save Ward and buy himself a few hours to at least attempt a solution.

Years ago, Harry and Ward had designated the Cumberland Gate of Hyde Park as a rendezvous spot should they be separated amid what used to be nothing but pranks in Town. Harry cleared his throat and coughed twice, hoping Ward would recognize the signal Harry had ignored when Ward had used it earlier.

What he would not give to go back and relive the last few hours of his life. Last few years, maybe. He heard Ward's sharp intake of breath as the larger man stepped forward.

Harry threw his coat at the men to buy a few seconds and yelled, "Run!"

Chapter Four

*S*abrina startled from sleep and lifted her head from the window pane. The moon was still bright in the sky. There had been too many late nights these last weeks. She stood to stretch her arms over her head when movement drew her eye to the street below. She lowered her arms and leaned forward as a man, dressed in a dirty shirt—she did not think he even wore a cravat—ran hard down the center of George Street.

The height and thickness of her windows blocked the sound of his boots on the cobbles or what she assumed would be his ragged breath torn from his heaving lungs. His quick pace and heightened color in his cheeks showed his fear, however, which made Sabrina wish she could help him.

It was nearly four o'clock in the morning—far past the time a woman could act on her compassionate feelings for a golden-haired stranger.

As quickly as he'd entered one side of the frame of her window, he was gone through the other side.

Sabrina knelt on the window seat and leaned forward to see

if she could catch an additional glimpse, but the other houses on the street blocked her view.

Another man, this one dressed ominously in black, entered the frame on the same course. Clearly the man in the dirty shirt had not been running *to* anything, but rather *from* this man.

The large man slowed near the center of her window view, then stopped. He bent forward, hands on his knees as he gasped for breath. After several seconds, he shook his head and stood up again, though not fully. He kept his hand pressed to his side for another minute as he walked in slow circles, looking in the direction the other man had gone. Finally, he turned back the way he had come and walked out of view.

"And the fox outfoxes the hounding hounds," Sabrina said quietly. Men like that would not give up, however. The fox for this hunt looked very much like the kind of man she attempted to save when she could: young, gentle born, with enemies he could not outrun forever.

Would that she could save this one.

The night returned to motionless dark. Sabrina raised her eyes to the moon again, grateful for this fox having reminded her of her purpose and her determination to use her position for something of good.

"But for grace," she said, turning to her bed.

Another night.

Toward another day.

May God bless the poor foxes.

Chapter Five

*H*arry peered cautiously through the curtain of the window in the parlor of Ward's parents' house in London. The street was clear, as it had been for the two days he'd been in hiding. No men in black coats looking out of place in Belgrave Square. No Ward either, however, and Harry felt near to bursting with anxiety over how long he'd been gone. Hours, now.

They'd gotten away from Malcolm on Saturday night by running different directions at Chapel Street and meeting up at the Cumberland Gate. Waiting for Ward to join him had been the longest hour of Harry's life. It had been almost dawn when they had pounded on the servants' entrance to wake the staff. A bellyful of rum had softened Harry's nerves enough to allow him sleep.

He'd slept through the noon deadline and awoken to a world in which he had officially defaulted on Malcolm's loan, which meant a five-hundred-pound late fee had been added to the balance that was now due in two weeks. Thirty-two hundred pounds in total. And Malcolm would go to great lengths to make sure Harry didn't leave London before every bit was paid. The amount of money made Harry dizzy, and two days later, he was still off-balance, drinking to stave off the terror of what was going to happen to him.

Harry peered through the pink lace curtain again, then let it fall back to hide him from the street. Ward's parents did not yet know he and Ward were staying at the house. When they found out, it would not go well. They did not think Harry a good influence, and as Harry faced more and more of the reality of what he'd become, he was beginning to agree with them. Ward was the only real friend he had left; he was even now seeing into Harry's affairs in hopes they could find a way for Harry to get out of this alive, preferably with both legs operational.

How have I come to this? Harry fell into one of the pink velvet chairs and dropped his aching head into his open hands.

There had been a time when fleeing a set of thugs would have brought a delicious rush of energy; Harry had lived for those rushes as a younger man. He used to race his phaeton outside of Hyde Park, *hoping* a constable would try to stop him so that he could outrun him. That was before the gambling had taken over every thought in his head and replaced it with fear of losing. Of not winning enough. The only way to keep his paralyzing fear at bay was to keep a bottle at hand. All the time. He'd sold the phaeton last month for half what it was worth in order to pay Malcolm's interest payment.

Harry heard movement behind him and twisted in his chair toward the door, ready to bolt if necessary. Ward's butler merely blinked at Harry's reaction as he entered the room with a silver tray.

"I did not request a tray," Harry said, suspect of anything out of the ordinary. Though perhaps he had ordered something and not remembered. The last few days had blurred together, and he struggled to keep his thoughts in order. He eyed the pot of tea and the assortment of sweets and savories. His mouth began to water.

"Young Ward asked that I provide tea at two o'clock." The butler set the tray on the low table and set about pouring. When he finished, he stepped back. "Will there be anything else, Mr. Stillman?"

"No."

The butler closed the door behind him when he left, and Harry gave all his attention to the tray. There were scones and clotted cream, biscuits, and a plate of fruit and cheeses.

Harry started with a caramel shortbread, and the first zing of sugar on his tongue reminded him of how little he had eaten these last few days—maybe a week. He chewed faster, picking up a biscuit before he had even finished the shortbread. A young man in rented rooms who no longer received invitations to society events rarely got food of this quality. He had stuffed the last scone into his mouth when the door opened again. Harry was instantly on his feet, chewing quickly as Ward entered the room.

Finally.

Harry drank the last of his tea to wash down the scone. "So?" he asked eagerly once he could speak, searching Ward's face for any indication of what he'd learned.

"Your landlord agreed to take the pocket watch as settlement on your rooms. Your clothes and other items will be sent over this afternoon."

The watch had belonged to Harry's grandfather, the fourth Viscount of Howardsford. It was the last material possession Harry owned aside from the estate and furnishings in Norfolk, which he had not seen for years. "And my solicitor? What had he to say about the sale of the parcel?"

Ward frowned and lowered his bulky frame into the other

pink velvet chair. The chair's ability to hold him was a testament to the fine craftsmanship of the piece, never mind the nauseating color scheme. Harry looked around the room, wondering if there might be silver or jewelry on the premises capable of earning thirty-two hundred pounds. Perhaps they could sell some of the furniture in the house?

When Ward spoke, Harry turned his attention back to him. "There is difficulty in splitting the land. He said he sent round a note last week."

Harry did remember some sort of note now that he thought of it. He'd thrown it on his writing desk with the intention to read it later.

Ward continued, "Something about the impact on the tenants. That the loss of the fields would make it unsustainable to keep them and that it would affect water access or something like that. He wants to send a clerk to survey the property lines and see if another division might be feasible, but he needs written consent from you . . . and twelve pounds to cover the clerk's expenses."

Harry cursed and began pacing, pushing his hands through his hair. Was that all the information Ward had gathered in all the time he'd been gone?

"I cannot pay him twelve pounds," Harry said, humiliated that what had once been a mere trifle was completely out of his reach. How did one sell their clothes? He owned a few quality pieces, though he was down to only two pairs of boots. "What of a loan? Did Mr. Jennings have anything to say about a loan against the sale?"

Harry *had* to sell. If not the exact parcel he'd submitted, another version. And quick. Men were making fortunes in industry, and old estates were being broken up to accommodate new money all the time. Harry had once felt this a tragedy to the generational lands and the overall economic structure, but now he was desperate to sell, sell, sell.

Ward scrunched up his face and shook his head. "I believe his exact words were 'Are you mad?' Your solicitor has been fielding payment requests from your creditors for months. The only way for him to arrange a new lender would be to lie to them about the level of risk, and he isn't going to do that for you, Stillman. And before you ask me again for money, my pockets are empty until my next allowance, and I'm surely not going to ask my parents to extend you credit. I am one folly away from them cutting *me* off completely."

Harry fell back into the chair, weak as reality descended like a blade at his throat.

You did this, Harry said to himself for the thousandth time. *You earned it, you pathetic wastrel.* All the times his father had bludgeoned him with cruel words and predictions that Harry would amount to nothing rang in his ears. Only drink would make those memories stop. Harry felt the burning need for more rum, but this conversation needed to be finished first. Then he could chase the voices away.

"And what of Malcolm? What did you hear about his intentions toward me?"

Ward crossed his arms over his chest. "The only reason I can make any inquiries into your situation is because Malcolm does not know the name of your *friend* from the alley Saturday night. If that changes, he'll find you here, and your time will be up. As it is, I worry your landlord would give up this address should Malcolm come around, though I pleaded with him not to." He spied the decanter and pushed himself out of his chair in order to pour himself a glass.

"You learned *nothing*?"

Ward spread out his arms, a glass in one hand and the decanter in another. "What more is there to know than you are in default and full payment of your loan is due in twelve days?"

Silence permeated the room, and Harry leaned forward, elbows on knees and hands in his hair. If he couldn't divide the parcel, he would have to sell the estate in its entirety. An estate that had been in his family for four generations. An estate that was supposed to help provide for his sisters but hadn't because Harry had needed every cent it produced to support his gambling habit. The thought brought a lump to his throat. He would lose everything . . . for nothing.

"What of your uncle?" Ward asked as he dropped into his chair once again, the half-full glass in his hand. He finished the drink in one swallow, put the glass on the table beside his chair, and pulled a silver-plated snuffbox from his inside pocket. He took a moment to inhale first through his right nostril and then his left.

Harry wished he dared ask for some himself, but a man's snuff was sacred. Harry had not been able to afford his own for weeks, and then he'd sold the box—a mother-of-pearl oval imported from India and given to him by his mother on his twentieth birthday. He'd once owned such nice things. He'd once had people who cared for him enough to celebrate the day he'd been born into this world.

Ward wriggled his nose like a rabbit and sniffed again to finish the routine, then looked at Harry expectantly.

"My uncle will never lend me another farthing." When Uncle Elliott had presented his financial plan to Harry last year, he'd said he would no longer contribute to the ruination of his family. And yet here was Harry, ruination all around him. If he went to his uncle in absolute humility this time, gracious and pleading, might his uncle be swayed? Would he believe Harry was truly at the end of his rope despite all the other times Harry had said that same thing?

"I meant that perhaps it is time you reconsider the wedding inheritance," Ward said.

Was Harry desperate enough to do such a thing? And where would he begin to find a woman of genteel birth with good character, family, and manners? He could not remember the last society invitation he had received, but he knew most doors would never let him in. Young men were given some latitude in their behavior when they found themselves surrounded by the excess of London for the first time, but after six years, the underground had become Harry's society. His connections consisted of club dwellers and drunks: men like him, whose reputations proceeded them like one of the hounds of hell.

I have squandered everything, Harry thought darkly.

Even if he were able to find a willing bride, Harry would make a terrible husband. Uncle Elliott believed that commitment and family connection would keep a person on a path to fulfillment and decency. If Harry could indeed focus on a family of his own, could he rise above and become the man his uncle thought he could be?

There was a knock at the door, and Ward ordered a cold luncheon to be brought to the dining room as soon as possible, along with two large mugs of ale.

When the door shut behind the footman, Ward cleared his throat. "There is one other option," he said, watching Harry. "Lord Damion."

The momentary hope Harry felt at Ward proposing an additional solution deflated just as quickly. "Lord Damion is a phantom."

Ward shook his head. "When I hit dead ends with your solicitor, I tracked down Basham, who'd mentioned that Bartholomew Hopkins was back in London."

"Hopkins?" Harry repeated, trying to place the name within their circle of acquaintances. "That skinny little fop?"

"He's finished with pink satin breeches and high-heeled shoes, Stillman. He didn't even have face powder when I found him at his house about an hour ago."

Harry snorted. Hopkins was a fool, whether he dressed the part or not. "Was it Lord Damion who told him to dress like a man now?"

There had been a great deal of talk about Lord Damion when he first came on the underground lending scene a few years ago. Unlike the usual money-grubbers like Malcolm who slinked in and out of the shadows when a man needed money in a hurry, Lord Damion required an application process that included odd terms that referenced the Bible, if the rumors were to be believed.

"You do not have so many options that you can afford to sneer at this one," Ward reprimanded. "Hopkins confirmed that Lord Damion is not a phantom. He said that without his intercession, Hopkins would have thrown himself off London Bridge."

Harry stared into his hands, humbled. He was in no position to turn his back on any viable option. Selling his estate or pursuing an acceptable marriage could take months. Harry didn't have months. He didn't have weeks, and even if some miracle freed him from his debt to Malcolm, what did life hold for him once he'd made one of the only two extreme decisions left to him? No land or secure a good wife—what a choice.

"Hopkins was a changed man, Harry," Ward said, his tone tinged with respect for this man they had used to make sport of.

"And to hear him talk, you would think Lord Damion was the prophet Moses himself leading Hopkins to the Promised Land."

Harry remembered that story. Moses had built a boat that saved his family when the floods came. Or, no, Moses was the man thrown into the lion's den, wasn't he? Harry shook his head in frustration. Why did people like those Bible stories so much anyway? They'd never made much sense to Harry.

"What were the terms set by Lord Damion?"

"Hopkins had to leave London for six months, write letters to the people he had lied to or cheated in the months leading up to his surrender, incur no additional debts, and either pay off the balance of the loan with five percent interest by the end of the year or sell his London house to Lord Damion for a hundred pounds. Hopkins is back in London to finalize the sale of the house since he was unable to raise the money otherwise."

"A hundred pounds for a house in Mayfair?" There was nothing magnanimous about Lord Damion if he was buying desperate people's property at ridiculous prices.

"No," Ward said, shaking his head. "Hopkins found a buyer for the house who offered a fair price. Hopkins will pay off the debt to Lord Damion and use the remaining profits to improve his country estate. What's more, he's quite grateful to have two legs to stand on, along with the peace of mind of no longer owing anyone anything. He believes that without Lord Damion, he would have continued to chase winnings to pay his debts, which were only leading to more debt. Does that not sound familiar? He plans to focus his attention on his country estate from here forward, and he's courting the daughter of a squire in his county."

Harry saw a flash of that kind of future, and it looked like freedom for a split second before his thoughts turned back to the bleak present. "How much did Lord Damion lend him?"

Malcolm had been one of the few backstreet lenders willing to lend more than fifteen hundred pounds without collateral. Harry's current debt to Malcolm, including the additional fees, was more than double that.

"He did not give me a sum, but I have a feeling it was extreme. Maybe not as high as what you owe, but higher than some of the other lenders. Lord Damion's terms seem meant to give a man a future rather than to bury him." He pulled a paper from the inside pocket of his coat and tossed it onto the table between them. "Lord Damion's solicitor manages the arrangements. This is his information should you want to see if your situation warrants Lord Damion's notice. Hopkins says he takes only one of every ten men who apply."

Harry took the paper—Mr. G.R. Gordon of 16 Garner Street, London.

"And now, after doing your business all afternoon without receiving a word of thanks," Ward said, an edge in his words, "I am half starved. Join me in the dining room if you choose, but keep in mind that you cannot live in my parents' house or continue to drink through their stores for much longer. Whether through Lord Damion or some other way, you must find a solution, and I have done all that I can do."

Ward left the room, and Harry immediately began a letter to Mr. Gordon.

By the end of the day, Harry had received a response that included a list of information Mr. Gordon needed in order to continue. Over the next few days, a flurry of letters were sent back and forth, exposing the full account of Harry's assets, debts, inheritances, and family connections. Each letter from Mr. Gordon ended with the same note: "Should any part of this be proven false in the due diligence of our work, all expectations will be forfeit."

Friday afternoon—nearly a week since outrunning Malcolm's men—a note came from Mr. Gordon inviting Harry to meet with Lord Damion to finalize their agreement on Monday morning, alone.

Harry sighed in relief. Earlier that very day, Harry had spotted a man in the shadows between two town houses on the other side of the street. He was dressed as a gentleman and reading the paper, but what gentleman read the paper outside a town house for over an hour?

The thought of leaving the safety of the house for his appointment with Lord Damion terrified him, but Harry replied immediately that he would be there. This madness had to come to an end, and Lord Damion seemed to be the only route left that would grant him a second chance to do better.

Chapter Six

$\mathcal{E}$lliott Mayfield, Fifth Viscount of Howardsford, was reviewing accounts when Brookie brought him a note, his old hands trembling as they held the silver tray.

"From London," Brookie said. "Messenger's waiting for a response."

"Really?" Elliott broke the seal quickly and unfolded the paper. He did not get many urgent letters from London. And he'd never had one where the messenger waited for a response.

> *Dear Lord Howardsford,*
>
> *By way of introduction, I am Lord Damion, a nom de plume I use to protect my true identity in order for my work to move forward. The work of which I speak is to help dissolute men who have reached the end of their options through any number of vices, but most specifically, gambling. I function as a lender, for the most part, but with terms that require a change in lifestyle and behavior that I hope will then continue throughout the young men's lives.*
>
> *To date, I have assisted eighteen men find a place*

of secure dignity, only two of whom have returned to their fetid ways. Most of the applicants have not yet destroyed every relationship to the point that they won't be saved by some well-meaning relation should they go back to their poor choices. The necessary humility and determination it takes to start anew has no space to grow so long as these young men have any other mode of rescue.

Your nephew, Harold Stillman, finds himself in a place where I believe my help can assist him to find a better way of life, which is my purpose in writing to you—his only relation in a position to rescue him, as you have in the past.

Mr. Stillman has told me of an inheritance that awaits him should he enter into an approved marriage. I would like you to clarify the situation so I am sure I understand it. My help needs to reach him at a time when he is ready to spend the next several years putting his energy toward building a future, not biding his time until a future falls into his lap.

Please do not think I am holding your inheritance as a reason not to help Mr. Stillman. I am only making certain I know the full situation before I make my decision.

He has also said you have refused to pay off his debts, something I applaud as, in my experience, a man who knows his accounts will be paid has no reason to think of the consequences of his choices. I would like confirmation that you are truly finished attempting to save him from his poor choices.

I have asked my messenger to wait for your response as time is of the essence.

Sincerely,
Lord Damion

Elliott read the letter a second time before leaving the room in search of his wife, Amelia.

He found her in the kitchen making bread, a task she insisted on continuing a few times a week despite the glares she received from the cook each time she darkened the kitchen flagstones. Mrs. Galloway had already had to make space for Mohammed, the cook Elliott had brought back from India, who prepared most of Elliott's dinners, and now she had to allow Amelia to make bread. She showed her displeasure at having her domain invaded in every sharp movement as she chopped vegetables for a meal for the servants. To Elliott's delight, Amelia quite liked the Indian fare that had ruined him for bland English food—though he still enjoyed a good English breakfast every morning and tea every afternoon. Nothing could compete with Mrs. Galloway's treacle tarts and lemon buns.

Elliott centered his attention on Amelia. "Ah, there's my countess."

Amelia looked up from the dough and gave him a wry smile as she pummeled the mass. "My *lord*," she said with as much derision as possible. But there was a smile there, and he winked to acknowledge it. She was not entirely comfortable with her rise in station since their marriage four months ago and seemed to feel it necessary to act put out by the formalities. He knew, however, that she did not mind having the best pew at church or a carriage at her disposal any time she liked.

"I've received a letter regarding Harry. Shall I read it to you?"

"Yes, please," she said, waving a flour-covered hand his way.

Amelia had not been supportive of the marriage campaign Elliott had devised to help his family rise to their potential when she first learned of it, but a great deal had changed since then.

Julia, Amelia's daughter who had married his nephew and

heir, Peter, was expecting a child. And Timothy now lived with his bride of six months in Somerset, having quickly developed a fondness for sailing and sea bathing. He wrote the most effusive letters to Amelia and Elliott every month and planned to bring his new wife to Howard House for Christmastide.

Amelia sometimes pointed out that the joy his nephews had found in love was *despite* the campaign, but Elliott would remind her that the campaign had played a significant role in each courtship all the same. She argued her position less and less as time went on and she better understood Elliott's concern for his remaining unmarried nieces and nephews.

He was not sharing this letter with Amelia for her own sake, however, but rather because he found it nearly impossible to make a decision without asking her opinion now that it was available to him. Even when they did not agree, the debate would bring him clarity that influenced his decision for the better. He'd been the lone head of his family for more than thirty years. To have a partner was manna from heaven.

Elliott cleared his throat and read the letter while Amelia's kneading slowed, then stopped.

"How very odd," she said when he finished.

"Yes. I'm not sure what to think of it."

"There's no request for money, so I don't see why you should be unsettled, aside from the fact that Harry is often unsettling."

Elliott nodded. Harry had written him last month—after nearly a year of silence—and all but demanded that Elliott step in and save him. It had been harder to say "No" than Harry would ever understand.

Amelia returned to her bread. "I'm relieved he's found what seems to be a good option and that he's been honest with her about the inheritance. Perhaps this is the beginning of some positive changes in his life."

Elliott stared at his wife. "'Her'?"

"Well, yes, surely you can see that Lord Damion is a woman." She waved toward the letter. "Her turns of phrase are very feminine."

Elliott looked back to the letter. "For the life of me, I have no idea what you mean."

Amelia smiled gently. "You read the letter without consideration that it could be a woman, while I—as soon as it said *nom de plume*—immediately suspected the possibility. That is the trouble with men: they think they know everything from the start and therefore miss the most obvious of clues. Surely you noticed she could have said what needed to be said with half the words she chose to use. Very much a female trait as well, saying more than is necessary, though I prefer to think of it as an expansion of ideas."

"I've not time for your female superiority on this, Amelia," Elliott said dryly, though he had to admit her suggestion made sense. But it was also impossible. Women did not lend money to wicked young men down on their luck and backed into corners. "There is a messenger waiting for my response. What is the right course?"

"I think you should confirm the details of the inheritance so that Lord Damion will know Harry will not be able to sweep some half-witted woman off her feet and land himself with thirty thousand pounds to clear his debts."

"You see no reason why I should not tell this . . . person such details?"

Amelia stopped kneading and cocked her head in his direction. "Your goal has always been to help Harry, and I believe your confirmation that you will not undo the good this woman is trying to accomplish would be the right course. If you do not give her that information, she may not help Harry. And it sounds like he needs the help and that this help will encourage what you want for him—respectability and a change of course."

"He could get married, inherit the means he needs to have a respectable life, and not need this Lord Damion's intercession at all."

"If he is truly so far in debt, then he is in no position to marry. But he might be in a position to think about it if he can get himself back on a straighter path. Tell her what she wants to know, and then pray that Harry is learning from all of this."

Elliott kept to himself that he was additionally uncomfortable sharing financial information with a woman. Amelia would not take that well, but was a woman capable of understanding the intricacies of finance and society well enough to be a lender of this caliber? And was it really a woman at all? Amelia could very well be seeing more than was really there. He knew better than to say any of that out loud, however.

Elliott returned to his study and pulled a fresh sheet of parchment from his desk drawer.

> *Lord Damion,*
>
> *I shall confirm what I am comfortable. I have indeed cut Harry off and will not pay any of his additional debts precisely because of what you expressed in your letter —as long as he knows that someone else will cover his debts, he will keep incurring them.*
>
> *I have also created inheritances for all of my nieces and nephews regarding securing a quality match. Should he make an acceptable marriage with a woman of high birth, he shall come into an inheritance, but it is not a*

cash asset. The enterprise he would gain will require him to educate himself in management and apply himself to something of value and purpose. The goal of this inheritance is to offer him financial security and create an opportunity for his children, should he have any.

I do not know what to make of your position in this, but I shall not interfere. Harry is more intelligent than he has ever cared to appreciate, and he has incredible potential that I hope he will discover within himself. Should the topic arise, please let Harry know that I care deeply for him and hope one day that he and I can heal the breach between us. My unwillingness to financially support my nephew's vices has nothing to do with my love for him.

Sincerely,
Lord Howardsford

Elliott reread his words, uncomfortable with how much he was revealing and yet assured that he'd been both honest and circumspect.

He took the letter to the messenger, a young man holding the reins of a rented horse; he'd have had to make a few different exchanges if he'd come straight from London. The man thanked him, put the response in his satchel, and swung himself into the saddle.

Godspeed, Elliott thought before turning back to his house. Elliott's greatest hope was to one day sit at a table filled with the people he loved with no animosity between them. That dream would never be complete if Harry were not at that table, but the power to make that happen was in Harry's hands, not Elliott's.

Chapter Seven

At four o'clock Monday morning, after a restless night, Harry slipped out of the servants' entrance and made his way through the sleepy streets of London. He looked over his shoulder continually, terrified of being followed, and avoided the coal vendors and street sweepers, who were already about their business in the dark morning.

When he reached the Waterloo Bridge, the meeting place stipulated in Mr. Gordon's invitation, a man was already there. He was bearded, slight, and dressed in the clothes of a common man. Lord Damion in disguise?

The man pushed away from the wall and approached him. There were too many lines around his eyes for him to be a nobleman playing a part. "Mr. Harry Stillman?"

Harry did not answer right away. What if this was one of Malcolm's men? "Who are you?"

The man smiled as though he'd expected Harry's distrust, revealing a broken eyetooth. He held out a piece of cream-colored paper like that used for the letters Mr. Gordon had been sending.

Mr. Stillman,

Jack will take you to the meeting place with Lord Damion. You can trust him.

Sincerely,

Mr. G.R. Gordon

Jack waited until Harry had refolded the letter, then began walking toward Covent Garden without looking to see if Harry followed, though he did. Harry's heartbeat sounded in his ears with every step. Jack led him first along main streets, then side streets, and eventually cut through alleyways, looping and turning until Harry lost his bearings.

Finally, they reached a door tucked in an alleyway somewhere east of Drury Lane, Harry thought. The streets weren't like the East Side locations of the best—or worst—gaming hells, but neither did the shops and offices cater to the upper crust. Was there such a thing as a middle crust?

Jack produced a key and unlocked the door, waving Harry to enter.

Harry ducked beneath the lintel, then straightened to his full height in a narrow kitchen thick with the smell of old smoke, fresh pork, and ripe beer. A single lamp on a sideboard cast flickering shadows on pots and knives hanging on the walls, which did nothing to settle Harry's nerves.

"This way," Jack said as he walked through the cramped space toward another door.

Harry followed the man into the interior of a pub set with tables and chairs made of dark wood. Front windows had been greased to keep people on the street from looking inside. It was exactly the type of establishment that would run a moderate gaming hell in the basement for those patrons who knew how to gain entrance. Harry wondered for a moment if all this effort could be an elaborate way to introduce Harry to a private gaming establishment where he could be given the chance to earn enough to pay off his debt. The instant hunger for the chance reminded him of Ward's comment that winnings were not wages.

Jack led Harry to a single chair set at a small table placed beneath a sconce on the wall—the only light in the room. On the table was a pencil and a sharpening blade. No paper.

"What of a chair for Lord Damion?"

Jack smirked and then leaned into the paneled wall, rapping three times in quick succession with his fist.

A portion of the wall set in the center of a square of wainscoting slid back, opening a space about four inches by ten inches just above the tabletop. A piece of paper was immediately slid through the opening.

Harry looked from the paper to Jack. "What is this? I was expecting to meet with Lord Damion."

"This is your meeting," Jack said, smiling and nodding at the paper. "Every communication with Lord Damion is writ. When all's done and said, you'll sign the sheets as contract between ya both." Then he turned and walked back through the door to the kitchen without another word.

Harry considered going after him—this was beginning to feel overly theatric—but instead turned back to the paper, waiting half in the wall and half out. He sat in the chair and hesitantly took hold of the paper, which was then released from the other side. As soon as he pulled the paper clear of the gap, the door snapped shut, making Harry jump, then look around to make sure no one had observed his reaction. His nerves were so tightly wound it was a wonder he hadn't squealed out loud at the sharp sound.

He pulled the paper closer so he could read the scrawled words written in black pencil across the top of the sheet.

This meeting is an opportunity for us to finalize the details of our transaction. All communication will be written between us so there is no question as to what has been agreed upon.

Do you confirm you are Harry Stillman, only son of Horace Stillman and Jane Mayfield?

Mr. Gordon had told Harry that his situation would be investigated, but it was eerie to see his parents' names on this page when he had not shared that information. He used the pencil to confirm the information was correct.

As soon as he set the pencil down, the partition opened. Harry put the paper into the slot, and it was taken quickly. The door slid closed with a snap. He'd need to be careful to keep from getting cut by the paper. He could hear the faint scratching of the pencil from the other side of the wall.

Harry and Ward had already deduced that Lord Damion was a nobleman; only a noble could have enough money and still need to protect his reputation from work such as this. In Harry's experience, noblemen were not as enterprising as this Lord Damion, but perhaps that was all the more reason for him to hide his identity. Harry imagined a middle-aged man with a paunchy belly and too much time on his hands. Orchestrating this covert meeting was likely a spot of excitement in an otherwise dull life. What would it be like to be so wealthy that you could have this type of hobby?

And yet "hobby" was not the right description. Though there were certainly profits being made, the extent to which Lord Damion had already gone in order to ensure Harry a secure future was beyond mere financial motivation or entertainment. Harry and Ward had wondered if the man behind the Lord Damion façade was someone they knew, someone from the *ton* who held extravagant parties and wore the finest clothes. Except Harry didn't know the *ton* anymore. He hadn't existed in that world for a long time.

The slot opened, and the paper was pushed through. Harry took hold, aware of the moment Lord Damion released his corner from the other side, and the door closed immediately.

> *Confirm that you have come to this meeting in hopes of repaying your debts to seven separate creditors totaling a sum of forty-two hundred pounds, which you are otherwise unable to pay. Pass the statements you have brought with you through the portal with this confirmation.*

Harry extracted the paper statements Ward had collected last week and smoothed them out on the table. Harry's curiosity was growing in equal proportion to his optimism that Lord Damion really would save him. This was all too precise—and too strange—to be a joke.

> *Please confirm that you, Mr. Stillman, own a property by the name of Falconridge in Norfolk, four hundred and eleven acres with an estate house and a number of outbuildings, including eight tenant houses. This estate is entailed on the next male heir in your family line and has no mortgages or liens attached, though there is surveying work*

to be conducted regarding whether or not there is a parcel that can be portioned off for sale in order to pay off your debt, which will soon be owed only to me.

The exchange continued, Lord Damion confirming all of Harry's debts and assets he had revealed to Mr. Gordon in the week's letters. Harry had also divulged his marriage inheritance from Uncle Elliott and confirmed it in the exchange. The idea of marriage still made his stomach unsteady, but he had only one year to raise the necessary funds to pay off Lord Damion, so he had not dismissed the possibility that he may have to take advantage of that opportunity. So help him, after he had put all this misery behind him, he would never touch another set of dice no matter how strongly the hunger begged for satisfaction.

The single paper was covered on both sides before Harry was told to sign and date it. Once he'd returned it to the other side of the wall, a fresh piece was sent through and the conversation continued. Lord Damion did not leave a single detail open to interpretation, instead spelling out each step and expectation to ensure no future claim of ignorance or misunderstanding.

Midway through the second sheet of communication, Lord Damion left the slide open after taking the paper. Harry lowered his head in an attempt to get a look at his benefactor. He saw red leather gloves and black cuffs before the door was snapped shut.

Red gloves, he mused, thinking of Hopkins. Was Lord Damion also a fop?

Another half an hour passed, during which Lord Damion explained his terms, which were almost exactly what Hopkins's had been: Remove from London for six months, write letters of apology—to be posted by Mr. Gordon after review—to anyone he had cheated, hurt, or taken advantage of, no additional debts, no gambling, limit drinking to social levels. Payment in full, plus five percent interest, due one year from today or Harry would sell his country estate to Lord Damion for five hundred pounds.

Should it come to that, Harry would have nothing. Well, aside from his life and five hundred pounds, which felt like a fortune right now. He would do anything he could to keep from losing the estate, however, and he was eager to get out of the city and away from the life he'd thought would make him happy but had only brought him to ruin. Once in the country, he would have time to consider his options and plan for his future.

> *This concludes our business. Please review all that has passed between us on this sheet and sign to confirm that all is correct.*

Harry confirmed the terms and signed and dated the paper. The paper passed through the slot and almost immediately a different paper was passed to him and the slot closed. Obviously, this letter had been written ahead of time as it was in ink.

> *Dear Mr. Stillman,*
>
> *This letter concludes our business. Mr. Gordon will send receipts as your individual debts are paid off in full. You are required to stay in London until all such transactions are concluded, after which you may commence your six-month removal to Falconridge. I hope that you recognize the opportunity this transaction has afforded you to choose a different path than the one you have chosen thus far. Like*

the prodigal son, you have squandered your inheritance. I am extending you the chance to learn from those mistakes rather than be defined by them. Whether or not this second chance proves to be worth my efforts will ultimately be up to you.

I wish you the best in regard to the new future ahead of you. Do not forget, Mr. Stillman, that my faith in you is based upon my belief that you are worthy of my investment. Change your life.

The world needs good men. I hope you will choose to become one of them.

Sincerely,
Lord Damion

The Harry Stillman of even a few months ago would have scoffed at such arrogant instruction. The Harry Stillman of today read the letter twice and felt tears rise to his eyes.

This Lord Damion, whoever he was, believed Harry capable of better things, and Harry could not remember a time when he'd wanted to rise to such an expectation. Actually, he could not remember a time when he'd wanted to rise to anything outside of wanting his father's praise, which he'd learned to live without. One of the letters Harry needed to write as part of the terms of Lord Damion's rescue would be to Uncle Elliott for him having paid off several debts before drawing the line. What would Harry say? There was enough pride left in him to find the prospect uncomfortable.

Harry folded the letter carefully and slid it into the inside pocket of his coat so he could read it again. Often. The way was outlined ahead of him—he must curtail his irresponsible behaviors, learn to manage his estate, and bring the remaining portion to profitability. Lord Damion believed him capable, and Harry felt a swelling desire to prove him right. Hope was a powerful thing he hadn't known he would recognize when he saw it again.

Chapter Eight

*H*arry remained in his chair for a solid five minutes, waiting for Jack to fetch him. Nothing happened. He listened for movement on the other side of the wall but heard nothing from there either. Had Lord Damion already left?

He knocked on the partition, but no one responded.

Gray morning light filtered through the opaque windows, but everything was still, save for the occasional shout from the street outside or the rumble of a carriage wheel on the cobbles as the city came to life. Without his grandfather's watch, Harry could only guess at the time, but he suspected it was nearly seven o'clock in the morning. Markets would open soon, and maids and manservants would start going about their duties. Harry needed to get back to the town house. Until the debt to Malcolm was settled, Harry was still at risk.

He finally stood and walked toward the kitchen door he'd come through a lifetime ago. He paused, looking back at the small table beside the wall through which he and Lord Damion had corresponded. From here, the panel was invisible. How many people came to the pub and ate and laughed and drank without realizing there was a portal that led to some mysterious, hidden room?

The kitchen was empty, the lamp that had been there earlier put out. The only light came from a greasy window set upon the back wall. Harry ducked out of the door, blinking twice to help his eyes adjust to the light, though the brightness of day was not yet upon the alleys. It was a relief to see Jack leaning against a wall several feet away, smoking a pipe. He nodded at Harry but made no move to lead Harry away the way he had led Harry in. It seemed that Jack's services were at an end.

Harry left in search of a main road he could use to get his bearings. He ended up on the street that ran in front of the pub where he'd sat for the meeting. "The Lost Tartan" was painted on a wooden sign hung out front; Harry had never heard of it before. The pub shared a wall with a snuff shop where heavy drapes had been pulled over the windows. That had to be where Lord Damion had been during their exchange.

Did Lord Damion own both businesses? How did he orchestrate meetings like this without anyone discovering his true identity? And yet Harry was beginning to understand the loyalty that protected him. It seemed wrong to want to know more about Lord Damion than Lord Damion wanted Harry to know. How many men had Lord Damion helped the way he was helping Harry now? Harry felt no temptation to wait around the snuff shop to see who Lord Damion really was.

Red gloves, fine penmanship, and loyal partners in Jack and Mr. Gordon was enough for Harry to know about his mysterious benefactor.

Harry turned and walked down the street feeling lighter than he had in weeks and capable of thinking beyond what tomorrow may bring. He tried to remember his favorite parts of growing up at Falconridge—miles of country to ride through in the early morning mist, fresh milk each morning, and that wide banister perfect for sliding down on the seat of his pants. A moment before he would hit the knob at the bottom of the staircase, Harry would push himself off and land perfectly on the bottom step, feet flat, knees bent, weight in his heels. He was likely too big to do it now, but he'd give it a try just in case. He could find happiness in being a country gentleman, surely.

He could find *happiness*.

That alone was incredible.

He did not hear the footsteps until they were upon him. The club hit him in the middle of his belly and bent him forward at the same moment his knees were kicked out from behind him, pitching him headfirst into the cobblestones. Air burst from his lungs, and as soon as he rolled to his back, a man stuffed a thick rag into his mouth.

His kicking did nothing to slow the men as they each hitched an arm under one of his and dragged him through a narrow alley between two buildings, around one corner and then another. They threw him to the ground beside a pile of broken barrels, and Harry only managed to get halfway to his feet before his arms were grabbed again and twisted behind him so quickly that Harry's right shoulder popped.

He screamed against the rag as searing pain shot through his arm and back. Rather than ease up, the man pulled harder. The world swam in front of Harry's eyes until he managed to focus on the black club in the hand of the large man standing in front of him; the same man he'd seen a week ago standing beside Malcolm in an alley much like this one. The man who had chased him through a maze of winding streets before Harry had managed to lose him.

The large man lifted the club over his bulky shoulder, and Harry shook his head, his pleas muffled by the rag. He needed to explain that he'd just arranged to have the debt paid—Malcolm would get a letter of settlement that very afternoon. The club stayed lifted, and the man from behind spoke into Harry's ear, the words hissing through his teeth. "This can go easy or this can go hard."

By all the gods, he would go easy! Harry nodded fast enough that the world began to swim again.

The large man lowered the club to his side and pulled the rag from Harry's mouth. Harry coughed against the dryness left behind.

"Malcolm has some questions for you, Mr. Stillman," said the man holding his arms, his breath hot in Harry's ear. "Where was Lord Damion's meeting place?"

"I-I don't . . . Lord Damion?"

The man with the club moved faster than Harry would have guessed possible, cracking the weight against Harry's ribs on the right side. Pain exploded through his body, but the other man covered Harry's mouth to muffle the resulting scream.

"Let's try this again, shall we, Mr. Stillman?" the man from behind asked. He moved his hand from Harry's mouth, and Harry gasped, saliva dripping from his bottom lip.

The man with the club leaned close. "We know you was meeting with Lord Damion, don't do no good to lie to us about that, and we know the meeting spot must be nearby. Where did you meet him?"

"Hoof and Groom," Harry lied without hesitation, referencing a pub located near Covent Garden but reasonably close, he thought. There was an entrance through the kitchen of that club to a members-only gaming hell that Harry had once frequented.

He wasn't going to betray Lord Damion, the man who'd saved him. Except Lord Damion hadn't saved him from *this*, had he? How did these men know that the meeting place was close by?

"M-Mal-colm w-will be p-paid," Harry gasped. "T-today."

"Who is Lord Damion?"

"I d-don't know." It was a relief not to have to lie about that.

Then his mouth was covered again, and the club whistled through the air, ending with a crack against Harry's left thigh that buckled Harry's legs. The man holding his arms kept Harry from falling, but the pressure on his popped shoulder split the pain into equally excruciating parts. Harry could no longer focus his eyes, and his stomach rolled with nausea.

"Don't lie to us," the man behind him said. "Who is Lord Damion?"

He moved his hand, and Harry gasped, unable to draw a full breath as vomit rose in his throat.

"Y-you have to . . . b-believe me. He was on the other side of a w-wall, and I never . . . s-saw him. No, don't!" The club cracked against his right shin. Harry twisted hard to get away, sending him and the man holding him into the pile of crates. His head hit against something harder than the club, and his eyes rolled back as everything went dark.

Chapter Nine

*L*ady Sabrina flipped open the silver pocket watch—a man's version rather than a woman's because the larger face was easier to read. It was 8:06, and Mr. Stillman had been gone for an hour, which meant it was safe for her to leave the snuff shop that shared the wall with The Lost Tartan.

She owned both businesses, or, rather, Lord Damion did, and Jack worked as the manager. Jack also kept her up-to-date on information about the goings-on in Town that she didn't hear about in drawing rooms. As expected, Mr. Stillman had tried to get her attention when he realized he'd been left alone in the pub, but he hadn't tried for long before finding his way back to the alley. Jack had knocked three times on the door to the snuff shop some five minutes ago to assure her that all was clear.

Sabrina slipped the watch back into the sash of her charcoal-colored dress and stood, taking a few seconds to stretch her back, which was tight from four hours of sitting in an uncomfortable, straight-backed chair. She always arrived an hour early for her appointments with the foxes, and she always stayed an hour longer to make sure she did not accidentally cross paths with the client coming to or from their appointment.

An afternoon nap would certainly be in order before the Kirkhams' ball tonight where she would dance most of the sets. Despite her advanced age of thirty-two, men of the *ton* enjoyed taking the floor with a woman rather than a girl of the Season more often than she would have guessed when she had been one of the young ones.

Sabrina closed the leather-bound notebook in front of her. She had used her hour waiting for Mr. Stillman to leave to finish organizing the seating chart for Nathan's dinner party next week. At their weekly Monday breakfast this morning, she would show her brother the arrangement, guide him toward an excellent menu, and, upon approval of those plans, set about the hundred and five additional tasks she would need to delegate to his staff or complete herself before the event. Invitations would need to be delivered by Thursday, so penning them would be a good task to fill the hours between dinner and bedtime. And after tonight's ball she had no more evening engagements until Friday.

The Season was winding down, and she was ready for a slower pace, even though it intensified the loneliness that had begun to plague her. Soon enough, however, she would set sail for Naples. And she had Mr. Stillman's case to occupy her thoughts in the meantime. He was the fifth and last case this Season. In Mr. Gordon's opinion, she should not have taken him on at all, but she'd recognized his name as the man who had helped her all those years ago in the Gilmores' garden. When Mr. Stillman had explained having run from Malcolm's men to Hyde Park on the evening of the twenty-eighth, she'd realized the impossible truth that he had been the golden-haired fox in a dirty shirt she'd seen from her window. Between the debt she owed him from years ago and the sympathy she'd felt for him more recently, she felt driven to accept him.

Sabrina slid the notebook next to Mr. Stillman's folio in her satchel—also a man's version, which was roomy enough to hold ledgers and papers—then changed out of her red gloves. If anyone managed to catch a glimpse of "Lord Damion" during these meetings, they would only remember the gloves. She pulled on black leather ones that matched her black coat and dress befitting a widow in mourning, put the red gloves into her satchel and fastened the straps. The letter she'd written to Mr. Gordon with an account of the meeting was in the pocket of her dress and gave the official go-ahead to begin settling Mr. Stillman's accounts. By the end of the week, the threat Mr. Stillman was living under would be lifted, and his way would be cleared.

Sabrina felt sure that Mr. Stillman, once he was out of debt, away from London, and off the tables, would begin to want those things that were natural desires for a young man in the prime of his life—respect, family, success. Contrasting his new life with the old one would show him more fully the error of his ways and hopefully motivate him toward responsible citizenship in a country where he'd been given every opportunity to thrive. Whatever bit of good a person exercised in the world was a step toward making it a better place for everyone. Helping Mr. Stillman was one more way in which Sabrina was fulfilling that measure for herself while helping him to do the same. The brief encounter with him all those years ago proved that he was capable of better things than what he had chosen of late.

Sabrina arranged her bag so the satchel lay against her hip, then retrieved her cloak—also a man's—from the hook near the door and threw it over her shoulders. She tied the strings at the neck and then pulled the hood over her ebony hair so her face would stay in shadow.

Lady Sabrina always wore rose-colored stain on her lips—just enough that it *could* be her natural color. As a widow, she could get away with eccentricities, but not too many if she also hoped to maintain her reputation as a woman of character. When working as Lord Damion, she disposed of the trademark color so as not to draw any unnecessary attention.

She opened the door a few inches, smelled Jack's pipe smoke in the air, which verified the way was clear, and let herself into the alley.

Jack would have been coming and going as he ran his morning errands this last hour, keeping an eye on the shops while also preparing for the day. His knock always came when he was ready to take a smoking break, and it had been a long and busy morning for him already.

She crossed to him and handed him the letter for Mr. Gordon regarding Mr. Stillman's accounts.

"I'll see it's delivered right quick, ma'am," Jack said with a nod as he tucked it inside his coat. He turned east, toward the wider street where the messenger boys would already be hanging about.

There had been a few instances where one of her new foxes had waited out of sight, hoping to discover Lord Damion. Jack usually found them before any risk was posed to herself, but once she had come face-to-face with the new fox. He'd been looking for a nobleman, not a widow in mourning trying to get a start on the day's errands, so he'd muttered a good morning while straining to see around her for the true object of his curiosity.

Mr. Stillman struck her as more grateful than curious, and

she sensed he was eager to return to the safety of the hole where he had been hiding for over a week now. Malcolm's men were likely seeking him, and she did not think he would take chances.

Sabrina kept her head down as she followed her feet out the south end of the alley, across the terrace and through another narrow walkway that would lead to the location where her unmarked carriage had been waiting for quarter of an hour. She was halfway down the corridor when she heard a scraping across the cobbles, like a dragging shoe.

She froze and then looked over both shoulders in turn. The walls of the buildings created an echo chamber that made it impossible to determine what direction the sound had come from. She pulled the hood of her cloak forward to hide her face, took a step, paused to listen again, and then took another. There was no good time of day for a woman to be alone in London, but outside of business hours was the most unsafe. She gripped the strap of the satchel concealed by her coat. She must not lose the satchel.

The unmistakable sound of a groan turned her around, and she scanned the barrels and crates stacked on one side of the alley.

The moan sounded again.

With another glance to make sure no one was watching her, she moved toward the barrels, then gasped when she saw a foot, or, rather, a boot, sticking out. As she moved around the pile of crates, she inhaled sharply when a man's body came into view. His face was a patchwork of bruises and blood that made his hair look as black as hers in the shadows of the alley. Hurrying forward, she dropped to her knees beside him.

"Sir," she said in a soft voice, leaning close to him. "Sir, can you hear me?"

He groaned again. His shoulder was set at an awkward angle, and she cringed; a dislocated shoulder was relatively simple to fix, though the very devil for pain. The wound on his forehead was no longer actively bleeding, so Sabrina ran her hands up and down the man's arms first—no breaks—then his legs to check for additional injuries.

He tried to pull his right leg away when she attempted a tactile assessment, but she could already see the fabric of his trousers tight around his calf—possibly broken. The upper portion of his left leg was tender too. Could he have two broken legs? One upper and one lower? Other than having fallen from a great height, there was only one explanation for such injuries.

But it was an early Monday morning, not a late Saturday night when a man would have to be on his guard against a robbery. His clothing and boots marked him as a gentleman. What was he doing here this time of day? She tensed and looked about herself. Were his attackers nearby?

Sabrina felt a sudden urge to run for her carriage and get as far from here as she could, but she couldn't leave him. She would fetch Jack! He could take over as the rescuer and call for a doctor.

She started to rise, but the man groaned, drawing her attention and her sympathy back to his poor battered face.

"Sir," she said again, leaning closer so he could see her face if he opened his eyes—at least one eye did not look too swollen.

"Wha-what . . ."

He must be trying to ask what happened. It was a mercy that victims of such violence often did not remember it.

"I think you've been attacked. Robbed, perhaps." She looked down the passageway to where Adam would be waiting with the carriage. So close, and yet he'd have to leave the carriage to help her if she chose to go to him for help instead of Jack. "Have you a family member I can contact on your behalf? Do you live nearby?"

"No one," he said, the words slow and . . . sad. "P-please." He opened his eye, and the blue of it stood out clear and bright amid his damaged face. With his good arm, he reached toward her face. She took hold of his hand before he touched her, then pushed the hair from his forehead, catching the first glint of its actual color—golden-blond. He was a young man, not past thirty.

What on earth is he doing here this time of day? Perhaps he had not yet returned home from an evening of entertainment that had ended badly. *Oh, England*, she mourned, *do you not see what you are allowing to happen to your legacy?*

"There must be someone I can call on for you."

He shook his head and closed his eye, sending a tear to track through the drying blood on his face.

She felt her mother's heart rise up in her chest—all the love and protectiveness she'd have given to her own child bursting forth like it had so many times before when someone in need crossed her path.

"No one would come," he whispered.

No one? Could that be true? Unfortunately, Sabrina had known enough dissolute young men of society to know that it absolutely could be true. The poor foxes who did not outrun their hounds.

"I am Lady Sabrina," she said, wanting to give what comfort she could and earn his trust.

"S-Stillman," he said. "Harold Stillman."

Her breath caught in her throat.

Handsome, blond, blue-eyed. Just as she remembered him from years ago when they'd first met. Just as she'd pictured him when she had been sitting on the opposite side of the wall during their transaction that very morning. He did not seem to have recognized her name the way she'd recognized his, but he was only semiconscious, and they had been introduced only one time six years in the past.

She ran her eyes over his broken body again and felt a second hitch in her breath. He'd likely been attacked shortly after their meeting to still be so close to the snuff shop location. Had Malcolm followed Mr. Stillman this morning? Jack always made a trek of winding through streets; perhaps he had lost them before he had reached The Lost Tartan. How else could Malcolm have intercepted Mr. Stillman in this particular part of the city at this specific time of day? Mr. Stillman had not left his friend's house for nearly a week for fear of this very thing happening, but she'd insisted on the in-person meeting as she did with all her clients, regardless of their concerns.

Mr. Gordon had warned her often enough about the risk of interfering with the business of these predatory lenders. But Mr. Stillman owed so much money and had already defaulted on his loan, which had spurred Mr. Gordon to issue an even greater warning when they had first considered him.

Sabrina had discounted his concerns because this would be her last case for the Season, *and* she owed Mr. Stillman a debt from all those years ago. And now Mr. Stillman had been left for dead a short distance away from their meeting place. She felt sick. Was the beating meant to be a lesson for Mr. Stillman or Lord Damion?

Mr. Stillman was still holding her hand, clinging to her as

though she were his only hope in the world. Perhaps she was, and it was fate that had brought her to this particular place amid the labyrinth of alleyways and streets of this part of the city. She was a woman who dealt heavily in numbers and equations, and the likelihood of her finding him *here* was very low indeed. Thank goodness she had, however. She covered their joined hands with her other black-gloved one and considered the possible options.

Mr. Stillman did not know she was Lord Damion—nor did any of the staff at Wimbledon House since she conducted Lord Damion's business only when she was in the city. Taking Mr. Stillman to Wimbledon would get him out of London, hide him from Malcolm, provide him with care he desperately needed, protect her investment in his ability to pay back what he owed Lord Damion, and make up for this having happened to him. The risk to herself if she helped him was minimal compared to the risk to him if she did not. Her decision was made in a fraction of a second.

"I've a carriage and a driver just down the way," she said, her voice soft and soothing. "I can take you to my house and have your injuries tended to."

He tightened his grip on her hand as more tears leaked from his closed eyes. "Thank . . . you," he said on a gasp.

On impulse, she lifted his hand to her lips and kissed the back of it, light and sweet and, she hoped, comforting.

She released his hand and placed it on his chest. "I need to fetch my man and my driver. They can help you to my carriage," she said. "I'll be only a moment."

He nodded. She stood, her eyes on him as she rose, then she lifted her skirts and ran for Jack.

What are you doing, Sabrina? she asked herself as she went around one corner and then across the terrace. The hood fell back from her hair as she ran, and she did not take the time to fix it.

I am doing the right thing.

Aren't I?

Chapter Ten

*S*abrina took another sip of tea and glanced at the clock behind Nathan's head, which was currently bowed over the seating chart she had arranged for his fast-approaching dinner party. After finding Mr. Stillman in the alley yesterday morning, she'd sent a note to Nathan canceling their usual Monday breakfast by claiming she'd had to go to Rose Haven on "urgent business." It was the sort of excuse men used all the time, but of course Nathan had interrogated her when she'd arrived today in order to determine what could possibly be more important than breakfast with her brother—well, half brother—and dear friend.

"That was a good move to sit Sir Bryan to the left of Lady Litchfield. She won't ignite his political fires."

"He's one of only three Whigs on the guest list. I tried to space them an equal distance from one another so as avoid too much concentrated fury in any one sector."

"Three?" Nathan looked up, his eyebrows pulled together. "Who else other than Sir Bryan?"

"Mr. Manning."

Nathan nodded with sudden recognition. He needed to

improve his ability to remember names and details; Sabrina would not be his hostess forever.

"And Lady Louise," Sabrina continued. "Rumor has it she's trying to find a place for her son in the party leadership as she believes he will be the one to save the party in the long term."

"Little Daniel?" Nathan said incredulously. "Is he even out of his Eton collars yet?"

"He's in his last year of university and has been recently coming to London for party events. Apparently he's quite the political debater at Oxford." He was not only showing interest in political rallies, however. Little Daniel had also become an increasing presence in the gaming hells of London when he was in Town, buoyed by the same ego and wealth that had been the downfall of too many men just like him. She hoped he would not one day need Lord Damion's help, which is why she'd placed herself next to Lady Louise on the seating chart in hopes she could drop a few subtle but well-placed bits of advice.

No one of the *ton* knew of Sabrina's secret persona, but she'd gained a reputation—especially among mothers of young people —as someone who knew about the underground workings of the youthful aristocracy. They believed she got her information from Nathan, which served her purposes. No one questioned why or how Nathan knew such things, and their own embarrassment of being connected to the darker corners of Town kept them from speculating.

When Sabrina kindly cautioned a woman to pay greater attention to the man courting her daughter, or made a discreet comment about a woman's son having been seen regularly in St. Giles, mothers listened. Sometimes they even came to her with questions of their own, and she used her sources to find out if their son or nephew or daughter's beau had lifestyles that did not show in more polite company.

"Excellent work on the party, Sabrina," Nathan said, grinning at her after reviewing the chart one more time. They each had their mothers' eyes—hers brown and his green—but shared their father's full lips and wide smile, which made them look like full-blooded siblings. "You never cease to amaze me with your understanding of people, sister mine."

Sister, she repeated in her mind, feeling a rush of tenderness.

When Sabrina had been brought into the Old Duke's household after Mama's death, she had been immediately sent to school in Brighton, then Dublin, and finally Bath. She came "home" to the Old Duke's principal estate on school holidays but never forgot her shameful place. Most of the time, the duchess had already removed to a different estate before her arrival.

Sabrina had never sat at the same dinner table as the duchess or ridden in the same carriage. The Old Duke had suggested Sabrina call him "Your Grace" rather than "Father," as his legitimate sons did. Sabrina had known, even then, that she had no place for complaint. She had tried to make herself small and quiet and unnoticed. She'd missed her mother horribly.

Nathan, however, had been thrilled to have a sister from the start and sought her out even as everyone else pretended she was invisible. Over time, he became her advocate in the household and breathed esteem back into her feelings about herself. He insisted she get a new wardrobe when he did before each term, and he introduced her as his sister despite the way it infuriated his mother and raised the eyebrows of nearly everyone else. If he received an invitation to an event while Sabrina was at the estate, he asked to bring her along. If they refused, he did not attend. "We are together in this," he would say when Sabrina objected or tried to beg off out of embarrassment. In time, the invitations included her name, she made friends of her own, and her confidence grew.

When Sabrina had turned nineteen, she was sponsored for a Season by the Old Duke's cousin—Mrs. Ambrose—who had been as accepting of Sabrina as Nathan had been. A natural daughter could never be presented at court the way a legitimate daughter could, but having a powerful father and an accepting brother had attracted a few suitors who, in exchange for her dowry and family connection, could give her a *legitimate* place in the Polite World. Richard Carlisle had seemed to be the best choice of the men who came calling—older, wealthy, from a good family, in need of an heir, and eager to move up the social ladder. If only she had known . . .

"Sabrina?" Nathan asked.

She shook herself back to the present and repaired her smile. "Sorry, woolgathering."

Nathan eyed her suspiciously. "Is everything all right?"

"Of course." She avoided his eye by leaning forward and plucking a macaron from the plate of identical pink confections. Father employed a French chef here at the London house. Raspberry, she concluded as the chewy confection filled her mouth with sweetness. She adored all things raspberry.

"Would your distraction have anything to do with your missing yesterday's breakfast?"

She laughed to cover her annoyance at his return to the topic and picked up another macaron. "I miss one breakfast, and you're practically apoplectic. I have told you I had to reschedule our breakfast due to matters I needed to attend to in Wimbledon. I am—as I've said three times now—very sorry."

There had been only one thing to attend to in Wimbledon, however: Harry Stillman.

Therese, as Sabrina's housekeeper, had determined she could manage Mr. Stillman's injuries without calling for a physician—she was all but one herself—and settled him in one of the east bedrooms. He'd been bathed and splinted and forced to drink broth every few hours before being dosed with laudanum to help him sleep. His shoulder was back in socket thanks to Joshua—the lone footman at Wimbledon House and Therese's son. Mr. Stillman's lower right leg was, in fact, broken, but the bone had been easily set—thank goodness—and he had cracked ribs on one side. The other injuries amounted to cuts and bruises that needed only cleaning and bandaging.

Sabrina had looked in on him before taking the carriage into Town. He'd been sleeping, his hair tousled and his face bruised but his color improved.

"Well, see, that's just it," Nathan said, leaning forward and resting his elbows on his knees as he stared at her. "In all the years I've known you, you have never—not once—forgotten *anything*." He had not been in London much during her marriage to Richard or he would have had to withstand numerous notes of regrets and rescheduling when she was forced to stay home to hide the evidence of how her marriage had been failing.

"Then one would think I've earned the right to change my plans this one time. Goodness, you act as though I've turned my allegiance to France."

Nathan kept his posture of interrogation, but Sabrina remained unruffled. His expression was serious, however, and that made it difficult for her to stay still in her seat. She did not want him to worry about her or wonder too much about the parts of her life he was not privy to. He was a soft, safe place she did not want to compromise.

"Are you sure you're all right? You seem anxious."

"I'm just tired," Sabrina said, though she was touched by his concern. She took another sip of her tea, long cold. "I'll be relieved when Parliament ends. It's been a very busy Season. Enjoyable, of course, I have had a wonderful time, but the blush does fade from the rose over time."

"Are you truly going to be in Naples all the way past Christmas?"

Sabrina felt a flush creep up her neck at the reminder of the trip she'd thought nothing about since discovering Mr. Stillman in the alley. He would need different accommodations before she left in five weeks. Could he find such a place? Would he be healed enough to travel?

Nathan furrowed his eyebrows as he continued to stare her down.

Sabrina recovered herself by putting on a bright smile and leaning toward him. "I am so very excited about this trip," she said as though admitting a secret, exaggerating her feelings in hopes of hiding the other thoughts filling the spaces of her mind. "Months amid vineyards and new society and my dear Meg—I wish I were leaving tomorrow."

Nathan relaxed some, leading her to believe she'd convinced him. "Except that if you were leaving tomorrow you would miss my dinner party, and I would be gaping at everyone like a fool for not knowing how to manage it."

Sabrina laughed, loving that, despite the pomp that accompanied his position, he was still humble enough to be insecure sometimes. "Well, yes, for that reason alone I must bide my time. Will you return to Hilltop when the Season ends?" Hilltop

Manor was the sprawling mansion of the Old Duke's principal estate. Sabrina had never felt at home there.

Nathan leaned back. "I might go on to Peterborough. Lady Carolyn will be summering in Elton with an aunt there, not far from Crawford."

Sabrina's smile widened as her eyebrows came up. Crawford was little more than a cottage set on land where their father liked to hunt now and again. For Nathan to stay there indefinitely said volumes about his interest in Lady Carolyn. "Oh really," she said sweetly. "Have you made a decision, then?"

He feigned a casual position, crossing his ankles and leaning to the side. "I invited her for a stroll through the park after you did not show up for yesterday's breakfast, and she did not balk at an early appointment. The city is still too populated for me to be able to go out like that at usual hours. Her parasol did not match her dress, and when my hat was blown off, she ran after it with me." He smiled at the memory. Nathan took comfort in things being less than perfect; he said it made him feel more comfortable in his surroundings. Perhaps that explained his devotion to Sabrina all these years. He continued. "I like her more and more each time I have the pleasure of her company. And Father approves."

"So my cancellation turned out to be a boon for you," Sabrina said with a touch of authority, keeping her distrust of their father's judgment to herself.

Nathan did not know the particulars of the falling out between Sabrina and the Old Duke, and for her part, he never would. When forced to be in the Old Duke's company, which happened a few times each Season, Sabrina treated their father with polite respect, but that was all. That the Old Duke did not seem to notice the change in her response to him was another testament that she had never been all that important.

"Perhaps you will be more tolerant of happy accidents that take place in your favor from now on," she said.

They made plans for Sabrina to attend an informal dinner on Sunday night to do a final review of the dinner plans slated for the following Friday—the night Parliament was expected to close—then they said their goodbyes.

Sabrina walked through Hyde Park toward her London rooms, stopping to converse with a few acquaintances also enjoying the summer day.

No men were allowed past the common parlor on the main floor of her apartment building, and the tenants—all unmarried women like herself—shared the expense of a butler and housekeeper, Mr. and Mrs. Billings, and the services of the girl of all work, Clara, who often filled in as a lady's maid when needed.

Mr. Billings came out from his quarters on the first floor when he heard the front door open.

"Lady Sabrina," the gray-haired man said, removing a handful of letters from his pocket and sifting through them before selecting two. "These have come for you the last two days."

"Thank you, Mr. Billings," Sabrina said, trading him her cloak—the light-blue one that looked particularly nice with her yellow-and-blue pin-striped walking dress—for the letter.

As soon as she saw Mr. Gordon's name, her smile fell. He'd expected her to have been in London following her meeting with Mr. Stillman so that he could keep her apprised of his work settling the accounts. What did he think of her not having responded? How had she managed not to think about him at all these last thirty hours or so?

"Is everything all right, Lady Sabrina?" Mr. Billings asked.

She repaired her expression immediately and smiled at him with feigned reassurance. "Yes, of course. Thank you, Mr. Billings."

Sabrina lifted her skirts but did not allow herself to run up the stairs despite her anxiety.

Once she'd closed the door to her apartment behind her, she quickly broke the seal on both letters, determined which had been sent first, and read them in order.

Yesterday's letter included a report of the notices sent to all of Mr. Stillman's creditors. By the time Mr. Gordon had written the letter, he'd already heard back from three creditors eager to have their accounts settled. Each had furnished him with a statement confirming the amounts Mr. Stillman had given Lord Damion at their meeting. Mr. Gordon planned to settle those accounts immediately, and he ended by telling her he would send a letter with his updated progress tomorrow—which was now today.

The second note had a very different tone and had been sent that morning.

> *Lady Sabrina,*
>
> *A gentleman by the name of Mr. Clarence Ward contacted me early this morning regarding Mr. Stillman, who did not return from his appointment with Lord Damion yesterday. Mr. Ward's attempts to locate Mr. Stillman have led him to no additional information, which brought him to me, since he was aware of Mr. Stillman's correspondence.*
>
> *Mr. Ward is quite anxious about whether or not Mr. Stillman arrived at his appointment and wishes to know where that appointment took place so that he might trace his route that morning. I have assured the man that*

I will ask Lord Damion on his behalf and relay the infor-
mation to him as soon as possible. I've asked him not to
speak with anyone else about this situation.

 I shall not move forward on this matter until I hear
from you.

Sincerely
G. R. Gordon

Chapter Eleven

Sabrina was pacing by the time Joshua let Mr. Gordon into the parlor of Wimbledon House Tuesday night. She had fretted all day about how to go about this meeting and still feared she'd chosen poorly.

"Joshua, please see that Mr. Gordon and I are not disturbed."

"Yes, ma'am."

The door closed, and Sabrina turned apologetic eyes to the older man she'd known for the better part of a decade. "I am so very sorry to have made you come all this way, Mr. Gordon. I simply did not know how best to manage this meeting."

They kept to strict rules about their communication. She visited his offices on Garner Street only once a month, a reasonable time frame for an enterprising widow to be updated by her man of business who also worked for a number of wealthy people in the city. All necessary communication between meetings was done via notes sent through messengers. Sometimes weeks would go by without the need to be in contact, and then, such as this last week, there were several notes back and forth as they conferred about a client's situation. Lord Damion made the decisions, but Mr. Gordon was the contact point. He was also the one who would be watched should someone come snooping.

Fear that Mr. Stillman may have been followed to the Monday meeting, coupled with Mr. Ward's inquiry about Mr. Stillman's present location, had left Sabrina paranoid. Mr. Ward may have already asked questions of the wrong person, which could ignite speculation that could invite unwanted attention on Mr. Gordon's office. They could not meet anywhere else in the city without risking exposure. The only safe way to conduct this meeting was to take it out of London entirely.

Mr. Gordon's ring of gray hair stuck out in a dozen different directions. "I do not mind the distance as much as I am concerned for your disposition, Lady Sabrina. I have never known you to be quite so worked up."

Because she had never had such cause. "Mr. Stillman is here," she said without preamble as though it were a race to get the words out.

Mr. Gordon blinked, then tilted his head slightly. "I'm sorry, did you say Mr. Stillman is *here*?"

"Yes, he is here. In my house." Her tone was pleading and scared. She shook her head at the folly of it all and pointed to the ceiling. "On the third level, the east bedchamber."

"Right," Mr. Gordon said in a slow exhale of sound and breath. As always, he was perfectly calm. "And why, may I ask, is he here?"

Sabrina explained what had happened yesterday morning, relieved to be able to confide in someone. "I could not leave him there. He had nowhere to go."

"Except, perhaps, back to Mr. Ward's house."

"Malcolm must have followed him from there, which meant

he knew where Mr. Stillman had been staying, just as Mr. Stillman had feared."

"Yes, that concerns me too, but for a different reason than it seems to have concerned you. The beating Mr. Stillman received rendered him incapable of escaping London, which was surely the point. Malcolm has no reason to debilitate him further, so allowing Mr. Stillman to return to where he'd come from poses no additional risk."

Sabrina blinked. "I had not thought of that." *Why had I not thought of that?* "But he also needed care. I had no way of knowing he would receive it if his friend were to take responsibility."

"I suppose not." Mr. Gordon's tone was conciliatory rather than agreeable to the justification. What he did not say was that Sabrina had taken on unnecessary risk to herself by bringing him here. Which was true. There were doctors in London whom Mr. Ward could have brought in. Her taking on so much responsibility further complicated an already complicated situation. For a woman of sharp mind and wise instincts, she'd acted rashly.

"Regardless, he is here now," Mr. Gordon said. "How is he doing?"

"He's been mostly sedated since his arrival. Therese felt the least movement possible would best allow the bones to knit. She will be lessening his dosage of laudanum over the next few days so he can properly withdraw from his addiction to drink, which we already saw signs of yesterday when he first arrived."

Mr. Stillman had been shaking and sick, begging for a drink, and seeing things that were not there. Therese suspected he'd been drunk for months on end. The laudanum would address his pain and help him taper from his dependency on drink, but he needed to find sobriety as soon as possible so his body could focus on healing.

"And he does not suspect you are Lord Damion?"

"I have not spoken to him since discovering him in the alley, but there is no reason he would suspect me. Therese, my house-keeper, is a bit of a physician and has been caring for him. No one here knows anything of Lord Damion." She glanced at the closed door. They did not know of Lord Damion because none of that work ever took place or was spoken about here. She'd broken that protection.

"What does your staff believe warranted this act of . . . charity?"

"I told them I came upon him in a London alley when I was in search of a particular cobbler shop in the area where I had an early-morning appointment."

"At eight o'clock on a Monday morning?"

She dropped her hands to her sides and sat heavily in a chair, her shoulders falling forward. "I know," she said. "The story felt inconsequential in comparison to a man who may have died without my help."

"Or been found within the hour by a shopkeeper who would have orchestrated a more natural solution. He'd have been taken to hospital, his friend contacted, and you would not be involved to this degree—or at all."

"I did not think of that at the time." She felt like a complete fool to have not seen all the flaws that were so obvious to Mr. Gordon. "And I cannot undo it for at least four weeks, according to Therese. Yet I set sail for Naples in five weeks, and I have no idea who might take him in after that."

Mr. Gordon waved away her concerns. "His uncle's response to our inquiry about the inheritance showed compassion for the boy. I'm sure he will take responsibility once Mr. Stillman is capable of travel. I will encourage that route when Mr. Stillman is once again communicating with me."

Mr. Gordon sat in the chair next to Sabrina before removing his glasses and pinching the bridge of his nose with his fingers. He didn't repeat his opinion that they should not have taken Mr. Stillman's case in the first place, but she felt sure he was thinking it.

The first fox they had accepted this Season had been Bartholomew Hopkins, who had owed eighteen hundred pounds to Malcolm. When Mr. Gordon had sent notice of settlement, Malcolm had required it to be paid in banknotes and in person by Mr. Gordon, whom he'd then interrogated about Lord Damion's terms and processes.

It was not the first time a lender had thrown a tantrum over the payoff; after all, a settled debt meant lost profit on the accruing interest. Due to Malcolm's reaction, Mr. Gordon had denied three potential candidates in part because they owed Malcolm. But Mr. Stillman's case had been different, in Sabrina's mind, at least. Sabrina had used Malcolm's unsavory ways as further reason to *help* Mr. Stillman, who would never otherwise be free of his debt.

"I shall order tea," Sabrina said, embarrassed she had not done so already.

"Do not bother with that," Mr. Gordon said, waving his glasses through the air. He put them back on and smiled sympathetically. "There is a solution to every problem, so we must focus our energies on finding the solution to this one without the staff posing interruption."

They parried ideas back and forth for the next half an hour, considering several options in turn. Eventually they determined that Mr. Gordon would tell Mr. Ward that he'd learned that an old friend of Mr. Stillman's had found him, beaten and bruised, and brought him to her home when he claimed to have no one she could contact on his behalf—most of which was true.

Deeming Sabrina and Mr. Stillman as old friends instead of having met only once lent credibility to why she had wanted to help him, but for this explanation to be believed, a few things would have to work in their favor:

First, Mr. Stillman would have to accept that he and Sabrina had known each other beyond that one encounter six years ago— an encounter she was not sure he remembered at all due to his heavy drinking.

The second aspect was that Mr. Ward would need to agree to keep the situation private in order to protect all the reputations involved. Mr. Gordon would not disclose Sabrina's identity unless Mr. Ward pressed. Hopefully, he wouldn't.

They would both be attentive to anything Mr. Stillman might say that suggested he'd made any connection between Lord Damion and Lady Sabrina, but they agreed he was the only person who might do so. They would have to wait until Mr. Stillman recovered enough to relay what he remembered to know if Lord Damion's identity remained secret.

They also both agreed it was imperative that Sabrina keep clear lines between what she knew and what Lord Damion knew. It would be easy for her to give herself away if she did not carefully guard her conversations with Mr. Stillman.

"It is fortunate this is happening at the end of the Season," Mr. Gordon said. "But we may need to consider how we move forward with Lord Damion's work next year. It is my hope Malcolm was only following Mr. Stillman and not sniffing out Lord Damion, but there is no way for us to know that for sure. And if Malcolm *is* this invested in discovering Lord Damion's identity, there will be other lenders wanting the same information. We may have done all the good we can do in this particular quadrant."

Sabrina felt a pit in her stomach at the idea of closing down an operation she felt so passionate about. Yet, they had always known there would be a point where the risk of discovery would be too high. She had not thought that point would be reached so soon, however. There were so many more men she could help. If she'd taken Mr. Gordon's advice about Mr. Stillman's case from the start, none of this would have happened. There was some comfort in knowing she had saved Mr. Stillman, though. Or, at least, she was still hopeful she could.

She nodded, "I think you are probably right, Mr. Gordon, though I am sorry for it."

"As am I, Lady Sabrina. We have done good work." He smiled kindly, and she tried to match it with her own but feared it did not look sincere.

It was after eight o'clock when Mr. Gordon climbed back into a hired carriage for the return to his home in London.

Chapter Twelve

Sabrina ate dinner alone in Rose Haven's dining room while trying to focus on the day's paper. She could not stop reviewing her conversation with Mr. Gordon and worrying about her ability to deal rationally with whatever might happen next.

What if Mr. Ward pressed for her identity and then exposed that she'd taken an unmarried man into her household? What if Mr. Stillman remembered he had met Sabrina only one time? What if Malcolm—who had not yet responded to Mr. Gordon's request for settlement—*had* followed Mr. Stillman that morning in an attempt to discover Lord Damion?

Mr. Stillman had to have been followed from Mr. Ward's house in Mayfair, and then Malcolm's men had waited for him during the entire appointment. The fear that Mr. Stillman had been beaten as a warning left a sour taste in her mouth.

The anxiety of the day compounded with traveling to and from London—two hours each way—had left her exhausted by the time she finished her late dinner. She longed for sleep, but at the third-level landing, where the stairs split, she came to a stop. Instead of taking the left stairs to the west wing where her bedchamber was located, Sabrina found herself drawn toward the east wing where Mr. Stillman was convalescing.

Therese had said that his awareness and discomfort was increasing in equal measure now that he was receiving laudanum every five hours instead of three. Most of his communication with Therese had been requests for brandy—first politely, then begging, then demanding, and, once, with tears. It was unfortunate that he had to come off the drink in circumstances such as these, but in Sabrina's experience, a man could not think clearly enough to rise above his mistakes until his body was free of the effects of alcohol.

Perhaps she should look in on the man she'd risked so much for and see how he was faring. Men were used to ordering women about and getting their way, but Therese had an additional difficulty in that she was merely the housekeeper, not the lady of the house. Sabrina might be the only person Mr. Stillman would view as more powerful than himself.

Therese kept four bouquets of roses in the house most of the year—one in the entryway, one on the table in front of the parlor window, one beside Sabrina's bed, and one on the dining room table. Since she'd become the owner of Rose Haven, roses had become Lady Sabrina's signature, a token of beauty that settled her with a sense of identity and calm. She made rose water from the spent bouquets and wore it every day, ordered rose-colored lip tint from Paris, and wore only shades of pink and red to formal events.

Richard's mother, Hortencia, had designed the remarkable gardens when the house had been built: concentric circular hedges of white, red, and three shades of pink, all set with a small pond at the center. Sabrina had loved her mother-in-law, though she had not known her long, and the roses held the woman's memory.

Sabrina returned to the entryway and picked up the bouquet there—a lovely collection of pink, white, and red blooms set in a porcelain vase. She would cut a replacement bouquet in the morning.

She tapped lightly on the door in case Mr. Stillman was asleep. When she did not hear a response, she let herself in, telling herself that the flowers would be a nice sight to see when he woke in the morning. The larger reason, however, was simple curiosity. It was not every day a woman had a strange man hidden under her roof; a man she'd saved, no less.

There was a single lamp turned low on his nightstand, and she was two steps into the room before she realized Mr. Stillman was not asleep. She stopped, held in place by those bright blue eyes until she unstuck her feet and approached the bed where he lay on his back, a pillow beneath his head.

She settled the bouquet on the nightstand, then looked back to find him still watching her, the lamplight reflecting off his hair and making it look like spun gold in the low flame. The ambience of the room was uncomfortably intimate, and Sabrina was careful to leave an adequate distance between herself and the patient.

"Good evening, Mr. Stillman," she said in a regal tone that sounded haughtier than she'd intended. Almost matronly. The five years between them in age felt wider due to the level of responsibility her life required and the opposite responsibility he had taken of his own. "I am Lady Sabrina Carlisle, mistress of this house. I wanted to look in on you now that I am back from London."

"You are the mistress of this house?" His tone was unreadable.

She nodded, and he continued to stare, which was rather

disconcerting. She turned up the lamp, but it did not remedy the tension as much as she had hoped it would. She clasped her hands in front of her and moved to the foot of the bed. "We grow our own roses here. Did you know?" She waved toward the vase.

"I did not." He glanced at the flowers. "They, um, smell very nice."

"Thank you," she said, able to study him now that he was looking away from her. The swelling in his face had gone down, allowing him to open both eyes, though the left one was not as wide as the right. His face was still mottled with bruises, and a cut showed up black against his forehead. A painful-looking split cut through the perfect line of his bottom lip. "I came to see how you are faring."

He looked toward the fireplace, laid but not lit as the day had been warm. "I am unable to rightly answer that question, Lady Sabrina. I have never felt so . . . unwell in my life, never lain abed for an afternoon, let alone days, and yet I am beyond grateful for your help." He looked back at her, then away again as though embarrassed by his thanks. Or perhaps his dependence. "You saved my life."

"I did what anyone would have done."

He let out a punchy laugh, but then cringed and pressed a hand to his right side, where Therese had said he had at least two cracked ribs. Once he'd caught his breath, he continued. "You have a much higher opinion of humankind than I do."

"Perhaps," she said, though she needed him to believe that anyone would have done as much to make her motives look like general concern for her fellow man. "I believe that as I seek to create a world I would wish to live in, that world becomes more of a possibility. You told me you had nowhere to go, no one I could call for you. Bringing you here seemed the only option."

He stared at the covers pulled up to his chest and seemed to curl into himself. "I-I don't have other resources, and so I thank you very much for your kindness. I do not deserve it."

The sincerity of his words struck that tender place in her heart. "Everyone deserves mercy, Mr. Stillman."

He shook his head but said nothing. After a few moments, he cleared his throat. "Therese tells me that you and I knew one another once. I feel terrible, but I don't remember. I am sorry."

Did it hurt that he did not remember their meeting? It was silly to think he would. That night had been of far greater significance to her than it would ever have been to him. Besides, she did not want to be remembered as a scared woman hiding from her husband.

"Our acquaintance happened some time ago, when you were new to London. I had quite forgotten about the meeting myself until you told me your name."

"I am all the more regretful not to remember yours, seeing as how you have done me this turn."

"Do not worry yourself over it, Mr. Stillman. Your focus must be on your healing."

"Therese says it may be weeks before I am able to walk again."

"Yet you *will* walk," Sabrina said encouragingly. "Therese is remarkably skilled, and as you are young and . . . hale, I've no doubt you will impress all of us with your fortitude. You are welcome to stay here for the next month—that is how long Therese expects it will take before you are fit to travel—but there must be some additional arrangements in place by then."

"Yes, she told me. I am . . . considering my options." He paused, his expression thoughtful. "Could tell me how it happened? Your coming upon me?"

Sabrina regarded him warily and then crossed to straighten

the curtain on the rod covering his window. She needed something to do with her hands. "Do you remember anything of that morning?"

"I remember being pulled by my arms into the alley by two men, but then only fragments—flashes of . . . a black stick and a carriage and a big man. I think it might have been Joshua—he is a footman here?"

Sabrina understood his confusion. Joshua was not built like the typical footman, small-boned and elegant. Rather, he was quite tall, broad-shouldered, and looked as though he would better fit in the stable.

"Joshua is Therese's son," she said simply, not feeling it necessary for her to explain that he had trained under the former butler from the time he was thirteen. When Mr. Rawlins had retired last year, Joshua had taken on his responsibilities but kept the title of footman due to his age. "He helped bring you here. I'm afraid navigating the stairs was a painful process, and you were quite uncomfortable."

"Yes, I do remember that—lots of pain."

"Do you . . . um, remember anything else?"

On the drive from Wimbledon, she'd sat with him on the floor of her carriage, his head in her lap. As he went in and out of consciousness, she'd sung softly to him, stroked his face, and assured him all would be well. It seemed he did not remember that either, which was just as well.

Mr. Stillman wiped his forehead, and she noticed the tremor in his hands. The laudanum must be wearing off, leaving him susceptible to his body's demand for liquor. He shook his head. "I remember nothing else. Trying to remember . . . makes my heart race."

"Then do not try," Sabrina said. "It is rarely helpful to ponder on traumatic events. Pretend what you remember is a dream, and in time, the anxiety you feel will lessen." She spoke from experience. It was better to look ahead than back.

He nodded, looking relieved, then met her eyes again. "How did you find me?"

He watched her as she told the story, his eyes occasionally moving to her lips. The rose stain emphasized their fullness, but other people's notice did not often make her feel self-conscious. His attentiveness tempted her to adjust her neckline or smooth her skirts. When she finished her practiced version of events, his eyes remained on her lips for a few seconds until moving to her eyes again.

"Why were you in the area so early in the morning?"

"I'd had an appointment with a cobbler for a fitting. The early time did not conflict with my social calendar. I have an upcoming trip, you see, and am trying to get everything I'll need ordered in time for my departure."

"You did not send a servant on your behalf?"

"I am an eccentric widow, Mr. Stillman." She shrugged as though embarrassed. "I keep my own appointments and prefer to be measured in person rather than send papers for my shoes. I daresay it is lucky for you that it unfolded the way that it did."

She held her breath until he nodded in acceptance, then she carefully exhaled.

"And you . . . you are a widow?" he asked thoughtfully.

"Yes, and for that reason I hope we might keep your presence here . . . discreet. Only my staff and I know that you are here." *And Mr. Gordon. And possibly Mr. Ward by tomorrow morning.*

"I do not want anyone to know I am here either," he said quickly.

"Do you know who would have done this? Were you robbed,

for instance?" That would be the most obvious reason, if she didn't know about Malcolm, which *Lady Sabrina* did not know.

Mr. Stillman looked away from her as though trying to hide his shame, though she was relieved to see it. Shame could be motivation to improve.

"Do you know much of my . . . reputation? Since we were acquainted all those years ago, Lady Sabrina?"

This was dangerous territory. How much of what she knew about him could she reasonably blame on gossip? She had not returned to London for more than a year after having removed for her confinement, and by then Mr. Stillman had apparently worn out whatever welcome the *ton* had extended him.

"I have heard rumors of certain . . . excesses."

He nodded but didn't meet her eyes. "I fear it would be bad for you if your circle knew I was in your home. I . . ." He trailed off, and she wondered if he had been about to say that he would go elsewhere before remembering there was nowhere else for him to go.

"I have no concern that they will find out," she said with confidence she hoped would boost his own. "I live quietly here in Wimbledon, and my staff is loyal. Should I have to defend myself, I have no shame in saying I merely helped a young man in dire circumstances as any Christian woman would."

She shrugged to further demonstrate how unconcerned she was for societal judgment. It was mostly sincere. She tried very hard not to give *anything* worthy of gossip to the tongues of the *ton*. They'd already had their share at her expense.

"It is not only reputations," Mr. Stillman said after a moment.

She thought it humorous that he feared he could still be damaged by gossip. From Jack and Mr. Gordon's reports, Mr. Stillman was a rake as well as a drunk and a gambler, but he hadn't pursued female companionship over the last year as much as he had the tables and the bottle.

Recovering in a widow's house would have no bearing on what the *ton* thought of him—the damage had already been done on that score. A good many men would find it admirable.

"I owe a man a great deal of money," Mr. Stillman continued, "and he was quite insistent I not leave London before my debt was paid. I worry that puts you at risk should he find me here. I should hate to bring such things to your home. A lady should not even know of them."

She was touched by his concern and humored by his protectiveness. "I know more than my share about dark places and evil persons, Mr. Stillman, and, as I said, no one knows you are here. If you are right about it being an unsavory lender who rendered you so injured, he has done his work in keeping you from getting very far, and I do not imagine he is much concerned beyond protecting his investment."

"If no one knows I am here, it will look as though I have fled the city, which is what he was trying to prevent."

"Ah," she said with a nod. "I see."

Mr. Stillman's eyes were eager to share more information. "I have made arrangements, however, with a different sort of lender just before I was attacked. He may have already paid off the debt, which frees me from the man's interest—every sort of interest." He looked to the side. "I need to correspond with this second lender, however. He will be concerned about my disappearance too. I shall be prudent in revealing my exact location."

"I have an address in London that might be more discreet for such communications. Any messages sent there are forwarded here when I am not in residence. I transact a great deal of business that way."

Every few days, Mrs. Billings would put the delivered correspondence in a canvas pouch and send it on to Wimbledon. Sabrina would spend a day or so responding to the messages and then return them in the same canvas pouch. The messenger service she used between her houses considered her an excellent client. The process seemed cumbersome when she explained it to others, but she never fell behind on business or personal correspondence this way, and the Wimbledon staff remained ignorant of whom she was writing.

"A London address would be ideal, thank you." He held her eyes, then looked at his hands, which shook slightly.

He'd been two days without a drink; the effects must be increasingly uncomfortable. It would get worse before it got better, however, and the misery was an essential part of his healing as it would, she hoped, help keep him from ever repeating his indulgence.

He wiped at his brow, wincing when he accidentally bumped the cut.

Sabrina dropped her clasped hands and came to the head of the bed to inspect the injury. His eyes did not move from her face as she examined his forehead, then turned to the bowl of water next to the bed. She dipped a corner of a cloth into the water, displacing the few rose petals that floated on top. She gently patted the cuts on his face with the wet cloth.

He studied her until she began wiping along his temples, then his eyes fluttered closed. He let out a breath, and his body relaxed against the bed linens. She was so very close to him.

Richard had been forty-three years old when they married, and already paunchy and balding. If he had been kind, his physical aspect would not have mattered, but since he was not, every deficit underscored his broken character.

Mr. Stillman was a very different specimen of the male sex. His nightshirt settled upon defined shoulders, and his hair appeared thick and soft. Unable to resist the temptation, she brushed his hair from his forehead. The tingle in her fingertips against his skin caught her off guard, and she swallowed the awareness of how vulnerable he was right now—his eyes closed, letting her minister to him.

"You are in need of a trim," she said, taking a step back. She wrung the cloth out over the bowl, making the rose petals dance like tiny boats caught upon the waves. "I shall discuss it with Therese."

He nodded, but his eyes remained closed and his body remained in soft repose.

Sabrina took another step away, and his eyes opened, capturing her and making her feel as though they were the only two people in existence. If other women felt this same way when he looked at them, no wonder they had come so easy to him in the past.

Nothing that came easy in life was worth having, however. She would be wise to remember that.

"Thank you," he whispered.

She wasn't sure if he meant the rescue yesterday morning or the ministrations just now. "You're welcome." She looked toward his legs beneath the cover, the bulk of the right thicker than the left due to the splint Therese had applied. "How is your leg?"

"Painful," he said, sounding exhausted. "When I shift my position, even a little, fresh pain shoots up my leg." He waved from his hip to his feet.

She was glad to see his shoulder was doing so well. Once a

dislocated shoulder was returned to the socket, movement was no longer impeded, though the area would be tender for a few days. He would also be susceptible to reinjure it if he wasn't careful.

"Therese says that in another day or two you will be able to sit up more fully, perhaps even transfer to a chair. We are attempting to find a Bath chair that will allow you some ability to move around the room. I imagine a young man like yourself would have difficulty staying abed this way."

"I fear it will drive me mad," he said, then held up his hand and hurried to add, "though I am very grateful for the chance."

Sabrina smiled. "Grateful for the chance to go mad?"

He attempted a smile, though he could not manage much given the injuries to his face. "Madness is a fair trade for one's life, I suppose."

She laughed lightly. A man both handsome and witty was a powerful combination. "Is there anything I can do to make you more comfortable, Mr. Stillman?"

He cleared his throat and licked his lips. When he spoke, the higher tone of his voice and quick delivery made her think he'd been waiting for her to issue the invitation. "Yes, actually, I wonder if I might have some . . . brandy or rum or . . . s-something."

She had expected this request, and had planned to say no, but changed her mind. One drink a day would not set back his recovery, and it could help him sleep if administered at night.

"I shall have a glass of sherry sent up."

"Sherry?"

The disappointment in his voice was rather overt, but then he attempted a smile that she suspected was designed to charm her, though the effect was subdued because his face was a mask of bruises. "Might I request brandy instead? It shall help manage the pain." He clasped his fingers together, perhaps to contain the trembling, or maybe to show her how bad it was.

"You are being given regular doses of laudanum for the pain, Mr. Stillman."

"The laudanum is helpful, yes, but I would also appreciate something more, um, familiar."

She raised an eyebrow. "Are you not familiar with sherry?"

He attempted to smile again, but there was a tightness to his mouth. "Of course, I am familiar with sherry. Women drink it in tiny glass cups while discussing hats and springtime."

Lady Sabrina took his sarcasm as an opening. "If you don't mind my saying so, Mr. Stillman, from what I have heard, you are more than a bit familiar with liquor. Seeing how your body is coping with the lack of such drink these last two days"—she gestured to his trembling hands—"I would guess you are used to far more than is good for you."

His smile fell and a look of desperation entered his eyes. It was essential that she establish her authority, so she did not give him a chance to speak. "Ale with your meals and a glass of sherry each night to help you sleep are all I will prescribe. Any more would interfere with your healing."

"I *need* brandy, Lady Sabrina. Without it, I feel quite ill."

"You feel ill because you have overindulged, Mr. Stillman. I would go so far as to suggest that your condition in the alley yesterday morning was in part due to your overindulgence, since I've never met a gambler who did not also drink to excess."

He was not humbled by her reprimand. "Surely one glass of brandy will only help me toward healing. It's medicine, really."

Her tone was tight and sharp. "As the authority of this household, I suggest you discontinue this argument both with me and with my staff. They will not go against my orders, and I will not change my mind. Your body needs to heal in more ways than one, and none of it will be comfortable."

She turned and spoke the last over her shoulder on her way to the door. "The next few weeks are an opportunity for you, Mr. Stillman, to heal your body and overcome some of the vices that put you in this position in the first place. While I am dedicated to providing for your comfort, I shan't do it to your detriment." She opened the door, smiled—though she kept it tight—and delivered her final sentiments. "Good night, Mr. Stillman. I shall have that glass of sherry sent up shortly."

Chapter Thirteen

*H*arry shivered beneath the covers while sweat dripped from his face and into his ears, pillow, and sheets. His stomach rolled like a ship on ocean waves, and there were monkeys climbing the curtains. Mean ones that kept baring their teeth.

Therese had tucked a bowl beside him on the bed in case he vomited, but there was nothing left to retch. The remedy to his miserable condition was somewhere belowstairs in the house's liquor cabinet, but he could not have it. This was the fourth day, and though Therese assured him things would get better soon, they had only been getting worse.

The cloth that had been laid upon his head was removed and a fresh one put on. The welcome coolness relaxed him some, but it quickly warmed from his fevered brow, and he shook his head to make it fall to the side.

"Mr. Stillman," Therese said in patient reprimand as she replaced the cloth on his forehead. "This will ease your discomfort."

"A bottle of rum will ease my comfort," he said through clenched teeth. He looked at the woman who had provided for his every need these last days. "I am dying, Therese. Can I at least get tonight's sherry early?"

"No, Mr. Stillman. This misery is healing you."

"You are as bad as she is."

He didn't realize he'd said it out loud until Therese responded. "I am likely worse than Lady Sabrina, as I have cared for others facing your same demons. Do you even remember the last time you drank for pleasure and not to stave off feeling like this?"

Harry couldn't, but he wasn't going to admit it. An emotion he could not quite identify rose in his chest: anger or fear or maybe just gutting sorrow. He could not do this. Unless he got his hands on another bottle and could save himself, he was going to die. He was sure of it.

"It would do you well to eat something—toast, perhaps? Or some soup?"

"I should like to try some toast," Harry said more for her benefit than his as he did not think he would keep it down any more than he believed he could survive another day of this.

If he was going to die, he would rather it happen sooner than later, and yet the thought of facing his death brought additional terror. What if he had to account to God for his life thus far?

Lord Damion's letter had told Harry to work toward doing good in the world. Tears leaked from the corners of his eyes as he thought about how worthless his life had become. He wanted another chance, didn't he? But he couldn't imagine he would ever feel better, and yet he could not feel this way much longer because surely his head would explode.

He must have slept because when he next opened his eyes, the sunlight coming through the window was rich and bright. He had one moment of peace before the nausea washed through him again and his head resumed its pounding. He found himself wishing for death again, then fearing it. He heard someone rise from the chair beside his bed and turned, expecting to see Therese keeping a deathwatch over him. Maybe with his toast in hand.

Instead he blinked at the familiar but unexpected face before him. "Ward?" Was he hallucinating again?

Ward's expression was concerned as he leaned closer to the bed. "Good gracious, you look like death itself, Stillman."

Could a hallucination speak? He reached out and poked Ward's shoulder.

"It is really you," Harry said, nearly crying again.

Ward pulled his eyebrows together and laughed awkwardly. He sat back in his chair. "What's happened to you?"

Harry attempted to wriggle into a seated position, but between the dull ache in his shoulder and the sharp pain of his leg, he could not manage much.

"Can I help you?" Ward said, rising to his feet.

Had Ward any idea how lucky he was to be able to stand at will and walk wherever he wanted? Harry had been in this bed—and only this bed—for days, with Therese attending to his every bodily need, which was as embarrassing as anything he'd ever experienced in his life. Yet Ward could move about like it was nothing.

"I would like to sit up," Harry said, still watching Ward carefully. He might disappear at any moment. "Could you put some pillows behind my back?"

Ward was not as efficient as Therese, but he was also not a hallucination, apparently. It took some doing before Harry was upright, but it made him feel less of an invalid to be at eye level.

Only then did it occur to Harry that Ward was *here*. In Lady Sabrina's house. "What are you doing here?"

"I've been writing back and forth with Mr. Gordon. He was

dashed vague about what happened to you, and I wasn't about to sit for that." He huffed. "I finally received a letter from Lady Sabrina yesterday, revealing where you were and offering me the chance to visit if I would promise to keep your location private. She even provided a carriage." Ward leaned in. "Well done, Stillman. Rumor has it she's one of the wealthiest women in England, never mind that she's a by-blow."

Harry pulled his eyebrows together. "What are you talking about?"

"She's the illegitimate daughter of the Duke of Anglesey. Surely you knew that?"

Harry shook his head. Lady Sabrina was illegitimate? Yet she had such a regal air.

Ward continued. "Raised by the duke and everything, but her mother was only a mistress before his marriage. She married into money and then inherited everything when her husband died. As I've heard it, she manages his holdings better than he did—there's a mine and a sheep farm and a number of holdings she's expanded since." He winked at Harry. "Many a man would like to find themselves at the *mercy* of a woman like her. She's not bad to look at either, eh?"

Harry felt his face flush as Ward's meaning sank in; his mind was still soggy and slow. "She's a tyrant, Ward. I've only spoken with her once since coming here, and she yelled at me for asking for brandy." He huffed and shook his head, powerful in his position of authority in regard to *Lady* Sabrina. "Pretty? Yes. Appealing? Not in the least."

He heard the lack of gratitude too late and hurried to fix it, since he was trying to be a better man and all that. "Don't get me wrong—I'm very grateful she came upon me, and she's been incredibly generous, but there's nothing more to my stay here than that. I'll leave as soon as I can."

A thought occurred to him, and he leaned forward, though it hurt his side and he had to suppress a groan. "Can I come back to London with you today? I'll be an exemplary patient, I promise."

Therese had suggested he ask Uncle Elliott to take him in once he was well enough to travel, but there was so much disagreement between him and his uncle. Had he written a letter asking his uncle for sanctuary? He couldn't remember.

"I'm back in my rooms, Stillman," Ward said. "And I don't think you are in any condition to travel. My parents learned we stayed at the house and sent me a scathing letter." He made a face. "I've decided to punish them by not speaking to them for the rest of the year."

Harry wasn't sure that would be much punishment, but he had little space to sympathize with his friend. He slumped against the pillows. "I'm glad the gargoyle let you visit, that's something at least."

"Gargoyle?"

"Lady Sabrina," Harry said. "I told you: she's horrid."

Ward laughed. "I will bring your trunk the next time I visit. I hadn't time to see it packed before I came."

That trunk contained all of Harry's possessions outside of his estate, and it humbled him to think of all he'd lost these last months. Why had he called Lady Sabrina a gargoyle? She'd saved him.

"That would be appreciated, Ward. Thank you," Harry said.

The men fell silent a moment, Ward watching him in a way that made Harry squirm. If Harry looked anything like he felt, it must be a gruesome sight.

"What happened with Lord Damion, Stillman?" Ward finally

asked. "You must have been attacked immediately after your meeting, right?"

Harry told him what he remembered of how the men pulled him into the alley and then recounted Sabrina's part of the story about how he got from there to here.

"I daresay she saved my life, Ward," he said. "But she is forcing me to come off the bottle, and I truly believe the attempts might kill me. I have never been so physically ill in my life."

"Not even after we ate those raw chicken livers on Christopher's bet that we wouldn't?"

Harry shuddered. They'd gotten some sort of illness from those livers that had rendered him the sickest he'd ever been—until now. "I'd eat two pounds of livers if I could wash them down with a swallow of brandy."

What a whiny baby he'd become. Here he was in a fine bed in a fine house, with staff who attended to his every need, food—when he could stomach it—and every bit of it at no expense to him. Two weeks ago, he'd been thrown from a club into the filth of an alleyway without a shilling to his name, and now he had fresh sheets and a vase of roses on his bedside table, for heaven's sake. Could he be more ungrateful?

Could he be more miserable?

The desire to cry gripped him again, and he fought against it with all he had. He was not so ridiculous to cry in front of Ward. For mercy's sake.

When he had gained control of himself, he opened his eyes to see Ward watching him.

"This is bad, man," Ward said softly. He reached into an inside pocket of his coat and withdrew a silver-plated flask.

Harry was overcome with such extreme longing that he nearly cried again, and yet the memory of all that Lady Sabrina and Therese had said about his needing to get off the drink kept him from reaching for it immediately.

Ward held out the flask, and the tangy smell pushed Harry over the edge of his half-hearted resistance. He grabbed the flask and drank the whole of it—a fine, smooth bourbon that went down like hot silk. When he'd finished, he dropped his head against the pillows and reveled in the warmth that moved from his chest to his extremities, relaxing his tense muscles and easing the shakes. A single flask had erased the madness that had been steadily building. Magic.

"Praise the heavens." After a few seconds, he opened his eyes. "Have you anymore?"

Ward laughed. "How many flasks do you think the average gentleman carries?"

Harry nodded and tried to focus on how much better he felt. "You would think being beaten half to death would be worse than being denied the bottle, but it is not. I would not wish this on my worst enemy." His body was already demanding a second drink, and a third, and a fourth.

"Not even on Malcolm?"

Malcolm. What a despicable man. If not for him, none of this would be happening. Yet, if not for drinking to the excess Harry had done for months on end, would he have made the same choices that had led him to borrowing from such a man? Harry looked at the empty flask on his coverlet. The shame of having drained it competed with his wish that he had more. It seemed that the situation was precisely as he feared: he could not overcome this. He *was* too weak.

"So, did Lord Damion agree to pay off your debts?"

"Yes," Harry confirmed as though Lord Damion's benevolence were only a side issue now. He stared at the flask as though it might refill itself if he wished for it hard enough. "Mr. Gordon is settling all my debts per Lord Damion's instruction. What day is it today?"

"Saturday," Ward said.

"Right," Harry said, though he wasn't sure he had known that. "By Monday, all the accounts should be settled. Mr. Gordon will send me a letter confirming that." He paused, gratitude washing through him. "To have two rescuers as I have had—Lord Damion and Lady Sabrina . . . It is a miracle, Ward."

The empty flask glared at him in reproach. He could think clearly now, but at what cost? And for how long? Had he undone Therese's ministrations? Slapped away Lady Sabrina's caretaking? Delayed his body's abilities to heal from the beating? A lump rose in his throat that he tried to swallow.

"What was Lord Damion like?" Ward asked, leaning forward, elbows on knees.

Harry thought back to the early morning meeting. "He wore red gloves."

Ward wrinkled his nose. "Red gloves?"

Harry nodded, looking at his friend. "And a black coat. I saw his hand when I managed to peek through the slide in the wall."

"Slide?"

Harry described the pub and the process of passing the paper back and forth through the opening in the wall.

"And all you saw was his hand?"

Harry nodded again. "I would guess him to be a gangly man from that minimal view."

"What did he say to you?"

"He didn't speak. Everything was written out on a paper I had to sign and date." He shook his head. "It was all very odd."

Ward sat back in his chair. "I cannot believe you were that

close to him and did not see him or hear his voice. Are you not curious? What if he is someone we know?"

"I do not care who he is," Harry said, closing his eyes to relish the ease he felt in his body, though not in his mind, where his shame continued to grow. "He took a chance on me. Let him keep his secrets." Lady Sabrina had taken a chance on him as well, and yet he had betrayed her. His eyes opened as he remembered something. "He gave me a letter."

"Lord Damion?"

Harry nodded, flushed with excitement. His mind worked so much better with just a little liquor. "After the transaction was finished, he gave me a letter confirming the terms and congratulating me on making a decision to change my life."

Ward chuckled, and Harry turned to him, wanting his friend to understand. "It was so . . . sincere, Ward. I don't think I had realized until that moment what his motivation truly was. He wants to give me the chance to be a better man. I have a second chance, Ward."

Where was the letter? He patted his chest as though he were wearing a jacket, but of course he was in a borrowed nightshirt. He would ask Therese to search the jacket he'd been wearing when he'd arrived. Maybe reading Lord Damion's words again would help give Harry the fortitude to continue.

"That is good, then," Ward said, then leaned in and lowered his voice. "Shall I bring you a supply when I bring your trunk?"

Harry opened his mouth to say no, but different words came out. "Would you?"

The idea that he could temper his misery overwhelmed every other thought. He knew he needed to give up drink, it had come to rule him, but he did not agree with Lady Sabrina's methods. He would not overindulge. He would just take the edge off, so he did not feel as though he were being eaten alive from the inside out. A drink or two a day was so much less than he was used to. In time, the sherry and the ale might even be enough to get him through.

Ward shrugged. "I could manage a few bottles so long as the wardens here don't do a search. Perhaps request mint leaves to keep beside the bed for your breath. Remember how we did that in school to keep the teachers from finding us out?" He gave a nostalgic smile.

Harry was glad for the suggestion as he would never have thought of such a detail on his own. "Bless your ever-living soul," he breathed in the manner of worship. "I shall count the hours until your return, my friend, and live forever in your debt."

Chapter Fourteen

abrina carried a vase of newly cut roses toward the "sickroom," as Mr. Stillman's bedchamber had become known among the household. It was Saturday evening, but this would be only her second visit to the patient. She thought it best that they not become too well acquainted, especially before he was off the drink.

She still wasn't certain it had been a good idea to allow Mr. Ward to visit earlier today, but refusing his request might have led him to raising his voice in London about what he already knew. She had met Mr. Ward briefly when he arrived, and he seemed amiable enough. On his way out, he'd asked if he could visit again the next day and bring Mr. Stillman's things. She'd felt unable to refuse him even though she would be in London by then.

She knocked lightly on the door to Mr. Stillman's room, and, after he issued the invitation, let herself in.

He lay abed, literally twiddling his thumbs on top of the bedclothes. He looked at her and smiled somewhat tightly. From Therese's reports, he had been having a hard time of it, but he looked as though he'd turned the corner.

"Good evening, Mr. Stillman," she said, crossing to set the roses on the bedside table. He looked at the roses with a neutral expression, just as he had the first bouquet she'd brought on Tuesday night. When he looked back at her, his irritation was clearly visible. Perhaps he had not turned a corner after all. She braced herself for confrontation.

"I thought I would see how you were faring before I left for the weekend." Though she'd avoided the sickroom, she'd been at Rose Haven since Thursday, and Therese had kept her updated on the news she needed to know. Sabrina had spent the days writing out the invitations to Nathan's dinner party, reviewing the last quarter's accounts for both the pub and the snuff shop, catching up with friends and neighbors here in Wimbledon, and attending to Hortencia's roses, which was her only real hobby.

During the first year of Richard and Sabrina's marriage—back when Sabrina had believed their difficulties would sort themselves out—Hortencia would sit on a chair and explain to Sabrina what a blind shoot was and why too much greenery would result in too few blooms. She had been a lovely woman—the best part of Sabrina's marriage—and tending to her roses helped keep her influence strong in Sabrina's life.

"How are you feeling tonight, Mr. Stillman? Therese said you've had a hard few days but seemed improved this afternoon."

"I have been improved for a short time, yes," he said, his tone cantankerous. "But then this evening the misery has returned." He wiped at his forehead rather dramatically. "I believe it would be better for all of us if I were to taper off slowly. Five years of hard drinking is not something to be undone in a few days."

"Ale with your meals and a glass of sherry at night is sufficient to take off the edge."

"It does barely that, if it does anything at all!"

Sabrina raised her eyebrows at his harsh tone. "Oh, then perhaps we should discontinue even those considerations."

"No," he said quickly—desperately—his tone softened by fear. "I do not wish to seem ungrateful, but my misery is beyond the extreme. If you had ever experienced this type of situation personally, you would know that this is nothing short of torture."

Such dramatics, Sabrina thought. "Did you enjoy your visit with Mr. Ward?"

The change of topic seemed to confuse him, then he nodded. "Yes, it was very good to see him."

"I imagine his visit was a welcome distraction."

A flash of something—guilt? regret?—crossed his face before he lowered his eyes to the bedcovers. "He brought to me the best improvement I have had for days." His tone was flat, and Sabrina wondered if Mr. Ward had brought bad news.

"I am glad to hear of your improvement. Did you remind Mr. Ward to keep your whereabouts a secret?"

Mr. Stillman raised his head, his expression serious. "I did, and he gave his word."

"We can trust him, then?"

"I would trust him with my life, Lady Sabrina."

"Good," she said with a crisp nod. She looked about the room in case there was something she could use to initiate further conversation. Some part of her wanted to stay, which made no sense at all since she had already done what she set out to do, which was to see how Mr. Stillman was faring and deliver the fresh bouquet. "He will be bringing your things tomorrow, I believe."

"Yes," Mr. Stillman said simply.

"Very good." Since Mr. Stillman had been so very down on his luck, the clothing Mr. Ward was bringing would most likely not be clean. "We shall have everything laundered, pressed, and hung so it will be ready when you are capable of dressing in regular attire."

Mr. Stillman would be dependent for a while yet on the nightshirts she'd provided. They were new, from a seamstress in London who kept such things on hand. After Richard's death, she'd emptied the house of anything that reminded her of him, including his clothing, and redecorated every room, except the rose parlor which Hortencia had designed years earlier.

"That would be fine," Mr. Stillman said, "but I should like to sort through the trunk with his help first and make sure all is in order before turning over my clothing to the staff."

"Certainly."

"I asked Therese earlier to check the coat I had been wearing when I arrived. There was a letter in the inside pocket—do you know if she found it? It was without an envelope. Cream paper, folded in half, then in fourths to fit within the pocket."

"A letter?" Did he mean Lord Damion's letter? One was given to every client at the conclusion of their meeting as a receipt of sorts that also included encouragement toward the betterment of their lives.

"It is very important to me," Harry said, smoothing the bed-covers across his hips.

Fearing she might look too concerned, she forced a smile to make sure she didn't betray any knowledge of this letter. "A love letter, then?"

"No." Mr. Stillman shook his head. "A letter from a . . . friend. A friend who was assisting me in some matters of business."

"Ah," Sabrina said. "Is he the same friend you have been corresponding with these last days—one Mr. Gordon of London?"

It would be silly to pretend she did not know about the letters going back and forth in her messenger pouch. Of course, they were all sealed, so she did not read them herself, but Mr. Gordon sent her daily updates of their communication. It was absurd that all this was happening in one household. Maybe one day she would laugh about it, though she would be laughing alone, which made it far less funny.

"No, a different friend. Therese has not found the letter, then?"

"She did not mention to me that you had asked after it, but I shall follow up with her. It was in your coat, you say?

"Yes, the letter offered some encouragement I would find helpful to revisit amid all this." Mr. Stillman picked at the bedspread and then looked up. "I would like to be reminded that at least one person has faith in me."

She watched him, suspecting his humility might be manipulation on his part. "You do not have faith in yourself, Mr. Stillman?"

He shrugged. "I'm not sure if I have faith in anyone. Or anything." He met Sabrina's gaze, and, as before, she felt pinned by the intense blue. "Are you a woman of faith, Lady Sabrina?"

"I am," she said.

"Then you believe people can change?"

"Change how, exactly?"

"Their character, who they have become, what they want from life." He took a breath, then looked back at the coverlet, perhaps to hide the vulnerability his musings were bringing to the surface.

"I do believe people can change, Mr. Stillman, but I believe it takes more than a circumstance or even the desire. It takes work and fortitude and the willingness to be . . . uncomfortable as the changes take root."

He looked at her. "You do not think being left for dead in an alley is enough to change a person?"

"No," she said quickly and firmly. "Once you have regained your health and functionality, you will have choices to make day by day, sometimes hour by hour, in regards to the man you want to be. You will have to face the hardships of life without the vices that have cushioned you from the struggles. That will be the true test. This—" She waved toward him lying in the bed, incapable of doing anything for himself. "This is a chance to prove that change is *possible*. Your choices and abilities are limited now, so it will not be until after you leave here that you will know for certain if you can do the work necessary to live differently than you have so far."

Had he paled slightly as she'd shared her advice? She took a step toward him. "Are you all right, Mr. Stillman?"

"Maybe there are those who cannot overcome their nature, no matter how badly they want to."

That soft place inside her heart became softer. How frightening it would be to think yourself incapable of improvement. "I believe the only people who cannot change are those who are unwilling to face the pain behind the poor choices they have made. Certainly, there *are* those people. You, however, are not one of them."

He startled. When he spoke, it was a whisper. "How can you know that?"

"Because you are asking the right questions." She smiled. "And asking the right questions will lead you to the answers that most men do not really want to find."

They looked at one another, and she waited to see him soften, but he continued to look unsure.

"You are very wise, Lady Sabrina," Mr. Stillman finally said.

Sabrina felt herself blush at the compliment and had the unwelcome thought that perhaps she could earn further appreciation by straightening her back and showing her figure to its advantage. The thought was a sure indication that it was time to leave this room. She forced her eyes away from his.

"I will ask the staff to look for your letter. Is there anything else I can do for you before I leave for Town, Mr. Stillman? I shall not be back until Tuesday."

"No, thank you."

She quit the room and checked that the carriage was ready before locating Therese in the housekeeper's office. "Mr. Stillman mentioned he'd asked after a letter that had been in his coat when he arrived."

Therese finished a note in the daily log and put down her pencil. "None of the staff I've spoken to has seen it. We will keep looking."

"Very good. It seems to be rather important to him. I hope it is found for Mr. Stillman's sake."

And her own.

If Lord Damion's letter *wasn't* found, then it had either been lost within the household or removed before she'd discovered Mr. Stillman in that alley—she'd have seen it if it had fallen in the alley or carriage. The second possibility brought to mind her concerns about what Malcolm might have learned about Mr. Stillman's meeting with Lord Damion and about Mr. Gordon's concerns about Malcolm's difficult nature.

Mr. Gordon had said Malcolm was not responding to his messages thus far, so he had been focused on settling Mr.

Stillman's other accounts before demanding a response from the disreputable lender. She would talk to Mr. Gordon about her concerns and get his opinion while she was in London.

As Sabrina settled in the carriage across from Molly, she took a calming breath. There was nothing revealing about the letter Lord Damion had given to Mr. Stillman. She used a practiced penmanship she had developed solely for Lord Damion's correspondence, and she never included anything that could identify her.

For the first time since Mr. Gordon had said they would need to discontinue Lord Damion's lending, she felt a sense of relief to put the disguise behind her. The fear of discovery had existed from the start but had not surpassed her determination . . . until now. Now she felt responsible for Mr. Stillman having been beaten in the alley, and she worried about what could happen if Malcolm, or someone like him, became determined to find answers.

She reminded herself of what Mr. Gordon had said regarding the good they had done. The final letter she wrote to each of her foxes was about how every bit of good a person did made the world a better place. She'd done a bit of good and would find other ways to help people in need.

It was time for Lord Damion to hang up his cloak.

"Is everything all right, Lady Sabrina?"

Sabrina looked up, wondering what Molly had read in her expression. She quickly put on a better face. "Yes, of course. I am only thinking about what is left to be done in London. Will you be seeing your mother while we are staying in Town?"

"Yes, ma'am," Molly said. "Whenever you can spare me."

"I never heard how she was faring after your last visit," Sabrina said kindly. "Was she at all improved?"

Molly blinked back tears, then stared at her hands in her lap. "No, ma'am. Not at all."

Sabrina continued to ask questions, drawing from the young woman the hurt and sorrow she felt to lose her mother. By the time they reached London, Sabrina had already begun forming the ideas of providing a place for servants who could no longer work. Most of them relied on family, but Molly's mother was in a workhouse. She was not required to work due to the compassion of the patron who funded the house, but the conditions were poor.

Sabrina would not need to hide her identity for such an enterprise as a charitable convalescent home for elderly service workers, which would be a relief.

When doors closed, windows opened. Perhaps she might find a way to share that insight with Mr. Stillman. The harder portion of his recovery would be dealing with the demons that drink had kept at bay, but if he could vanquish those, life could be brighter than it had been for a very long time.

Chapter Fifteen

On Tuesday, Sabrina was preparing for a garden party—her last society event before Nathan's dinner on Friday night—when she received a letter from Mr. Gordon. The letter reported that all of Mr. Stillman's creditors had received their payments and signed a receipt stating as much—except Malcolm. The lender had finally responded to Mr. Gordon's message with a message of his own: he would sign a settlement agreement only if Mr. Stillman was present during the pay off.

Mr. Gordon was concerned. So was Sabrina. And both of them were ready to be done with Malcolm once and for all.

She penned a response, asking Mr. Gordon to offer Malcolm an additional fifty pounds if they could settle the account by Thursday. They had never overpaid a debt in this way, but since this was their last fox, she was eager to be finished. Her monthly meeting with Mr. Gordon was scheduled for next week, and she sincerely hoped the matter with Malcolm would be settled by then.

She caught up on a few other matters of correspondence before she ordered her carriage. If it made more sense for her to simply stay in London rather than travel back and forth to her country estate in less than two days, well, she did not look at that too closely.

Joshua greeted her at the door of Rose Haven that evening. Once relieved of her summer cloak and hat, she asked that Therese join her for tea in the rose parlor.

"Mr. Stillman seems to be doing quite well," Therese said when she arrived a few minutes later, bringing the tea tray with her. "Mr. Ward has been visiting, which has improved his mood."

Sabrina poured while Therese filled her plate. "I am glad to hear it. He is no longer ill?" She handed over Therese's cup.

"No," Therese said, nodding her thanks as she took the saucer. "He is talkative, joking. He asked Joshua to play cards with him after Mr. Ward left this afternoon. I prevented that."

"Well done," Sabrina said, sipping her tea. She stood and walked to the window to look outside at the pops of color amid the green foliage of the rose garden. Roses bloomed from May to September in this part of the country—half the year almost. No matter how long and cold the winter was, the roses would begin blooming in spring and keep up the celebration all summer long.

She turned back to Therese and their conversation. "The last thing Mr. Stillman needs—or Joshua for that matter—is to play cards."

"That is what I thought as well."

"I am glad to hear that Mr. Stillman is through the worst of the misery. I shall look in on him this evening." She returned to her chair across from Therese. "And how is the rest of the household faring? Has the excitement of Mr. Stillman's presence finally settled into routine?"

After visiting with Therese, Sabrina enjoyed a simple, cold supper of ham, cheese, and buttered green beans from Cook's garden. It was the height of summer, and the vegetables were at their peak. Mr. Stillman had venison stew for today's supper and was gracious about finally receiving meat.

Later, Sabrina knocked on Mr. Stillman's door but was met with silence. She paused, then let herself into the room.

Mr. Stillman was asleep against the pillows, his head turned away from the door. The light from the lamp beside his bed reflected off his golden hair. His nightshirt lay open at the neck and chest, and a shimmer of attraction got the better of her. She thwarted her embarrassment with an immediate justification. What woman would not feel attraction to a man as handsome as Mr. Stillman?

To keep herself from being *too* admiring, however, Sabrina crossed the room and evened the curtains on the rod, then straightened the rug that was a few inches out of alignment in front of the hearth. She expected her movements might wake Mr. Stillman, though she was careful not to be too disruptive, but he still had not stirred by the time she'd run out of things to do. Her eyes landed on the bouquet of roses she had brought to his bedside last Saturday.

The blooms were still vibrant, but some were beginning to droop at the neck. She rearranged the order so those with hanging heads were in the center and pulled off a few of the petals that had begun to dry at the edge. Rubbing the wilting petals between her fingers released a bit of fragrance, and she inhaled the perfume deeply. There was a small bowl filled with leaves set beside the bouquet, and she lifted one to her nose—mint. The plant was a remedy for nausea, which Mr. Stillman had certainly been experiencing, but a tea would be more effective than smelling or chewing the leaves.

Sabrina turned toward the door, thinking that she would look in on him again after she read the day's papers, but the sound of Mr. Stillman shifting spurred her to turn toward him. He was not awake, however, simply adjusting his shoulders as he turned his head to the other side of the pillow—facing her. His braced leg prevented him from moving much more than that. He smacked his lips and then settled back into sleep. What was it about sleeping that made everyone look so angelic?

She watched him for several seconds, then was turning back to the door when she noticed something peeking out from beneath the covers beside him. It was dark but smooth, reflecting the candlelight. Sabrina took a few steps closer to the bed, then stopped abruptly. The top of a bottle?

She marched across the remaining space, reached over him, and pulled at the neck of the bottle.

He woke suddenly, his eyes wide, and shrank into the pillow, to stunned to try to stop her.

"W-what?" He blinked at her, then looked at the bottle held in her fist, then back to her face and then to the place where the bottle had been. The stupidity of his reflexes spiked her rage another degree.

"Where did you get this?" she demanded. He had invited Joshua to play cards. Had he also convinced Joshua to bring him liquor? Had he worked his charms on a maid? No, she recognized the label as a brand a servant would not be able to afford. And Mr. Stillman had no money to pay for himself. She stared at Mr. Stillman, her chest prickling with indignation. "Where?"

"I, uh . . . You were not supposed to find that." He pointed at her, a bit wobbly. Is this what Therese had interpreted as cheerful? How had the nurse not noticed her patient's misery was alleviated because he was keeping himself in the drink?

"I'm sure that I wasn't."

"L-Lady Sabrina," he said in a nearly even voice. "Let me explain." He reached a hand toward her, and she glared at him. Did he honestly think she would return the bottle to him? "I have been very ill, more than you can imagine and—"

She had no tolerance for his justifications and lifted the bottle as high as she could, holding it long enough for Mr. Stillman to understand her intent. His eyes went wide, and his mouth dropped open right before she threw the bottle against the fireplace hearth. The brown glass shattered and a spray of brandy doused that part of the room, a few drops splashing far enough to catch her hemline.

She did not flinch as she glared at him, hands on her hips. "You ungrateful, dissolute, ape of a man!"

He stared at the mess on the floor, then turned frantic eyes in her direction. His mouth was open, but he had no words.

She, however, had plenty to say. "After all we have done for you, you not only defy my rules but you betray your own healing by going right back to the proverbial vomit that landed you in that alley in the first place!"

His cheeks were in high color as his expression tightened. "You gave me ale and one pathetic glass of sherry. I was dying!"

"*My* ale and *my* sherry given to you at *my* expense in *my* house," she snapped, wishing she could yell louder. "How dare you throw all that away. How dare you spit in the face of our compassion!"

He stared at her another moment, then crumpled beneath her rage. The look in his eyes went from shocked and angry to scared and pleading. "I just needed a little bit to help me through the shakes and the d-delusions—I was going mad."

"I should take you back to where I found you and retract the—" She stopped herself mere syllables away from saying she would retract Lord Damion's payment on his debts. Being that close to revealing herself cooled her enough to think more rationally. She took a deep breath as the door flew open. She turned to see Joshua, his eyes wide as he ran into the room.

"What is—Lady Sabrina?" He looked between Harry and Sabrina, who were both red-faced, and then to the glass all over the floor. The room reeked of brandy.

Therese appeared behind Joshua and took in the scene. "Gracious," she said in a tone of both shock and concern. "What has happened?"

Mr. Stillman hung his head petulantly. "I only meant to stave off the worst of the misery."

Pathetic ingrate! "Who got it for you, Mr. Stillman? I will have a name," Sabrina demanded.

"I thought I could manage. I only—"

"Who brought it?" she said between clenched teeth. Then she turned to Therese. "I want every member of the staff called here *right now*. We will find the culprit, and so help me, I shall turn them out and—"

"Ward," Mr. Stillman finally said like a cry.

Sabrina spun back toward him. When she'd met Mr. Ward before she had left for London, he had been all smiles and gracious thanks. But he was the only friend Mr. Stillman had left, which meant she should have realized he would have been a scoundrel himself. She had been so distracted by her fear that he might reveal their situation that she had not considered how he might compromise Mr. Stillman's care.

"When?" she demanded.

"O-on S-Sunday."

Sabrina looked at the shards of glass left from the bottle. Mr. Ward had smuggled in the bottle?

Therese cleared her throat. "Lady Sabrina," she said carefully. "Mr. Ward brought Mr. Stillman's trunk when he came on Sunday, and they requested privacy to sort it together before turning the clothing over to me to have it laundered. I hadn't even thought he would have brought drink into the house. I should have been more attentive."

"This is certainly not upon your shoulders, Therese." Sabrina glared at Mr. Stillman. The trunk! How could she not have anticipated such deception? "You trusted that Mr. Stillman *and* Mr. Ward would be as determined about his recovery as we have been, yet it seems that neither of them has half the consideration for what it means to be respectable."

Mr. Stillman held his face in his hands and began to cry like a child.

Sabrina remained unmoved, her hands clenched into fists at her side.

"Joshua," Sabrina said through tight teeth. "Search this room. If there is more liquor here, Mr. Stillman will watch all of it meet the same fate as this bottle has."

Mr. Stillman's head snapped up, and the panic on his face confirmed Sabrina's suspicions that one bottle was not enough to have sustained him this well for this long.

Joshua threw open the wardrobe doors, the creaking hinges echoing in the otherwise quiet room.

"It is here," Mr. Stillman said quietly.

Sabrina spun from watching Joshua, her chest heaving with indignation. "What?"

Mr. Stillman swallowed and then threw back the covers of his bed, revealing his well-muscled legs, which he tried to cover by pulling down the hem of his nightshirt, which reached his knees. Even his modesty was infuriating.

Sabrina strode toward him and pulled the covers down the rest of the way, hanging them off the footboard and exposing two bottles at the base of the bed. Each bottle had a string tied around the neck that was then tucked beneath the pillows at the head. The strings would allow Mr. Stillman to pull the bottles up from their hiding place, though she didn't know how he got them back down. Clever. And so very disappointing. A quick inspection revealed that one bottle was empty and one full.

"Joshua," she said, her voice calm.

The footman peered from behind the door of the wardrobe, then came to her as she held the full bottle toward him.

"Smash it on the hearth, just as I did the other."

"Ma'am?" he said, sounding pained.

She turned her look on him, and he snapped into action. He took the bottle and crossed to the hearth. Lifting it, he looked first at Sabrina, then at his mother, who stood near the door, her eyes wide and her hands clasped tightly in front of her.

"Do as she says, of course," Therese said, and while it bothered Sabrina that Joshua hadn't obeyed her orders, she understood why. The boy held half a year's wages in his hands.

Joshua lifted the bottle higher.

"Wait," she said, a sudden idea occurring to her.

Joshua fumbled to stop himself, pulling the bottle close to his chest to keep from dropping it.

"Go to Fordman's pub instead, Joshua," she said, "and ask Mr. Fordman if he would be willing to buy that bottle. If he offers a decent price, I want you to sell it. You and Therese will each get a quarter of the proceeds, and the other half will be split between the staff who have also taken on the responsibility of Mr. Stillman's care this last week."

She stared at Mr. Stillman, who was pulling the covers up as though that might protect him from her anger. He was bent over like an old man, shoulders curved in.

"At least that will give some benefit to these people for the care they have given you, Mr. Stillman. All of them will be starting over with the worst of it come morning when you once again will be denied the liquor that is killing you."

He did not look up at her. "I am so sorry. I just could not—"

"An apology followed by a justification is no apology at all! But you will have plenty of time to feel the error of your choice. You will have nothing going forward. No ale. No sherry."

She watched him swallow. She lifted the empty bottle and crossed to the mantel, glass crunching beneath her shoes. She placed the bottle dead center, pleased with the way Mr. Stillman stared at it. She hoped that every time he saw it, he was assaulted with a fresh wave of longing.

He turned frightened eyes to her. "Are you going to turn me out?"

"And to whom would you go, Mr. Stillman? Your family, who will have nothing to do with you? Your friend, Mr. Ward, who would rather put you in the gutter himself than support your care? You are in the household of a stranger because you have created a life empty of anyone who would come to your aid!"

She could see the barbs of her words cutting through him, and she evened her tone, wanting to deliver her message as directly and surely as she possibly could. If all he heard was her anger, he would learn nothing. "I brought you to my home and bid my staff to care for you as I would a member of my own family, and you repay us this way."

"I am so sorry."

Surprisingly, she believed him. A sincere apology did not undo what he'd done, however. "Should you defy my orders again, you will be taken to the nearest church and left to their mercy. I can promise you that, while their hearts might be bigger than mine, their capacity to help you will not be."

He raised his hands to his face, and his shoulders began to shake.

She held herself hard against his crying, knowing she could not trust it as sincere, and turned to Joshua, whose eyes were huge in his round face. She had never lost her temper in front of her staff, and she hated how much like Richard she likely appeared to them right now.

"You may go to Fordman's now, Joshua. Bring what you can get for the bottle to my study when you return." She turned to Therese. "I want Mr. Stillman left alone for the next hour. After that, you may bring him a glass of *warm milk*. Constance can come with you to clean up the mess of the brandy and the broken bottle after he's had plenty of time to smell it."

Joshua and Therese nodded their agreement to her orders and left the room, the door standing open behind them.

Sabrina turned back to Mr. Stillman. "Have you anything to say, sir?"

"I'm sorry," he said, still crying behind his hands. "I just . . . I just c-can't do this. I am n-not a s-strong man."

"You *can* do this, Mr. Stillman. Whether or not you *will* do it, however, shall ultimately be up to you. I shall write to Mr. Ward my exact thoughts on his part in this and make it clear that he is not welcome if he is not willing to obey my rules. One more step out of line from either of you and I will be finished with you, is that understood?"

He finally lowered his hands, the redness of his face competing with the lingering yellows and greens of his bruises. "Do not blame Mr. Ward. He was trying to help me."

"That either of you thinks liquor will *help* you shows both of you as the idiots you are."

He nodded pathetically, his shoulders drooping as he looked at his hands in his lap.

Sabrina squelched the sympathy rising up in her as his body curled inward and his head fell forward. The other men she had helped turn their lives around had faced their demons far away from her. She followed their progress through Mr. Gordon, who would receive letters from time to time. Seeing the difficulty up close made the struggle these men faced in changing their lives much more real.

If she could relay her sympathy without obstructing the process Mr. Stillman had to endure to achieve the wellness he needed, she'd have done it. But she needed to keep her authority in hand, so she turned on her heel and stormed from the room, slamming the door behind her hard enough to shake the entire room.

Chapter Sixteen

*H*arry's misery began anew the next morning. The monkeys were back, his belly burned, he both sweated and froze beneath the covers, and he wished he was dead all over again. Through it all, he took turns cursing Lady Sabrina and Ward but mostly his own pathetic weakness. Neither of the people he cursed came to see him, and he vacillated between fighting Therese's ministrations when she tended to him and thanking her through gracious tears. She remained steady and calm and hummed what he thought were hymns that lulled him to sleep.

The endless days of misery allowed him to ask himself how he had come to this, and it was as if he had lifted the lid of a very ugly box, the hinges corroded and bent as though to keep it closed.

Once the lid was open, however, remembrances of his life began to filter into his mind—things he had not thought on for years. He thought of the way his father's eyes would darken without warning before he would harangue Harry as worthless and stupid and a pathetic son. "What have I done to be saddled with such a son as you?"

Harry would run to his mother for comfort, and she coddled and cooed over him. Then his parents would fight—loud and long and horrible—and he knew it was his fault, and he would promise never to put his mother in that position again. Until next time.

As Harry got older, his father got meaner, and Harry grew to hate anyone in authority over him. His rebelliousness led to punishment at school, which only spurred on his defiance—a power in itself. Other boys were drawn to what looked like strength, and he reveled in the attention.

When necessary, however, he could be docile and attentive, which helped in his relations with the fairer sex. What a lovely distraction women had turned out to be, further drowning out his father's voice, which had kept up a steady berating in the back of his mind all of his life.

Harry stopped coming home on school holidays, going with friends instead and raising Cain wherever they ended up. He was young and full of furious energy and determined to be noticed.

Father died just in time for Harry to use his inheritance to fuel a raucous campaign through London—women and brawls, drink and gaming tables. The memories swirled like fire in Harry's head, faces of old friends who fell by the wayside when some scrape or another pushed their parents' patience to the brink. How many girls of fine family had he seduced in dark corners? How many women of low family had he never even looked in the eye? How many friends had he humiliated in one way or another, left behind when he had no use for them, or poked and kicked at until they left him for good?

Have I ever done a good thing? he wondered as scene after scene played out more pathetically than the last. *Have I ever been a benefit to anyone who trusted me?*

What if he continued to live the way he'd lived his life thus far? What if ten years from now he was still exactly here—friendless, hopeless, homeless, broken, alone? He had no doubt that was exactly what would happen if he didn't do what Lady Sabrina had told him to do—commit to make different choices. Every day. Lord Damion had believed in him enough to rescue him from utter ruin, and Lady Sabrina believed he could use the beating as a place to grow from. Be better. Do better. He had an opportunity right now to be what he'd never been before.

"The only people who cannot change are those who are unwilling to face the pain behind the poor choices they have made. Certainly, there are *those people. You, however, are not one of them."*

Lady Sabrina's words became a mantra. If he was the only person who could change himself, then he alone had to be different. He had to be fair. Honest. Trustworthy. He had to think of more than just his desires. He needed positive relationships. He needed accomplishments he could take pride in.

He had to find a different way to drown out the words of his father. It had been so long ago; why had he not outgrown the fear that he was exactly what his father had said he was? Lady Sabrina had said something about how pain drove him to live in such excess, and it was not difficult to admit how those childhood memories faded when he was drunk or flirting or gaming.

What if instead of running from that voice, he could prove it wrong? What if instead of being angry and hurt at the words, he lived a life that proved himself otherwise?

There was power in that. A new power. A power that drew him from the muck of his history until the thought of another drink sickened him. The image of another loose woman smiling at him made his blood run cold with shame. Cards would always be set against him. Friends he made in dark corners were there because of the darkness within themselves, just like him.

"Asking the right questions will lead you to the answers that most men do not really want to find."

"Dear God in Heaven," he whispered into the dark on a night that had blended and blurred with all the other nights until he did not know if there had been two or twenty. "Help me ask the right questions. Help me be a better man."

Lady Sabrina thought he could do it. Lord Damion thought he could do it. What if he believed them instead of his father, who had never actually known him and who had been driven by a darkness that Harry logically knew had nothing to do with him? What if the biggest step was *wanting* to be different, better, more?

Help me.

Help me.

Help me.

In the early morning, Harry woke up in a nightshirt not soaked with sweat in time to watch the sun rise through the open window. Therese believed the natural light was good for him.

First the sky turned from gray to peach, then pink, then a color he could not name. Orange, maybe, but still pink. And purple too. The birds began to praise the dawn, and he watched as the first brush of sunlight changed the sky to gold. The first day. The start of a new life.

Harry thought of Falconridge, his childhood home. He did not know when he'd last seen a sunrise in Falconridge, but he knew he'd admired more than one in his past. His memories of any other sunrise could not compete with witnessing this event afresh, however. The gauzy reverence of the experience washed through him with every breath, and when a hawk, or some such similar bird, came into view, and the morning sunlight reflected off its wings, Harry felt as near a spiritual epiphany as he'd ever felt in his life.

There was beauty to be seen if one simply took the time to behold it.

The past was not greater than the present.

Who he had been was not stronger than who he was now.

Who he could be in the future would grow from who he chose to be today.

He watched the morning light grow until the sun was a ball of fire that possessed the sky, forcing him to move his gaze to the ceiling so as not to be blinded. The way the sun bathed him in light felt like a sacrament.

He took a breath, stretched his fingers and toes and appreciated the parts of his body that still ached from the beating. His mind felt better than it ever had. Than he could ever remember.

"I will not forget this," he said to the ceiling and to the God he wanted to believe was above it. "O Lord, thou hast brought up my soul from the grave: thou hast kept me alive, that I should not go down to the pit."

He did not know where he remembered the psalm from—he'd never been a churchgoing man—but the words of it felt seared into his mind and into his chest. Another phrase followed the first: "weeping may endure for a night, but joy cometh in the morning."

He felt tears in his eyes at the realization that he was not completely alone. Not yet. Perhaps it required his invitation for this God he'd never quite believed in to reveal Himself.

Chapter Seventeen

When Therese brought him toast for breakfast, Harry dared to eat it and asked if he might also have eggs. For lunch he had soup, then he slept through the afternoon and woke up feeling even better than he had that morning.

Hopeful. Alive. Strong.

Forgiven?

Therese brought him tea, and he was able to pull himself to a seated position, his splinted leg hurting only a little. Performing the task by himself made the discomfort worthwhile.

"Thank you, Therese." His mouth watered as she set the tea tray over his lap. He lifted the thick slice of bread spread with butter and took a bite, relishing the taste of salty butter that filled his mouth and slid down his throat. He felt so much more aware of everything—the colors of sunrise, the smoothness of butter, the kindness of Therese.

"You are welcome, Mr. Stillman." She watched him with a wariness he understood. He'd lost the trust of all these people. He hoped he would be able to earn back some portion of it.

He watched Therese move about the room, setting out a

clean nightshirt—she always helped him dress in a fresh one before bed—and straightening the room. She was humming again.
Servants in Harry's life had always been silent creatures who attended to his needs without his awareness most of the time. The
only servant from his youth he remembered by name was Mrs.
Horace, a cook whom he could charm into giving him an extra chicken leg now and again. The rest were faceless forms who
moved out of a room when he came into it, fetching trays and
clearing linens.

"How long have you worked for Lady Sabrina, Therese?"

"I came with the house." She moved to the opposite side of
the bed where she straightened the bedclothes on that side and
fluffed pillows he did not use.

He smiled at what he thought might be banter. "And how
long has Lady Sabrina had the house?"

She paused, looking at him as though weighing what she
ought to tell him. Was it loyalty or fear that kept her from sharing
information? From his interactions with Lady Sabrina he suspected fear; she was as intimidating as any woman he'd ever met.

"I am only curious," he said, hoping to put her at ease.
"Where did you grow up?"

"Here in Wimbledon, off Avondale Road," Therese said. "My
father was a surgeon here in town. I very much wanted to follow
in his footsteps, but, alas, I was far too female."

The prospect of conversation coupled with her humor was
invigorating, and Harry grinned. "England's medical association
lost that round, then. You have been very attentive to me, even
though I've been quite a terrible patient. Thank you for your
ministrations and patience." It felt remarkably good to tell the
truth for no other reason than wanting Therese to know. He
didn't want to manipulate her or impress her. Just thank her.

"You have not been a terrible patient," she said, but she did send him a direct look. Her steel-gray hair was gathered into a knot at the base of her head, with a few locks that hung in soft waves about her face. Wire-rimmed spectacles framed hazel eyes set within a lined face that reflected an age near to his mother's when she had passed. "When you are sober, you are quite gracious and accommodating, Mr. Stillman. Most men, in my experience, resent being cared for. You have taken to it rather well, save for the parts surrounding drink."

That her mention of drink did not make the hunger rise up was encouraging. He took another bite of bread, nearly moaning in the pleasure of it. After he swallowed, he spoke again. "Perhaps I simply like to be taken care of by beautiful women."

"Do not try to charm me, young man," she said, wagging her finger at him, but smiling all the same. Therese was in her fifties with a lovely smile and very nice bone structure. He told her so, and she blushed. Again, he told her the truth for the sake of it, and again, it felt good.

"I've never been to Wimbledon before, but what I have seen is quite lovely." All of this one room. And a sunrise. "Tell me about growing up here."

Therese surprised him by not waving off his questions and instead sat in the chair beside his bed. For nearly half an hour she talked of her childhood as he crafted one question after another that drew her story out. The more she said, the more . . . real she became. She'd lived a whole life, with relationships, a fine son, and work she enjoyed. The pride she took in her accomplishments showed on her face as she spoke. She seemed happy with her life.

Happy.

A servant.

Harry did not need to think about if he had ever been happy. He'd always felt the need to do something, go somewhere, get away, feel this pleasure, best this man, prevail in this situation or that one. Perhaps you could not be happy if you only ever wanted something different than what you had. Perhaps being happy with what you had was the first step.

" . . . then I was hired on as a caretaker for the late Mrs. Carlisle when the house was built," she said when Therese's story reached her young adult years. "My husband was hired as a driver, and we were given the quarters behind the carriage house."

"Who is Mrs. Carlisle?"

"Richard's mother."

"And who is Richard?"

"Lady Sabrina's late husband."

"Not Lord Richard or some such title?" Harry asked. "Didn't he have to have been a lord for her to be a lady?"

Therese's expression flattened as she looked at him. "I won't speak of Lady Sabrina, Mr. Stillman."

"Oh, no, of course," Harry said, waving his hand through the air as though he understood. But he didn't. If she didn't wear her husband's title, then it would be her father's, which would make him at least an earl in rank, or higher. Gracious, who was her father? Ward had said something about Lady Sabrina's history, but Therese looked as though she might be preparing to leave so he hurried to ask another question. The bread was long finished, but Harry sipped his cold tea slowly to prolong Therese's company.

"What year was the house built?"

She considered a moment and must have decided it was not a threatening question to her employer. "It was 1804."

Harry lifted his eyebrows, though his skin seemed to have lost its ability to move in all the ways it used to. He would be grateful when his bruises healed and faded. "You have worked in this household for twenty years?"

"Twenty-one."

He nodded. "I was estimating. Will I meet your husband?"

Her smile fell slightly. "He passed away when Joshua was eight years old. He'd never had strong lungs, and when typhus came through . . ." She looked at the floor.

"I am very sorry, Therese," Harry said quietly, wondering if anyone would mourn him should his lungs not be strong and typhus come through again.

"It was a long time ago," she said, then stood. "We all have our trouble."

"You must like it here," he added quickly. "To have stayed on, I mean."

"I do," she said, nodding as she straightened her gray skirt. "The Carlisle women are the best of them."

Harry noticed she did not mention the Carlisle men. Something niggled at him, something about Lady Sabrina's late husband, only he could not pluck it from the pot of his jumbled memories. The details were mixed in with the other ones about her parentage. He would need to sort it out later.

"You think quite highly of Lady Sabrina." Her rage last week had been so much like his father's that he felt unsettled at the thought of seeing her again, though it was inevitable.

"She is remarkable, sir. As generous as the day is long and as smart as those Tories in Parliament, mark my word."

"She does, um, have a bit of a temper, though, doesn't she?"

Therese's face closed off like the turning of a spigot, and she straightened. "I should warn you, Mr. Stillman, that no one speaks a cross word about Lady Sabrina in this household. I withstood your rantings these last days because you were out of your mind. Now that you are restored, I would caution you against speaking too freely. We will not tolerate anything said against her."

"I meant no offense," Harry said quickly, not wanting to damage the accord he had felt building throughout their conversation. "I am very grateful to her. Most women would not do any of what she's done for me."

Therese looked at him as though trying to determine if he were sincere or not. She softened slightly, nodded, and took the tray from his lap. "I shall return in an hour to ready you for bed."

"Could I bother you for a pen and some paper?" Harry said quickly.

He'd been thinking all day of the letters he needed to write to the people he owed apologies per Lord Damion's instruction. He should have written them before now, but then there were a lot of things he should have done before now.

He had written to Uncle Elliott last week about needing a place to go when he was fit to travel, but his words had been hasty and desperate as he'd still been sick. He'd not apologized to his uncle the way he needed to, only begged to be cared for when he had to leave here. Harry wasn't sure he could repair the relationships he'd let break around him these last years, but it would feel good to at least try, and his mind was finally clear enough to make the attempt.

"I will send Joshua up to help you into a chair," Therese said.

Instant fear shot down Harry's spine at the thought of leaving his bed. "I-is that wise?"

"I'd hoped to have you sitting up in the first week," Therese said. "And it will be more comfortable for you to write at a desk than in bed." She nodded toward the small writing desk set beneath the window. "I'll follow with the instruments and paper you will need." She smiled at him encouragingly. "Do not worry, Mr. Stillman, I am quite sure you will triumph against this challenge."

He looked at her, serious despite her attempt to be light. "I will take your confidence in me as my own, then. It seems beyond me, truth be told."

She laughed. He did not.

Chapter Eighteen

*S*abrina returned to London the morning following her tirade against Mr. Stillman and threw herself into the details of Nathan's dinner party regardless of whether or not those issues actually required her attention. She obsessively reviewed every element with every staff member overseeing every portion of the event, followed up with suppliers, and even folded all the napkins herself into the shape of a swan. One of the schools she'd attended had spent three weeks of classes on napkin folding instead of math, of course, because why would a woman need to factor interest payments or forecast expenses or determine the price per square foot of a factory in Leeds?

On Friday, Sabrina gave orders, fussed over the flowers when they were delivered, and rearranged the centerpieces four times before the guests began to arrive and she transformed from the organizer into the hostess. Nathan's staff was likely ready to hang her for overmanaging the situation, but she needed the distraction, and there had not been a better option of focus. Besides, overmanagement was hardly a capital offense.

The dinner consisted of separate courses of bouillie, entree of sole, a cucumber salad, and braised beef with burgundy sauce for the entrée, all paired with the perfect red wine. The dessert was a fresh strawberry tart—a simple but delicious dessert to balance the elaborate flavors of the other courses. After dinner, there were two musical performances, a harp piece and a vocal ensemble, that everyone seemed to enjoy. No one was in a hurry to leave after the performances, and the party continued for hours.

Whether or not it was Sabrina's attention to detail that made the party a success, she could never know, but she chose to believe so as she began saying goodbye to their guests. It was after midnight when she walked Mr. and Mrs. Proctor to the door.

"I hope you have a wonderful time in Naples," Mrs. Proctor said, giving Sabrina a quick embrace.

The Proctors were not the first friends to mention the trip, but once again, Sabrina had forgotten all about it. She could blame the Season coming to a close as the reason behind her distractibility, but she suspected her lack of focus was mostly due to Mr. Stillman. He had become such a large presence in her mind that the travel she'd spent months planning had been forced to give way.

After the door closed behind the Proctors, Sabrina turned and let out a breath, allowing herself to feel the pride of a job well done. She made her way to the library where Nathan and a handful of his friends were still laughing and talking. They would likely continue through the early hours of morning, then wander off to their rooms amid the city and sleep half of the day away tomorrow. After that, the four winds would take them wherever it would.

"Ah, there she is."

Sabrina stopped a step into the room and lifted her eyebrows toward the speaker, Lord Towershod. All the men stood in belated chivalry.

"I'm pleased to know you are not so drunk as to not recognize me, Lord Towershod. What a positive step toward your reformation. Your mother will be so pleased to hear it."

The men roared with laughter and flopped back into their various chairs and sofas.

"Lady Sabrina," Mr. Lawson said, "would you *please* marry me before I have to leave London? *My* mother will be ever so disappointed when I return, yet again, without a wife."

Sabrina tsked and shook her head. "My answer will always be the same, Mr. Lawson. You could not possibly match a wife like me, not with wealth nor wit."

Another bout of laughter erupted, and Sabrina smiled at the men's good humor as she crossed to Nathan, sitting in one of the chairs near the fire, looking exhausted but happy. He'd kicked off his shoes, at ease now that he could be. She leaned in to kiss him on the cheek.

"You are off, then?" Nathan said as she straightened.

"I am back to Wimbledon first thing in the morning." What would her first interaction with Mr. Stillman be like? Should she keep a firm position or soften? Would he be sufficiently dried out by now for them to interact reasonably?

Nathan pushed himself up from the chair. "Let me walk you out, then."

"No, let *me* walk you out, Lady Sabrina," Mr. Lawson said, springing to his feet and bending sharply at the waist.

"No, no, let me," another man said.

Nathan did his best to click his stockinged heels together as he looked down his nose at the roomful of men. "She is *my* sister, and I shall defend her against you devils to my last breath. *I* shall keep my right to walk her to the door." Nathan jutted out his elbow, which Sabrina took while rolling her eyes.

The men groaned in good-natured protest and called out their goodbyes as she and Nathan exited the room.

"I cannot thank you enough for all you have done for me these last months, Sabrina," Nathan said as they passed through the great hall. "I would not be half the man I am without all the effort you have put into establishing me here in London. Thank you."

"You are welcome," she said, squeezing his arm and then letting go. "But you have done me far more good than I have ever done you."

"Do not speak that way," Nathan said, shaking his head.

"I won't, then, but only because I know it makes you uncomfortable. I am grateful, though, and glad to be a part of your life."

She would have been little more than a whisper behind hands if not for Nathan having treated her like a full sister. After losing the baby and then Richard's death, she'd hidden in Wimbledon, but Nathan had drawn her out, and the ways she had grown through that challenge had made all the difference. It felt good to be able to return some of his favor through acting as his hostess.

They reached the foyer, and Nathan touched her arm, indicating he wanted to say something else. He would be on to Cambridgeshire by Monday, and the hushed seriousness of his expression reminded her that this was their goodbye.

"Did you have chance to speak with Lady Carolyn tonight?" Nathan asked.

The anxiety in his expression made her smile. "I did. She's a lovely woman, Nathan. I like her very much."

"You approve, then?"

"Completely," Sabrina said, touched that her opinion meant so much to him.

"We are thinking of a February wedding. Will you be returned from Naples by then?"

Sabrina's eyebrows shot up. "You have discussed timelines?"

He nodded nervously. "I know it is not usually done, but does that not seem to be a silly thing? I did not want to pursue a match if she did not welcome it, and we are living in a modern age after all. I also wanted to make sure she would be comfortable with such a wait."

"Seven months is a very long engagement, Nathan."

"You do not return until January, I believe, and then we shall have to be back in London for Parliament."

Sabrina swallowed against the sudden thickening of her throat. "You are waiting on the wedding for my return?" she said quietly.

"Of course."

"Nathan," she said, putting her hand on his arm. "You should not wait so long on my account. It is not fair to Lady Carolyn, and the duchess will be displeased."

"Lady Carolyn had no hesitation when I explained my reasons, and Mother is not a consideration. She knows my regard for you and has even acknowledged the service you have done for me these last years. I am telling you this only to confirm when you will return so that we might move forward with the planning."

The duchess had acknowledged Sabrina's help for Nathan? Sabrina had not seen Lady Anglesey for nearly ten years—she'd been traveling the month Sabrina had spent at Hilltop Manor, the only time Sabrina had returned to the family estate after her marriage. The unexpected acknowledgment did not lead Sabrina to think their relationship would change, but it was nice to hear all the same.

"So, when do you return?" Nathan asked again.

"I am supposed to arrive in Brighton near the middle of January; I don't know an exact date."

"Then if we were to plan for, say, February 20, you would be here in time to help me pick my wedding clothes."

"The duchess will help you pick your wedding clothes," Sabrina said.

Nathan shook his head. "She will dress me in the fashion of fifty years ago, you know how she is. That date will give you time, though?"

Sabrina laughed. "It shall be my first priority upon my return."

"Excellent." His smile softened. "I worry that my marriage will change the accord you and I have developed these last years, Sabrina. Will you promise not to stay away from London? I shall still need you and want your company. Lady Carolyn would benefit from your help as she steps into the household."

Sabrina laid a hand on his cheek. "You shan't be able to keep me away."

"Things will change, though, won't they?"

Sabrina lowered her hand and looked past him as if searching for the footman who had gone to fetch her cloak, but truthfully, she was avoiding Nathan's eyes. She didn't want him to see her fear for the future. "Things are always changing, Nathan, but we shall adapt."

"I worry for you, you know."

Sabrina smiled against the tightening inside her chest. Worrying felt like he did not trust her to manage herself.

"I know you hate for me to say such things, but I would feel such relief if I could see you settled and cared for."

Sabrina let out a hard laugh that broke the tenderness of their exchange. "I care for myself just fine, Nathan." She turned toward the door and began walking, but Nathan hurried to keep up with her.

"I know that as well as anyone," he said, speaking quickly. "If you were to marry, our lives would be in tandem once again, and we could move forward together. Our children would be cousins, go to school together, and—"

"No, Nathan," Sabrina cut in, looking from one side of the foyer to another. Where was the footman with her cloak?

"Sabrina." He took her arm and turned her toward him, lowering his voice to a whisper. "I know he was not good to you. I know you are frightened—"

"I am not frightened," Sabrina said, though that was a lie. "I am content with my situation as it is, that is all."

"There are men who have asked after you, you know," Nathan continued, dropping her arm. "They wonder how determined you are to remain independent and if it might be worth an attempt to capture your attention." He nodded toward the library where his friends were waiting for him, their laughter barely audible. "Mr. Lawson may seem to be joking, but he asks after you continually."

"Because he has no land and wants mine." She said the bitter words before she thought better. Nathan pulled back in surprise. She closed her eyes and shook her head, then tried to soften her tone. "I appreciate your concern for me, Nathan, but I have a full and rich life. I want for nothing, not in material or friends and connections."

She paused, considering how much she wanted to say, and

then chose to say a bit more than she was comfortable with in hopes it would help Nathan avoid this topic in the future. "Richard ruined me, Nathan, in more ways than I hope you can ever understand. I have never wanted to burden you with details, but my determination to remain independent is not a flippant decision. Trust me and allow me to find joy in all the beauty of my life, of which beauty you are a part."

She went up on her toes and kissed his cheek again, which was slack with surprise from what she'd told him. She did not share her burdens with the people she cared for because she did not want anyone to suffer for her sake any more than they already had.

"Lady Carolyn is a lucky woman to have the affection of such a good and kind man, Nathan. I shall look forward to the wedding in February, and I am touched that you would wait for me so that I might witness the happy day." She smiled, then turned and walked to the front door.

The footman finally appeared, hurrying forward to help her with her cloak.

Nathan followed her silently, then said gently, "I didn't mean to upset you, Sabrina. I am sorry."

Sabrina smiled brightly as she tied her cloak at the neck. "You did not upset me, Nathan. You never could. I wish you safe travels when you go on to Peterborough."

"Perhaps I could come to Rose Haven for a few days before I go."

"No," she said with a laugh to hide her panic at the idea. Nathan and Mr. Stillman in the same house? "That is silly."

"You do not want to spend time with me?" His face fell as it had when he was young and she was sent off to another faraway school while he remained at Hilltop Manor.

"It is not that," she said quickly. "I simply have to prepare for my trip, and you need no delay. We need Lady Carolyn's family to fall in love with you as much as she already has so they will not refuse a seven-month engagement."

Nathan nodded, though he remained petulant, and Sabrina patted his arm before heading through the door held open by the footman. It was raining, which would keep Nathan from following after her.

She pulled the hood over her head and hurried down the steps. She could not see Nathan clearly through the rain-streaked glass of the carriage window, but he stood in the doorway until the carriage pulled away.

The secrets she kept felt especially heavy as the carriage rumbled toward her apartment. Would there be a day when she no longer kept parts of herself hidden from the people in her life? Would it be possible for someone to truly see her, know her, and understand her?

Chapter Nineteen

When Sabrina returned to Wimbledon, she asked Therese to join her for afternoon tea so she could get an update. Things had apparently turned a corner for Mr. Stillman the day before, and he was like a new man, Therese said. The more she praised Mr. Stillman's charm and thoughtfulness, the more suspicion Sabrina felt toward the man. Was he fawning over her staff in order to earn their devotion that he could then use to his advantage?

"I mentioned you were returning today, and he asked if you might come speak to him," Therese said as she completed her update. "I think he wants to apologize for the row on Tuesday."

"You mean the row where he cried like a child because I took away his brandy?" She smiled, but Therese did not smile back. Sabrina sobered her expression appropriately.

"You know what drink does to a man, Sabrina. You cannot hold him completely accountable for his actions when he was under its control."

Sabrina bit back an argument partly because Therese was right—to an extent—but mostly because of how much she respected the older woman's opinion. Therese had been Hortencia's companion when Sabrina first came to Wimbledon as an anxious bride. She had tended to the bruises Sabrina had first blamed on narrow stairs and overall clumsiness.

When Richard "accidentally" dislocated Sabrina's shoulder shortly after his mother's passing, however, there had been no hiding the truth. Therese had Joshua help reset her shoulder—thinking on the pain of that still took her breath away—and then hid Sabrina in her quarters for three days, telling Richard that Sabrina had gone to stay with a friend. No one could hide a man's wife from him for long, however.

As things had become worse, Therese had asked Jack, the groom at that time, to show Sabrina how to break free from a man's grip on her arm and the proper way to hit a man at the bridge of his nose to cause the most pain.

Richard's violence did not stop—in fact, fighting back had made individual attacks worse—but when Sabrina was no longer an easy target, Richard began spending more and more time away from Rose Haven. Until he decided it was time to have an heir.

The six months following his return were the worst of Sabrina's life, though the months after that, once she was expecting, had been the very best. He'd been more careful with her, drank less, and she'd had such hope for the future.

After she lost the child, Sabrina could not stay at Wimbledon, and Therese had helped smuggle her to the Old Duke's principal estate. The duchess had been traveling, and the boys were away at school, leaving Sabrina with only her father. Sabrina had told the Old Duke of Richard's violence and the fear she felt for her very life now that there was no child between them. Though he was sympathetic for her position, he would not support a petition to Parliament for a divorce. Her very existence was scandal enough, he said, and he would not put the family through another one at her hand.

At *her* hand.

As though her illegitimacy was her fault. As though her husband's abuse was her fault.

That day had been a defining experience for Sabrina. Despite the financial care and education the Old Duke had extended to her throughout her life, what people thought of him was more important than her safety. He let her stay at Hilltop through the month to regain her strength, then planned to return with her to Wimbledon and give Richard a talking-to.

Sabrina had known the duke's "talk" would have no bearing on Richard, and she would suffer for having told. Her body was as broken from Richard's beating as her heart was broken from the loss of her baby. No one could, or would, protect her.

Sabrina had withdrawn to her room at Hilltop and stayed there. The doctor had told her there would be no more children. She had prayed and cried and prayed again. What could she expect from her marriage now that she could not give Richard the only thing he wanted from her? The only way out would be death, and she began to wish for it.

She had not considered that it would be Richard's death, not her own, that would free her.

Sabrina had returned to Wimbledon as the sole owner of the Carlisle family's holdings. Therese cried with her in relief, and then they had both knelt in the middle of the entryway and offered thanks to God for bringing Sabrina *safely* home. She became a new woman after that day, with a new life she herself could manage. She would not be a mother, but she would do what she could to make the world better for the lives she could reach.

Because of their history, Sabrina did not discard what Therese had to say on any matter. Even regarding Mr. Stillman.

"You think I should talk to him?" Sabrina asked, her own curiosity battling her hesitation.

"I do," Therese said. "With an open mind."

Sabrina furrowed her eyebrows. "An open mind?"

"I think you might enjoy his company if you would let down your guard."

Sabrina huffed, feeling oddly jealous of Therese's praise of him. Sabrina did not need anyone to tell her to have an "open mind" about anything. She was as open-minded as anyone she'd ever met.

"I have no interest in enjoying his company," she said as though the idea were preposterous and she felt no draw to him at all. "I simply need him to be healed so he might carry on with his life elsewhere. Have you heard from his family?"

Therese nodded. "Yes, his uncle has agreed to make his London house available as soon as Mr. Stillman is fit to travel. He will await our word on when he should meet him there. They will remain there until Mr. Stillman is fit for travel to Norfolkshire."

"Well, that is good news," Sabrina said. "How much longer do you feel he needs before he can remove?"

"Two more weeks at least," Therese said.

Sabrina nodded. She left for Brighton in three weeks and knowing Mr. Stillman would be gone before then was a relief. Right?

"Did you know he is a poet?"

Sabrina pulled her chin back. "What?"

"He writes poetry," Therese said, unable to hide her smile. "He wrote a poem for me after finishing his letters yesterday.

Would you like to hear it? It is not very long; he said it was Japanese."

"He knows Japanese?" Sabrina asked, wrinkling her nose, unsure what to make of this information.

Therese removed a small piece of paper from the bodice pocket of her dress and handed it to Sabrina, who took it tentatively.

> *Bold. Bright. Vibrant. True.*
> *Sunrise, and Therese will come.*
> *The summer starts anew.*

"It is a haiku," Sabrina said. "A form of poetry that originated in Japan."

Mr. Stillman's verse wasn't anything remarkable in Sabrina's opinion, other than the fact that he had written it at all. Haiku were not expected to rhyme, and she wasn't sure the pattern was correct either.

"I thought it was very sweet," Therese said. "It's been a long time since I've been compared to a sunset. He said the poem was the only means he had of showing me his gratitude." She shrugged as though she didn't care, but clearly Mr. Stillman was casting a spell on her.

"I am glad he expressed his thanks," Sabrina said, returning the paper to Therese.

"It proves he is more than a dissolute scoundrel."

"A scoundrel can still be a poet. One need only to look at Lord Byron to know that much."

Therese laughed, which made Sabrina laugh, then the housekeeper sobered. "Do you not think him handsome?"

"Therese! I'm sure I don't care if he is handsome or not."

Therese shrugged. "A handsome man who also writes poetry could make a woman very happy, I think."

Sabrina felt a flush in her cheeks. "I'll not hear another word about this, Therese. If I told you half of what I know about him, you would not let your mind wander down such paths."

Therese shrugged one shoulder and chose a shortbread from the tray. "A man's reputation is something to consider, but I do not think his past should define him completely. If he can prove himself able to rise above the foibles of his youth, of course." She shrugged again. "If I were twenty years younger, I might give you some competition."

"Therese!" Sabrina scolded again.

She laughed and popped the shortbread into her mouth before shooing Sabrina out of the room. If Sabrina had thought she had a good enough reason to stay, she would have, but she feared remaining would invite more of this conversation.

Designs on Mr. Stillman?

Really, Therese, do you not know me at all?

When she reached Mr. Stillman's door, Sabrina could not bring herself to knock. Therese's advice to have an open mind made her uncomfortable. What if Mr. Stillman had written her a poem as well? How should she react to such a gift?

What if he had *not* written her a poem?

Sabrina did not trust herself under the weight of her thoughts and so, after checking left and right to make sure she hadn't been observed standing before his door, she straightened her shoulders and went to her sitting room in the other wing of the house, where she kept herself busy until her mood settled.

As best she could, at least. It turned out that hiding a handsome poet in a spare bedroom was not something that lent itself to equanimity of mood all that well.

Chapter Twenty

Sabrina ate dinner in the dining room and worked in the study until Therese reported that Mr. Stillman was readied for bed and had asked again that they might speak. Sabrina, bent over a book laid open on her desk, nodded curtly and did not meet Therese's eye.

Once Therese had gone, Sabrina went to his room. She kept her back straight as she knocked, heard his invitation, and let herself into his room.

She left the door open, worried that if Therese had gotten the outlandish idea that Sabrina had designs on the man, the other staff could also fall prey to such nonsense if they noticed anything less than strict propriety.

He was sitting in bed, as always, and smiled at her sheepishly. The pink scars on his lip and forehead, and the slightest green tinge to the left side of his jaw, were all that remained of his facial injuries. His smile was radiant enough she could practically feel it on her skin.

She exchanged the wilting bouquet at his bedside with the new one she'd brought, and then she placed the spent one near the door so she could collect it on her way out. She turned back to him with her hands clasped before her, standing several feet from the bed. "You are looking much improved since the last time I saw you, Mr. Stillman."

"I believe I have finally moved through the worst of everything—the beating and my self-inflicted malady."

"I am glad to hear it. Therese tells me that yesterday and today have shown marked improvement."

He nodded. "Joshua helped me sit in a chair with my leg propped this afternoon. I looked out the window at your lovely roses. He says you tend them yourself."

"When I can, yes."

He paused, and his smile fell. "I wanted to apologize for my awful behavior last week." He closed his eyes a moment as though remembering just how awful it had been. "Both for having the bottles smuggled in and for not following the guidelines you had laid before me."

"You agree that you were wrong to have the bottles brought in, then?"

"Yes," he said with a nod. "Absolutely. Therese explained that I was through the worst of it when I began in on the bottle again—and thus suffered through the illness again. It was foolish and ungracious. I hope I have sufficiently paid for my folly."

"Yes, it was foolish."

He looked disappointed that she agreed so quickly, but she wanted him to feel every bit of his shame to ensure this never happened again. They fell into an awkward silence Sabrina refused to break.

Finally, Mr. Stillman cleared his throat. "I wondered if you had written to Mr. Ward as you had said you would. I have not heard from him."

"I did write to him and asked him to cease his visits if he could not comply with the standards of my household, but I did not forbid him to return. I pointed out that if he were any kind of friend to you he would be making choices in your best interest and not cowing to your dissolute vices that have done you no favors."

The way Mr. Stillman's face went slack made her think that perhaps she was being a bit heavy-handed, but she did not sit with the regrets for long. She had not wanted Mr. Ward's visits from the start, and it was his own fault that she now had cause to make him uncomfortable about returning.

"Did he respond?" Mr. Stillman finally asked.

"No, he did not. I assumed he would write to you, however, not to me. I was not particularly inviting about a response."

Harry nodded. "He is probably frightened."

She shrugged. She did not mind if Mr. Ward were frightened. Mr. Stillman was watching her as he always seemed to, and being the focus of his attention was disconcerting. She could not help but wonder what he saw when he looked at her with such intensity. A bitter woman of advancing years? An intriguing woman of grace and confidence?

The seconds ticked by until the discomfort was more than she could stand. "Well, I am pleased by your progress and commend you for your fortitude, Mr. Stillman. It is not an easy thing to break such habits. I am proud of you."

"You are proud of me?"

"Yes."

"As though I am a child?" His expression remained neutral.

She narrowed her eyes slightly. "As though you are a man having come through a hardship. Would you rather I were not proud of you?"

He seemed to consider that and then shrugged one shoulder.

She made a mental note not to be so patronizing. If she wanted him to respect her and her staff, she needed to show him the same consideration. She had wanted to discuss his poetry, but there was no space for it, and he had not offered her a poem as he had Therese.

"Well, I hope you have a good night and continue to heal." She turned to the door.

"Will you be staying here in Wimbledon for a time?" he asked quickly.

She faced him. "Yes. The Season is finished, and my responsibilities in Town are far reduced." She nearly told him of her upcoming trip but felt it too much an invitation into her privacy.

His face broke into a smile once again and, once again, she felt the change in the very air of the room. He was handsome without the smile; with it, he was absolutely disarming. She remembered having noticed the same thing on the first night they had met in the Gilmores' garden.

"That is wonderful news." He shifted, then winced.

She stepped toward the bed. "Are you all right?"

"Just a twinge. It happens when I move too quickly. You would be surprised how easy it is to forget that my leg is little more than a log attached to the knee."

The image of him having an actual log instead of a leg came to mind and, with his smile still casting magic, she felt a smile quirk her own lips. She cleared her throat in an attempt to hide it. "I imagine that is quite cumbersome."

"Very much so," he said, looking at the lump beneath the covers as though his leg were a foreign object. "It was wonderful to be upright today, but it has made the ache a bit more extreme tonight."

"You must be careful not to overdo it," Lady Sabrina chided, then wanted to roll her eyes at herself. Did she have to take the power position in every conversation?

"Yet it would be foolish to underdo things, would it not?" He did not wait for an answer and looked at her quickly with that disarming intensity again and just a hint of a smile as though waiting for her to permit a fuller one.

To test the theory, she smiled, and his full smile burst forth. Gracious.

"Do you play chess, Lady Sabrina?"

The change of subject surprised her. "Chess?"

He nodded. "Now that my brain does not feel as though it is nigh unto exploding, I feel a bit . . . restless. I remember liking chess a great deal when I was younger. There is a stone board at Falconridge—I hope it is still there—and my sister and I would wager all manner of things upon the game." He put up a hand. "I do not mean to imply a wager now; that is behind me." He lowered his hand and watched her expectantly.

"You want to play chess? With . . . me?"

"Unless you are either very good or very poor," he amended. "I am an average player and would not like to be too easily bested or make you feel inferior by beating you too soundly."

Goodness, he was charming—so much so that it was difficult to see the man from Tuesday within this man before her now.

He is a drunkard and a carouser, she told herself but then had to amend it. He *had been* a drunkard and a carouser. But he could also be thoughtful and funny. And a poet.

Circumstances could change a person if they chose to let them be the inciting incident of change.

"I have not played chess in some time," Sabrina finally admitted. "But there *is* a set here in the house somewhere. It used to be in the billiard room, which I've since turned into a second parlor. I could have it fetched. Perhaps we could play tomorrow evening."

His face fell, and she swallowed the instant desire to bring the smile back. "If you are looking for distraction at present, I can offer any number of books. What are your interests?"

"Well, to present my interests have not done me much credit. Books, I believe, are primarily focused upon things such as learning and improvement, which, as you know, has not been an area in which I have excelled."

She could not help but laugh, though the sound felt strange coming from her throat. In this room. Amid this company. "You are so very unfamiliar with books?"

"So *very* unfamiliar, I am afraid. I did read from the New Testament a few days ago, however. The language is too difficult to read all at once, I decided, and thought it would be best if I took time to mull over what I read."

She watched him carefully. Was this another attempt at manipulating her? Presenting himself as pious so she might lower her defenses? She would proceed with caution just in case. "I find reading a small amount of the Bible each day is the best way to become familiar with its stories and teachings. Perhaps you could do the same."

"That is good advice," he said with a nod and what sounded like true sincerity.

"The household's library includes an array of books on such topics as land management, agriculture, and animal husbandry. And history, primarily Grecian—the late Mr. Carlisle, my father-in-law, had a great penchant for all things Greek."

"Those topics sound exhausting," Mr. Stillman said.

She could not hold back her smile. "There are also a few

novels." She meant the suggestion as a joke—men did not read novels—but to her surprise, Mr. Stillman's eyes brightened.

"Have you something like *Gulliver's Travels*? I liked that one when I was in school."

"I do not believe so."

He lay back on the pillows. "Pity," he said.

"Indeed," she said. "Would you like me to make a list of what titles we have available so you might choose one to your liking?"

"That would only be effective if I had some idea of what I'm looking for, and I'm afraid I do not."

"What about . . . poetry?"

He narrowed his eyes. "Therese told you."

"She *showed* me," Sabrina clarified, tracing the curl of the footboard with her finger to avoid his gaze.

"It was not very good, but I did get the syllables right, or at least I think I did. It was supposed to be a haiku."

"You nearly got the syllables right," she confirmed. "And managed to incorporate the reference to a season, which many modern poets pass over. When did you first begin to write poetry?"

He smiled mischievously. "When all boys learn to write poetry—upon noticing the loveliness of girls for the first time and wanting to impress them." He shrugged self-consciously. "My literature teacher at the time loved poetry, practically crammed it down our throats, but I must admit—though you must promise not to tell any of my former schoolmates—that I grew to like it quite a bit. Then, of course, I grew older and wiser and knew it was folly to care for poetry, so I gave it up. Mostly. With my mind so much clearer than it has been for some time, however, it overtook my more practical thoughts, and I remembered that I have no will of my own when it comes to meter and rhyme and tempo."

He let out a dramatic sigh but did not laugh, which led Sabrina to believe he was being honest about his relationship to poetry yet stating it in a way that she could take it as a joke if she chose to. Many a truth was hidden in jest with Mr. Stillman, apparently. Though not well hidden—he was being surprisingly candid.

"There is a solid collection of Shakespeare in our library here," she offered.

He crinkled his nose.

"Donne?"

He brightened. "I do quite like Donne."

"I shall have Therese bring you a volume, then." His later work, she decided, after he'd joined the clergy. Some of his early work was rather scandalous, and Mr. Stillman did not need any more of that.

"That would be much appreciated," Mr. Stillman added. "Though a man cannot live on poetry alone. Do you think the chessboard could be found tomorrow? I think Donne can manage to keep me from madness if I have chess with you to look forward to."

With you, she repeated in her mind. "I shall see that it is found as soon as possible. Is there anything else I can do for you tonight?" She could have slapped herself—her offering to help him!

"Just having the chance to find accord with you has quite satisfied me. The only thing that could improve upon it would be a glass of warm milk." He smiled in such a way that the rake showed straight through.

She heard herself offer to tell Therese he was ready for his nightcap, then picked up the spent roses on her way out of the room. She paused in the hallway, holding the vase to her chest and reviewing the exchange. Even with all the associations she had enjoyed this week in London, none had left her feeling quite as light as this one.

Mr. Stillman is a dangerous man, she told herself, shaking her head. *A woman best be on her guard.*

He had managed to overcome one vice through Lord Damion's generosity and a second due to being unable to get his hands on a bottle. That left just one of his former vices for him to indulge in, and she would as soon swim across the channel as be the woman to fall in his way of becoming a better man.

Dangerous or not, though, she smiled on her way down the stairs. Only a little.

Chapter Twenty-One

*J*oshua located the chess set in one of the storage rooms at the top of the house. Made of mahogany and alder squares, the board fastened to a pedestal, making it into a small table. The matching chess pieces were individually wrapped in felt and stored in a latched cherrywood box.

Sabrina inspected the set, imagining Richard's parents playing the game in the evening, though she'd never seen them do so. They had both been in poor health by the time Richard and Sabrina had married; she'd later learned they had practically begged Richard to find a wife before they died. Of course, they had wanted a grandchild from that union, but that was not to be.

Sabrina would never understand how such kind and devoted parents had produced such a cruel son. The best she could determine was that he'd been mistreated in his early school years and, over time, learned to be the bully instead of the victim. He'd also become a gambler and a drunk, which only fueled his baser traits. Saving young men on a similar course was in part an attempt to save them from becoming like Richard themselves.

"Please have this taken to Mr. Stillman's room," Sabrina said, stepping back from the chessboard.

"Yes, ma'am."

She fetched her wide-brimmed straw hat, the one with a tear in the center where she'd stepped on it a few years earlier, then found the leather gloves, clippers, and basket she used for tending Hortencia's roses. For the next three hours, she weeded, pruned, and inspected each shrub, taking immense pleasure in seeing how each one was flourishing while also planning out the things she needed to do before her trip.

That night after supper—chicken with wild mushrooms and new potatoes in garlic sauce—Sabrina made her way to Mr. Stillman's room, irritated by the nervous bubbling in her stomach. Until now, she had been the benefactress and he the patient. Playing chess with him could invite a change in their relationship, and she wasn't sure how to manage that.

He was not someone of high society, where she knew what topics of discussion were expected. And yet he was not an employee either, someone whom she could manage with demanding graciousness. Then she realized the other reason for her trepidation—beyond status and position, Mr. Stillman was a man. A handsome one, as Therese had pointed out, and a vulnerable one.

She knew more about him than he thought—or rather Lord Damion did—and it gave her the upper hand. Yet when he smiled at her and his eyes pinned her in place, she felt herself tempted to be submissive. It was not a comfortable feeling. Since gaining her independence, Sabrina had become strong and powerful, apt to take the lead when necessary, and confident in her capabilities. She would need to watch herself in his company and make sure she kept her place within their dynamic.

Mr. Stillman brightened when she came into the room, but

it took several minutes for Sabrina to feel as comfortable. Joshua had placed the chessboard next to the bed so the edge overlapped the mattress enough for Mr. Stillman to move his pieces easily.

Sabrina introduced politics as the first topic of conversation because it was a comfortable one for her. It was soon apparent that Mr. Stillman was terribly ignorant of the power dynamics of London. The discussion ended with her lecturing him on his civic responsibility to be mindful of the laws that governed the country in which he lived. He smiled politely and promised her he would improve his education of such things. She felt sheepish at her tone and focused on moving her bishop three spaces.

"So," Mr. Stillman said, studying the board for a few silent seconds. "Therese tells me you shall be sailing for Naples in a few weeks. That is extraordinary. Have you been there before?"

"No," she said simply.

"But you have traveled to other destinations, have you not?"

Therese was talking too much. "I usually travel when Parliament is out of session."

Mr. Stillman moved a pawn.

She took it with her knight.

He frowned and studied the board more closely. "Where else have you traveled?"

It was a casual question, a conversational one, and so she answered, explaining her other trips to Edinburgh and Southern France and how she'd spend months there each time. He asked questions, and she answered, which eased her comfort level until she remembered she had wanted to be cautious with him and not reveal too much.

"What remarkable experiences you have had," Mr. Stillman said. "I have never traveled. Meant to take the Grand Tour after I finished school but came to London instead and, well, never left."

"Perhaps one day you will have your chance."

"Hmm," he said noncommittally.

She made her move, and he took her rook. She should have seen that potential move before she left herself open for it.

After another minute of silence, Mr. Stillman cleared his throat. "Would it be improper for me to ask you some advice, Lady Sabrina?"

She looked at him, something she'd been trying to avoid. "Advice?"

"You are a businesswoman, are you not? Mr. Ward told me you inherited your husband's estate and business ventures and now manage them in his place—and with better success than he did, if it is not too bold for me to say so."

Was it too bold? Most of society did not speak much of her business interests, which made it seem as though they were unaware, but if Mr. Ward—who did not move in her circles—knew, then others must as well. She rather liked the idea that her success was not completely unknown.

"It is not too bold, and yes, I have been lucky in my success."

"It takes more than luck to be successful, Lady Sabrina. You need not be modest about it with me. I need to make some decisions regarding my holdings, and, as I have avoided being very studious, I am not sure where to start." He looked up at her. "Does it make you uncomfortable for me to ask your opinion on these matters?"

His tone was sincere, and she shook her head. Such topics were more comfortable to her than more personal ones. "It does not make me uncomfortable if you do not mind advice from a woman."

Mr. Stillman laughed. "Obviously I do not mind or I would not have asked."

She braced herself for him to add an aside such as, "You are all I have available" or "I'm sure you know *something* that might be helpful for my situation." But he didn't.

Instead he cleared his throat and shifted his position. "Upon my father's death, I inherited the Stillman family estate—Falconridge, in Norfolkshire."

He went on to explain everything Lord Damion already knew about the size of the land—how much was farmed and how much was used as pasture—and the number of tenants. He told her of the portions he'd sold off and the portion he was considering to sell. He confessed that his man of business felt the sale would affect the profits so dramatically that the remaining estate would no longer be able to support itself.

She listened without showing her surprise at how much he was revealing. To her, a virtual stranger, and a woman, no less. She never had the chance to talk business with anyone but Mr. Gordon. Most women did not know such details, and most men would never lower themselves to discussing them with a woman.

"It sounds as though selling off that parcel is ill-advised," she said, before explaining the profitability quotient of estates reliant on farming, to which he listened attentively.

"The further complication," he said after he had clarified some of her explanations, "is that I owe a substantial amount of money to the lender who rescued me from the original debt I owed to the man who left me in this condition." He gestured to his broken leg and shook his head. "Saying all of this out loud makes me physically ill regarding my disgraceful behavior."

As though to atone for his decisions, he moved his bishop directly in the path of her remaining rook. She had no choice but to take it, as he'd known she would. It seemed to make him feel better.

"I have one year to pay this new debt in full, and after thinking over the situation, I believe the best thing I can do is sell the estate."

Sabrina tried to hide her surprise. "In its entirety?"

He nodded. "I tried to sell it a year ago and was told it would likely sell for near eight thousand pounds, but I did not need that much. I sold off the first parcel, certain it would restore my situation, which I have told you did not happen. Selling it now would allow me to pay off Lor—the new lender—and have funds enough to invest in . . . something, which, in time, might prove restorative. It is how to manage the investment of the profits from the sale that I would like your advice on. Where would be the best place for me to begin learning about the markets and such? My uncle made his fortune in India some decades ago. Do you think I should take my money there?"

Sabrina feared she would have a headache from the effort it was taking to keep from showing her shock and dismay at his ideas. She spoke in careful, measured words. "India is certainly an option, but as I am sure your uncle has told you, fortunes are not as easily made now as they have been in the past. As trade routes improve, there are more and more people competing for the imports, and a man often has to compromise on his prices."

He looked at her, somewhat forlorn, which was adorable. "I didn't realize that. What would you recommend?"

"Well, I would first recommend being less hasty in selling off your holdings. If you keep the parcel you are looking to sell and find a way to improve the profits, then you should do everything you can to keep the estate. Nothing increases in value over time like land does." Their very country was founded on the economics of land ownership, and for one of the lucky few who owned land, to give it up was almost unheard of.

"I can't raise the money I would need in time otherwise," Mr. Stillman said, which Sabrina knew was true. "If I don't raise the money within a year, then I have agreed to sell the property for five hundred pounds to this lender to resolve the debt. It is more reasonable for me to sell the estate myself in order to increase my profits, and I am eager to have a clear way ahead of me without owing anything to anyone."

Sabrina had to bite her tongue to keep from telling him that Lord Damion had never actually purchased the properties for as small a sum as agreed to in the contract. Only four of her clients had been unable to pay off their debts by the end of the term, and she had created a mortgage for two of them and paid full value of their assets for the others, minus what they owed Lord Damion and the five percent interest. The point of such a low settlement in the contract was to motivate the foxes to be active in resolving the debt some other way.

Mr. Stillman, however, had no hope of raising the forty-two hundred pounds he owed Lord Damion any other way. It was simply too much money. She had anticipated Mr. Stillman would pursue the marriage inheritance, which would help him secure a mortgage before the end of the term. It was yet one more way she had not fully appreciated the depth of this situation.

"Do you not have any other sources of income available to pay off the debt? Could you get a mortgage, for instance? Or . . . perhaps there is a relative who could help you?" She could not believe what she was saying! Lord Damion was determinedly against family members coming to the aid of his foxes, and yet she was encouraging that very direction.

It is different now, she told herself. *He is taking responsibility. He is thinking of his future.*

Mr. Stillman set his jaw. "I am determined to resolve this debt and never find myself owing ever again. My poor reputation, both moral and financial, means a legitimate mortgage is not an option, and I have no family foolish enough to lend to me. I need to find my own solution."

Sabrina thought carefully about what to say, fearing she would reveal how much of his situation she knew. "What of your uncle who made his fortune in India? If he has done so well, then perhaps he would extend you some opportunity. I'm sure he would not like to see you lose this land."

Mr. Stillman shook his head. "He has assisted me before, digging me out of more than one pit of debt, each time believing his help would change me. It didn't, and he finally cut me off. He is already agreeing to see to my physical care when you leave for Naples—did Therese tell you that was arranged?—which is more than I deserve. I have written to him my sincerest apologies, which I hope will soften him toward me, but I will not follow that letter with one asking for financial help he was right to refuse me." He sighed and stared at the board. "I need to be a different man than I have been, Lady Sabrina. If I manage the profits wisely going forward, perhaps one day I can be a landowner again." He looked up at her. "Do you think that is possible?"

It was burning her throat not to ask him about the marriage inheritance, but he'd said nothing about it to Lady Sabrina. She swallowed and focused on his question.

"It is possible, if you proceed wisely," she said. "Have you considered textiles? With the cotton imports coming more regularly from America, there is more and more money to be made in that sector, especially if you can anticipate changing trends early on."

"I have not considered anything," Mr. Stillman said, then

pulled his eyebrows together in a thoughtful expression. "Where would I start in learning about textiles?"

Sabrina shared what she knew about the industry that was already well-established in Leeds and growing quickly in Manchester. Mr. Stillman listened intently as they continued their game.

"I could locate some additional information if you like," she said when she sensed he was beginning to feel overwhelmed. She made a mental note to ask for Mr. Gordon's help to address the selling of his estate—there had to be a different way to go about things.

"I would appreciate that very much. Thank you, Lady Sabrina."

They each made a few more moves in silence. The game was beginning to drag, and she wondered if he was prolonging it on purpose. If he *let* her win, she would be furious.

"Would you like to hear about the time I accidentally drove my father's carriage into Alderfen Broad?" Mr. Stillman asked in a jaunty voice.

"I most certainly would," she said, relieved at the change in topic. She gave him a smile that he returned tenfold.

He told her of the escapade in exaggerated language and with so much feeling that she had tears streaming down her face by the end from laughter. When had she ever laughed this hard? She was in the process of catching her breath when he moved his rook and captured her queen.

"Checkmate," he said with a grin and a wink.

She stared at the board, mapping out his last few moves to see how he'd done it. After seeing the route he'd taken, she raised her head to meet his eyes. "You used that story to distract me?"

"Yes," he said with a self-satisfied nod. He tossed her king into the air a few inches and caught it in his fist. "I did. Thank you for the game, Lady Sabrina. I am already looking forward to our rematch."

Sabrina leaned back in her chair, both frustrated and flattered. Yes, Mr. Stillman was someone she was going to have to keep her eye on.

Chapter Twenty-Two

$\mathcal{E}$lliott was in his study when Brookie brought him a letter. He recognized the handwriting and took a breath to prepare himself. Harry's letter from almost two weeks ago had been short and to the point. He'd been badly beaten and was recovering at the home of a friend but would need a place to go in a few weeks. Could he count on Uncle Elliott to care for him after his current placement could no longer keep him? It had not been arrogant, but neither had it been humble. Elliott and Amelia had crafted a simple response. Yes, they would help with his recovery; please send additional information.

Harry only ever came to Elliott when he needed something, and as soon as Elliott had stopped taking care of the need—which had always been financial until this last letter—Harry had ignored him. The last time they had spoken in person had been last year when Elliott had gone to London to see both Harry and Timothy; Harry had been insulting and rude before storming out of the pub where they had met for breakfast.

Elliott braced himself, broke the seal on the letter, and read. When he finished Harry's surprisingly humble letter of apology and contrite regret of his former behaviors, Elliott blinked and read it again.

Could this really be from his nephew? Elliott retrieved the letter from a few weeks ago to compare the handwriting just to be sure. A lump formed in his throat. If he trusted the words and tone of the letter, it seemed Harry had found the redemption Elliott had been praying for.

When he joined Amelia for tea a few hours later, he passed the letter to her. As she read Harry's words, he spread butter and jam on a slice of her homemade bread. They always had bread for tea.

"Well," Amelia said when she finished reading, setting the letter aside and picking up her cup of tea. "That is an unexpected turn."

"Indeed. What do you think of Harry's apology?"

"If his words can be believed, it's remarkable."

Elliott nodded, more confident of his impressions now that Amelia shared them.

"He still hasn't said where he's been recuperating, though, has he?"

Elliott nodded. "I noticed that too. Odd that he has not told us. I shall ask him directly."

"Excellent idea," Amelia said with a nod. "I worried after that last letter, afraid of what we might be getting ourselves into, though we certainly had to help him. This letter"—she waved at the paper on the table—"gives me hope that he might actually be on a better path. The only thing that could be more helpful would be if he could find himself a good woman." Amelia leaned forward for her own slice of bread.

Elliott laughed and shook his head. "And to think you were so very against my campaign."

"This is nothing to do with the campaign, only that the right woman can give a man purpose enough to change his behavior. If the right sort of woman could cross Harry's path at this time in his life, it could put his future into a new perspective. "

Elliott thought about how often he wore blue because Amelia said it looked well with his eyes and how he no longer removed his shoes when he was lounging in the study. He walked every day because Amelia said it was good for a man his age to be active, and he had not smoked a single cigar since the night before his wedding. She had certainly changed him for the better, and he could not think of what he wouldn't do to please her.

"Ah, yes," Elliott said with a nod. "There are few things more powerful than a good woman taking charge of a man."

Chapter Twenty-Three

The day after their first chess match, Sabrina returned to Mr. Stillman's room before dinner. Determined to win, she kept conversation to a minimum to maintain her focus. Once she captured his king, she sat back in her chair with a smug grin. It had taken only eighteen moves.

"Well done," Mr. Stillman said. "You beat me."

"Yes," she said, copying what he'd said the night before. "I did."

"And did not even need to resort to distraction in order to do so."

"Well, I have no stories to compete with driving a carriage into a lake." She paused. "I have been wondering about the horses pulling that carriage, though. What happened to them?"

"Ah, yes, I shall tell you," he said, his eyes sparkling. "Though I should warn you I come across quite heroic in that part of the story." He leaned forward and told her how he had jumped into the lake and cut through the harness straps so the horses could swim to shore.

"You are funning me," she said, trying to picture a fourteen-year-old boy doing such a thing.

He laughed. "I am not! It happened just as I said and is likely the only reason I survived the beating my father gave me for having destroyed his carriage. If the horses had not survived . . ." He whistled and shook his head. "I would not be here to tell the tale." He continued smiling but there was a tightness there.

Had he truly been beaten? Not that he didn't deserve punishment, but being physically dominated could break things inside a person. It was too heavy a thought for her to allow, not when she needed to be attentive to the present.

She wasn't sure she could believe he'd rescued the horses, and yet she could picture him doing just that sort of thing. A younger Mr. Stillman seemed exactly the type of boy who would walk the roofline twenty feet up, burn down sheds on accident, release a neighbor's pigs, and then brag about the triumph to his friends. Did that mean he had been punished for all those things too?

"I must tell you, Lady Sabrina, and I will understand if you find it hard to believe because there are so many virtues I have not taken to heart, but I have always appreciated honesty. In myself and in others."

"And yet if you are a dishonest man, saying you are honest is the very easiest lie to tell."

Mr. Stillman considered that for a few moments, then nodded. "I suppose that is true."

They held one another's eyes for a moment, then two, then several. He looked so sincere in what he said, so trustworthy and solid. His eyes were like a clear lake where a person could see all the way to the bottom, and she felt that if he were lying, she would see it. Know it.

Something shimmered between them. Perhaps it was only

that she believed what he said, but it felt like more. A knowing sort of feeling. But could you really know a person from looking in their eyes? Outside of a novel, of course.

Therese came with Mr. Stillman's dinner tray, which was the excuse Sabrina needed to break free of his gaze. She excused herself while Therese put a small tablecloth over the chess table. Sabrina imagined taking dinner with him here, in this room. Just the two of them. With the light turned low and . . .

"Will you return after dinner?" Mr. Stillman said to Sabrina. "We need to break the tie."

"I . . . shall see," Sabrina answered before quitting the room. It felt unwise to return when she'd already spent so much time in his company these last two days—and enjoyed it more than expected. She ate dinner alone in the large dining room, then caught up on the London papers for nearly an hour before her feet took her to his room seemingly of their own volition.

They played chess again, and she strove for a better balance between engaging in the conversation and remaining focused on the game. If she won this third game, she would break the tie, and it felt very important that she leave this room the victor. Paramount, really.

"Where did you grow up, Lady Sabrina?"

Personal questions always tightened her defenses. "Why do you ask?"

He laughed self-consciously. "I do not know. To start conversation, I suppose. Your focus on the game is a bit intense, and I must distract myself from my fear of losing to you again."

She looked up from her study of the board. She had three potential moves, but each of them would create advantages on his part, and she was trying to best plan which sequence to put in play that would be least damaging to her own campaign.

"I think it interesting that people give a fig one way or another where someone was born." He'd admitted last night that Mr. Ward had given a report on her, which meant he certainly knew of her illegitimacy.

Mr. Stillman considered her comment. "And I find it interesting that people use the cliché of 'giving a fig' in such a context. What is so great about figs, I wonder? Truffles, for instance, are far more valuable than figs, and truffle oil . . ." He let out an appreciative whistle. "That is something that would be hard to part with, assuming the information you sought was of equal value, which you could not know until after the deal had already been made."

"You misunderstand," Sabrina said. "A fig is of little worth, that is the point. Not giving a fig means that you care very little."

"Well, then, you used it incorrectly because I would give a truffle to know where you were born."

He had her there, but she rolled her eyes and moved her attention back to the game. She was down to choosing between two moves now, realizing the third move would give him too much advantage if he reciprocated with his knight.

"So, do they grow figs in the town where you were born?" he asked casually a few minutes later.

She laughed out loud. Why did no one else make her laugh like this? "You are quite determined, aren't you? Well, then, I was born in London."

"Really?" Mr. Stillman said, leaning against the pillows and lacing his fingers over his stomach.

She found her eyes drawn to the deep V of his nightshirt, the smattering of golden-blond hair of his chest just visible. An uninvited image of Richard with his shirt off pushed into her mind, and she replaced that unsavory memory with the imagination of how Mr. Stillman would look bare-chested. She entertained that image longer than was wise.

Mr. Stillman continued. "You seem much more a woman from the country than a city girl. What with your roses and such."

"Perhaps because you have known me only in my country house, though a growing number of people no longer consider Wimbledon 'the country.'"

"I think of Wimbledon as the country, though I've seen only a bit of it through the window." He waved toward his view of green hills and a few chimney stacks poking up from pitched roofs of other homes.

"And where were you born, Mr. Stillman?"

"At the same Stillman estate I shall have to sell within the year." He spoke casually, and Sabrina had to stop herself from repeating her opinion that he should not being too hasty taking such a step. She still needed to talk to Mr. Gordon about how they might better handle that situation.

"Have you brothers or sisters?" she asked, more comfortable with him being the topic of conversation.

"Two sisters," Harry said. "Hazel is the oldest, by ten minutes. Hannah came when we were three."

Sabrina blinked. She'd known he had sisters from the investigation she had done before agreeing to take him on as a client. "Oldest by ten minutes? You are a twin?"

He nodded but showed neither excitement nor reticence to talk of this interesting detail.

"I am not sure I have ever met a twin."

"Well, most twins do not survive childbirth." He shrugged, and discomfort entered his expression, lowering both his energy and his shoulders. "As it was, Hazel was born with a clubfoot."

She waited for him to expand, but he leaned forward and

focused on the board even though Sabrina had not yet made her move. The changes this topic had brought into his demeanor were poignant. She decided to test his insistence that honesty was the one virtue he had not cast by the wayside along with the other morals he'd dismissed.

"You and your twin sister do not get on?"

He flickered his gaze at her, then back to the board. "Not in so many words, no."

"How many words does it take to better explain it?"

He took a deep breath and let it out slowly. "Between Hazel's sex and her physical failing, she was all but invisible. The attention and support I received for *my* sex and my health cast a particularly long shadow that further hid her from view. When Hannah was born . . . Well, my parents had an able-bodied daughter to put their minds to. The difficulty this created for Hazel is something I did not realize for most of our life and have never remedied. She is, as you can imagine, rather resentful."

Sabrina stared at him. "I did not expect such an answer." It was humble and insightful and tinged with regret. And, perhaps most interestingly, honest. As far as she could tell.

Harry shrugged, still looking at the board for reasons she better understood. Honesty invited vulnerability, yet he'd still told her the truth when he could have given a different—and easier— answer.

"Where has life taken your sister?" Sabrina asked, feeling a kinship with this woman she'd never met but whose circumstances—through no fault of her own—kept her on the outside. But then, wasn't everyone a victim of circumstances in one way or another? Mr. Stillman's circumstances had spoiled him and left him irresponsible and hedonistic.

"The one good turn my parents did for Hazel was providing

her an excellent education. She finished her own schooling at the top of her class and immediately began teaching. Last I heard, she was teaching French and mathematics at a girls' school outside of Brighton."

"Mathematics? I have never heard of a woman teaching mathematics."

"She has a mind as sharp as her tongue; I know that as well as anyone. When we were children and home on holiday, my parents would quiz me on my studies, but she would beat me to the answer ten to one. It did her no favors since my mother would send her away so that she might praise me disproportionately to my successes, but I think the personal triumph of beating me was important to my sister. Learning was the only aspect of her life she had any control over."

"Is she happy as a teacher?"

He looked up at Sabrina, as serious as he'd ever been, and held her eyes for a beautiful eternity of four seconds.

"I believe she is bitter about the course of her life, but then I have also been bitter despite having many more advantages than she ever did. There was a great deal of discord in our household when we were young, and it stayed with my sisters and me as we grew. Each of us fled in one way or another as soon as we were able, and none of us has a great deal of trust in the others.

"I hope Hazel is content, but to expect happiness amid the circumstances in which she finds herself feels rather unrealistic. After all, she has a clubfoot and a worthless brother who has not supported her the way he should have, which means she has had to work for her own support.

"The last time I corresponded with her—other than the letter of apology I sent last week—was to ask to borrow money nigh on a year ago. How is that for brotherly kindness?" He let out a humorless laugh. "Her response was less than ladylike." He shrugged, perhaps to take the point off the painful truth. "Every word deserved, however."

"And your other sister? What was her name—Hannah?"

"Yes." His expression softened, leading her to believe that even if none of the siblings was close to the others, there was something more between Mr. Stillman and Hannah than he could claim with Hazel. "She is married, though it was not a good match. Her husband is a fisherman."

"A fisherman?" Sabrina could not hide the surprise in her voice. Hannah was a gentleman's daughter.

"Yes," Mr. Stillman said, looking at the board.

"And is *she* happy with her life?"

"I have not seen her since my mother's funeral, which took place a few months after Hannah's wedding. She seemed well enough, if not a bit disenchanted. Her fairy-tale expectation turned out to be a small house in a fishing village far away from anything, and anyone, familiar. She has a child, though I've never met her." He looked up from the game and met her eyes again. "Are *you* happy, Lady Sabrina?"

Chapter Twenty-Four

She opened her mouth to give a glib answer that would deflect his attention, but he'd bared his life far more openly than she'd expected when she'd begun asking questions. "I am not rightly sure, Mr. Stillman. I am . . . content and secure."

"Which can feel like happiness if it contrasts significantly enough against feelings that are the opposite of contentment and security."

"A contrast which then becomes . . . enough, I suppose."

He nodded thoughtfully and smiled. "You are a very intriguing woman, Lady Sabrina."

The compliment was like champagne, filling her with a fizzy warmth—but also filling her with the knowledge that she would need to stay on her guard.

"I am not intriguing," Sabrina said breezily, debating on moving her bishop two spaces. "In fact, I'm quite boring. I spend my days managing investments, following politics, and networking within society on behalf of my brother."

"Lord Hattingsham, heir to your father's dukedom?"

He did know of her family history, then, and yet his expression held no censure. "Yes. My brother is one of my dearest friends."

Mr. Stillman smiled. "You have done well for yourself."

She looked away, needing to hide her discomfort. She'd done well with what she had, yes, but she would never discount the grace that had brought her there. Nor the price she had paid along the way. From the outside it looked easy—a rich father followed by a rich husband who'd had the good manners to die before he'd spent through his inheritance. What luck.

"All that any of us can do is our best with the cards we are dealt," she said finally.

"And you enjoy living as an independent woman?"

"Very much."

"It is never lonely?"

Oh, but he had arrows aplenty tonight. There were a few ways his question could be interpreted, so she chose to believe he wondered if she were lonely living by herself. "I think anyone who lives alone is lonely at some point or another, but it is not so bad that I have plans to remedy the situation."

"You do not want to remarry, then?"

"No." The word came out strong and tight and bound up with the same determination she'd expressed to Nathan so recently. Why were the people in her life asking this question of her? Uncomfortable with Mr. Stillman's focus, she finally made her move even though she'd lost track of which was the better one.

Mr. Stillman's attention went back to the board. "I have no desire to marry either," he said, as though it were a white flag. "It feels so very confining."

"Marriage is not confining for a man," she said with a sharp laugh. "They are the party who reap all the benefits."

"And the confinement."

"What confinement?" she asked incredulously.

He looked up as though surprised by either the tone or the question, perhaps both. "Of responsibility," he said. "Of saddling themselves with one woman and taking on the burden of children."

She felt heat rising in her chest and tried to keep her voice calm. "Rare is the man who reserves himself for one woman, married or not, and children are a legacy, not a burden. Save for bouncing them on a knee every week or so, how are they a burden to the father?"

He held her eyes for several seconds, and though she wanted to look away, she didn't. "You have a very low opinion of men, don't you, Lady Sabrina?"

She looked back at the board quickly even though it was his move. "Perhaps I do," she admitted, though she'd never thought of it so directly as that. She thought well of Nathan, and Richard's father had been kind, but he'd been nearly seventy years old when she'd joined the family, and he was not necessarily inclined to form a bond with his son's nervous wife.

"And a man like me does little to improve your opinion of my sex."

She waved toward the board, her jaw tight. "It is your move, Mr. Stillman."

He tapped a finger to his chin. "I have tried and tried to remember our acquaintance from those years ago. Do you remember which party it was where we first met? I did not make the rounds in high society for so long that I have a great many to choose from."

Sabrina, distracted by the many conflicting emotions in her chest, said without thinking, "The Gilmores, perhaps."

"Lady Constance Gilmore?"

His excited tone caused her to lift her head, and her breath caught at the look of recognition on his face. What had she said? She had not really wanted him to remember. "Y-yes."

He smiled in relief. "She is the aunt of an old school friend of mine—Nathan Williams." He paused, looking to the side as though searching for the memory she fervently hoped he would not find. Why had she not been more careful with her words?

"I had only been in Town a few weeks, and she invited us to a party and I . . ." His eyes moved back to her, and she watched the memory bloom across his features. His expression turned instantly to confusion. "You were in the garden."

She swallowed against the sudden dryness in her throat as a flush shot up from her chest. She could not look away from him, though she feared he was seeing far more in her expression than she wanted him to.

"You were *hiding* in the garden," he clarified, his voice soft as realization connected to the memory. "You were afraid, and—"

"I was ill."

He squinted as though trying to focus on the details he had not yet captured in the net of memory.

She spoke before he could. "You fetched my friend, Lady Townsend, for me."

"Yes. She had a green ostrich feather in her hair. But there is something more."

She forced a smile and cocked her head to the side, determined to cut into his recollections. "I have always had a question about that night. The young woman you were escorting to the darkened corner when you came upon me—what was her name?"

His cheeks flushed with embarrassment, as she'd expected they would when she put the focus on his actions that night instead of hers. It was a mean trick, but it worked. He was the one to look away, and they were silent for a full minute until he made his next move. It left his queen open to her knight, which meant she could end the game in only a few more moves. She moved her bishop instead. What was she doing? What did she hope to gain by extending the game?

"Is that why you are set against me?" he asked quietly. "Because of who I have been?"

Sabrina should have ended the game when she'd had the chance. "I am no more set against you than I am any man, Mr. Stillman."

"I know I am not a good example of my sex, Lady Sabrina, but you must know that a good number of men are decent and kind—far better than I am."

"And faithful?" She raised her eyebrows in challenge.

"Yes, there are faithful men." He smiled, probably an attempt to lighten the conversation, but she found it patronizing.

"Name me one." She sat back in her chair and crossed her arms over her chest. "Give me the name of one faithful man you know well enough to be *certain* he can claim credit of that virtue."

"My cousin Peter," Harry said easily. "And my cousin Timothy as well. I've no doubt they will remain faithful to their wives. Peter's first wife passed away, and he's recently remarried. And Timothy . . ." Harry's smile grew larger. "He once told me he hopes to have ten children."

Sabrina thought back to the letter she'd received from Harry's uncle some weeks earlier, stating how he'd planned to bestow inheritances to each of his nieces and nephews upon marriage. Had Peter and Timothy already claimed theirs? That seemed reason enough to question the virtuous intention of these men, but only Lord Damion knew those details, so she bit her tongue.

"Well, 'tis a shame they are both married already. I'd have liked to have a chance with one of the only two men of virtuous character left in England."

Mr. Stillman laughed. "So if there were a man of virtuous character, you would consider marriage? That means it is not that you don't *want* to marry but that you do not *trust* to marry."

Sabrina felt herself bristle like a cat, but to react with claws would be contrary to the confidence she wanted to convey. What a mess she had made of this conversation! She took a long, deep breath, determined to give him her undivided attention. Though uncomfortable, this was still a better topic than their first meeting in the Gilmores' garden.

"When a woman marries, she becomes an appendage to her husband. Anything she owns or has built for herself becomes his, and she is left to live at his whim. If he should choose to gamble away money she brought into their marriage, she cannot say a word. Should he choose to take a mistress, she is powerless against it. He can cheat her, use her, abuse her, cut her off from family and friends and treat her as wickedly as he wants without accountability or reproach.

"If a woman found herself in a situation of equality, perhaps she, too, would take advantage of the same power and freedom men take for granted, but that is not how our society operates. If there were a guarantee that only good men were in positions of power, it might be different. But any kind of man can run this country and their homes, while women are considered barely human. Men pat us on the head and compliment our stitching while denying us education and occupation that would free us to make decisions toward our own best interest.

"I managed to find a break in the wall meant to keep me in. I was widowed without an heir for my husband and nothing he owned was entailed upon a male relative. The fact that he died before he found a way to keep me under someone else's power gave me a freedom very few women will ever know. I will *never* give up my power again. The very potential of the risk that would be is unacceptable to me. So, yes, I am lonely sometimes, but, no, that loneliness will not drive me to give up my rights to myself ever again."

She'd said too much. She could feel it in the air between them as he held her eyes and absorbed her words. She braced herself for a rebuttal—either something easy and light or insightful and pointed; he'd shown himself equally capable of both.

After enough time for Sabrina to feel foolish and vulnerable for having said so much, Mr. Stillman smiled at her, and then moved his bishop without looking away from her.

"Checkmate."

Chapter Twenty-Five

*S*abrina arose the next morning feeling foolish about her rant that had allowed Mr. Stillman to win the game. Again. She wasn't sure how to talk to him now—she'd left rather abruptly last night—so she tried to distract herself with work. She went over the household accounts in detail, planning out the months she would be gone week by week.

Joshua, Maria, and Constance had all made arrangements for temporary work at other homes in Wimbledon, though she would continue to pay a percentage of their wage to ensure they returned to her when she was back from Naples. Therese would manage the house on her own, with Steven maintaining the grounds and stables.

The planning moved naturally into Sabrina making detailed lists of what she needed to do before she left, what she would pack, exact times she would be leaving one place for another, and even setting out most of the dresses she would be packing to make sure the trunks she'd chosen were the right size. Poor Joshua ran up and down the stairs to the attic storage half a dozen times helping her find the right luggage. She decided on the yellow trunk; it was the right size and would be easy to identify amid the other passengers' luggage. Eventually she ran out of lists and packing, though she would not leave for Brighton for another fortnight.

She took a walk and tended to her roses, which did not need her tending. Later, when she lay down to take a nap, she only stared at the ceiling and wondered what Mr. Stillman was doing and how it would be perceived if she looked in on him during the afternoon. It would be two days in a row she'd visited before dinner. Would it give the wrong impression?

Had she given the wrong impression already?

What did he think of her?

Did he think of her at all?

If he had other companions to choose from, would he still want to play chess with her?

Even after her rant and quick departure last night?

Did she owe him an apology?

It was nearly five o'clock before she gave in, deciding it was late enough in the day that she could claim having finished her work in time to look in on him. Therese was adding new levels of movement for his routine every day, including the use of a Bath chair so he could maneuver around the room. In a few more days, Joshua planned to take Mr. Stillman outside in the chair so he could get some fresh air and practice with the crutches Steven was making for him. Sabrina could reasonably ask Mr. Stillman how the activities of the day had gone and how his leg was faring.

At the door she knocked twice before pushing open the door in time to see Mr. Stillman quickly stuff something under the bedclothes.

The taskmaster within her instantly wielded a willow strap.

"What are you hiding?" she demanded, taking authoritative

strides across the room. If he had talked one of her staff into giving him a bottle of wine, so help her . . .

"Nothing," he said with a nervous laugh. He smiled wide, and her suspicions deepened. He knew what effect his smile could have on a woman.

"I saw you put something under the bedclothes," she said as she reached his side. "Show it here." She put out her hand.

His smile fell. "Lady Sabrina, it is nothing."

"Then you won't mind showing me."

"I would prefer not to."

"I'm sure that is true." She reached over and pulled back the covers, revealing . . . a skein of pink yarn, a square of stitches, and wooden knitting needles. After a moment, she reached forward and stripped the covers all the way from the bed as she had the night she'd found the brandy just in case there was something more.

His nightshirt was high on his legs, exposing a portion of the lingering bruise on his left thigh, but there was nothing else hidden beneath the bedclothes. Sabrina stepped away from the bed as Mr. Stillman leaned forward and pulled the coverlet back over himself, restoring some level of decency. He then extracted the yarn and needles and set them on his lap.

"Knitting?" she asked after a few seconds.

"Therese has been teaching me," he said with a touch of defensiveness as he squared his shoulders. "She claims I am a quick study. I was hoping to surprise you, but apparently you still distrust my assertion that I am a new man capable of more noble pursuits."

Sabrina blinked. "Knitting?"

He gave her a wounded look. "You said I needed to find constructive things to occupy my time."

"Well, yes, reading and . . . whittling perhaps." Wood shavings would be intolerable in a bed, however.

"Appropriate *male* pastimes, you mean?" He raised a single eyebrow in reprimand. "You are the one who says a woman should have the same opportunities as a man, so why can't a man knit? Especially if he is inclined toward the skill of it, for it most certainly takes skill to do well." He paused his work to look at her, then lifted his chin defiantly.

It seemed he had listened to her rant about the inequality of the sexes with greater attention than she'd expected.

"I owe you an apology, Mr. Stillman," she said once she'd swallowed her pride. "Well, two, now, I suppose. I became rather . . . energized last night and left abruptly; I am sorry for the rudeness. I am also sorry for assuming the worst just now."

He grinned in obvious triumph.

"Apology accepted—for the knitting. But I *earned* your overall displeasure last night so there is no need to apologize for that. Would you please call me Harry?" he asked.

The invitation took her off guard and sent a shiver through her. To call him by his Christian name was an invitation for a more casual connection. "I fear that would be undignified, Mr. Stillman."

"I am wearing a nightshirt and knitting," he said slowly. "Dignity is no longer an option. Also, you remind me of a schoolteacher when you address me as Mr. Stillman, though that is better than 'Young Stillman,' I suppose. However, if you continue to refuse, I must press my suit. As the reigning champion of our chess matches, I ask that you satisfy this demand and call me by my name."

She pressed her lips together in an attempt to maintain some dignity of her own, but she could not seem to keep her serious attitude when he was so very light in his. "You demand I call you by your Christian name as the prize for having won our matches? Though I use that term loosely due to the fact that you distracted me in order to win both games."

"Yes," he said. "When you are champion, you can make a demand of your own, and I will comply so long as it is within the same boundaries of propriety." He winked and smiled, and she felt it in every nerve of her body. What did he mean by it?

She cleared her throat. "I do not think it proper for me to call you by your Christian name, Mr. Stillman. I am your caretaker."

He set his work in his lap and looked at her pointedly. "Therese is my caretaker, and Joshua assists. *You* are my chess partner and . . ." He pursed his lips thoughtfully. "Well, since you are mistress of the house I can't really tell you what to do, so let me go about this another way." He smiled his overwhelmingly bright smile that made her feel wobbly on her feet. "Will you *please* call me Harry?"

"Absolutely not," Sabrina said, not only because she was a woman of principle but also because if she played along with his masculine wiles, she could find herself falling under his spell.

He sighed loudly and picked up his work. "Would you like to see what I am working on? It is nothing too elaborate—just a lap rug—but then I've only been a knitter for a few days, and no one can expect to build Rome in such a short time as that, now can they? Therese says that once I have mastered a single color, she will show me how to do alternating ones. Have you seen the checked scarf she wears? The yellow-and-purple one? I should like to make something like that, only with colors more befitting my sex. Blue and green, perhaps."

Sabrina pressed her lips together again to keep from laughing at the boyish excitement in his voice. "It is remarkable, Mr. Stillman. I am very impressed."

"And surprised," he said with a knowing glance. "Admit it—you did not think me capable."

"You are exactly right," Sabrina said, no longer holding back her smile. "I have not once considered what a master knitter you could be."

He smoothed the partially knit rug across his lap, looking as pleased as a hound before the fire. Then he let go of one of the needles and waved her toward the chair. "And how was your day? What adventures did you have?"

She felt too tense to sit and instead walked around the room, straightening and resetting the room as she told him about her day, trying to make it all sound more interesting than it had been.

"When will you be returning to London?"

"I have an appointment on Friday," she said, turning toward him. She'd run out of things to do, and since he was busy with his knitting, it didn't seem right to ask that he put it aside so they might play chess. "But the Season is finished, and my brother has removed to the country for the winter, so I shall return Saturday afternoon."

"I shall miss your company," he said, giving her a heartfelt smile before lowering his gaze back to his knitting.

She was unsure how to respond to that. Did he really mean it? And what, exactly, would he miss?

He looked up at her. "Would you have some time to read to me?" He nodded toward the book on the nightstand beside his bed.

"No chess?" She hoped she didn't sound disappointed—she hadn't meant to.

"Is that all right? Nothing against the game or the time we

have spent playing, but I think you are on to my strategies of distraction now, and a man who knits cannot also lose at chess."

"Lose to a woman, you mean?"

He let go of his needle and put up his hand, palm facing her. "Do not put words in my mouth. Can we leave it at my not being able to accept losing at chess to a *person* and let me get back to my needles?"

Sabrina smiled. "Well, when you put it that way, I suppose so. But if we are not playing chess, then perhaps I ought to return to the papers and—"

"The only part of knitting that I find tiresome," he broke in, winking at her when she closed her mouth, "is the silence of it. I tried for a time to put the book on my lap and knit in between turning the pages, but I kept dropping stitches, so I had to give up one for the sake of the other. I would very much like to get a bit more work done today, and I can do it better if I have something to listen to."

She crossed to the book and read the title gilded across the front cover. "*Clermont?*" She looked from the gothic novel to him though he remained focused on his yarn.

"I am abashedly ignorant of what makes up good fiction, but I read the first book of *The Children of the Abbey* after a friend bet me I could not read an entire book in one sitting if that sitting was done in a bath. I am proud to say that I won sixpence, though I also caught a cold so it may not have been a worthwhile venture, save for the bragging rights—things like that can really boost a young man's reputation in school—fortitude and all that."

Sabrina shook her head at the ridiculous, yet entertaining, folly of this man.

He continued as though she had not reacted. "I asked Therese if you might have any Regina Roche in your library, and she came back with this." He waved toward the book in her hand. "I only made it through the first chapter before realizing that I could not be attentive to both activities, as I have already explained." He picked up his needles and smiled brightly at Sabrina. "If you would be so good as to start at the top of chapter two, I would be most obliged."

She pulled up the chair and turned the pages to the start of chapter two, amused and entertained in equal amounts. She had just opened her mouth to begin reading when Mr. Stillman spoke again. "Before we start, did you notice that I chose pink for your lap blanket?"

He lifted the square of tidy stitches.

"*My* lap blanket?"

"Yes, did I not mention that? I have so few ways of showing my thanks, it seemed fitting that my first completed project should be a gift to you to thank you for all you have done for me." He glanced up at her, his expression humble and gracious. "I really cannot thank you enough, Lady Sabrina." He rested the needles in his lap. "The clearer my mind becomes, the more I realize the level of sacrifice you and your staff have made to accommodate me."

He looked toward the window, turning his perfect face into profile. "Being away from the places where it was easy to be my worst self has given me a view of the future I have never considered before, and while I am eager to heal and get to work on making a life worth living, I am truly trying to make the most of this time here, in your home, surrounded by good and generous people. I am not sure you can know what a remarkable experience that is for a man like me, but it has changed me."

He looked at her, and she—yet again—could not look away.

Her heart was beating in her throat, and she felt as though he could surely hear it.

"You have changed my life, and I want you to know that I will never forget that. I will do all that I can to make you proud of the sacrifices you and your staff have made on my behalf."

Sabrina could not think of how to answer him, and so she just nodded and waved toward the knitting now piled in his lap. "It is a lovely shade of pink."

There was silence for a moment, and then he spoke as though he had not just laid his heart bare. "It represents your roses. Therese brought me an entire basket of yarns to choose from—your late mother-in-law's, I believe—and I was completely tickled to have found this exact shade."

Completely tickled?

Sabrina complimented the color, and the neat stitches again, earning herself another radiant smile, then settled in the chair beside his bed and opened to chapter two. She cleared her throat at the same time his needles resumed their clicking.

Chapter Twenty-Six

When Therese arrived with Harry's dinner tray, Lady Sabrina helped him put the needles and yarn into the knitting basket he kept under his bed, though he did not need to hide it anymore now that she knew. He wished she would stay and eat with him, but it seemed out of place for him to ask.

As Lady Sabrina was leaving the room, however, he could not help but offer a parting invitation. "If you feel up to a game of chess after dinner . . ." He trailed off. It seemed presumptuous to invite her to his room, which was actually her room. Yet in just a few days he'd become so accustomed to spending time with her in the evening that he could scarcely imagine doing without her.

Lady Sabrina stopped near the door and turned to him, cocking her head as she regarded him. He'd noticed her eye color yesterday—brown, but not just brown. Chocolate brown. Deep brown. "You said earlier that you might not be able to tolerate losing to a woman now that your knitting secret is known."

"Person," he emphasized. "Sex is of no consequence. And I think I may have come up with another way to win."

She pursed her lips slightly, emphasizing their perfect shape and rich color, the sight of which sent something like a shiver through him. "Aside from winning through better skill?" she asked.

"Well, of course," he said with a laugh, ignoring the sensation the sound of her voice ignited in him. He winked at her specifically to watch her catch her breath. He did not think she was aware of her reaction, and it worried him that he had noticed. What worried him even more was that he continued to deliberately elicit the reaction, which now seemed to be creating a reaction inside himself.

She laughed and shook her head. "I shall return in an hour, then."

"Brilliant."

Therese set up his dinner—pork and new potatoes that made his mouth water—and he thanked her when she stepped back.

"Is there anything else you would like, Mr. Stillman?"

Aside from a better understanding of Lady Sabrina? "No. Thank you for all you've done."

She excused herself, and Harry began cutting his meat and replaying his conversation with Lady Sabrina. It had been so . . . easy. They had bantered back and forth the way friends would. But she was a woman. Men and women could not be friends—or at least that was what he'd always believed.

But then he'd believed he could never give up drink, never humble himself before his uncle and sisters. Never learn to knit. *This*—whatever it was—was different from those things, however.

Harry had spent a great deal of time with women. Flirting and . . . He shook his head away from those thoughts. He'd never talked to a woman the way he talked to his male friends, and he'd never enjoyed talking to his male friends the same way he enjoyed conversation with Lady Sabrina.

Spurring a physical reaction in a woman, such as her catching her breath and blushing, was a tactic he'd employed when he wanted a woman's particular attention for a particular reason. Such as convincing a tailor's wife to make him a new shirt against her husband's wishes. She'd blushed and simpered and finally agreed. Harry had always had that sort of effect on women. And he'd taken it much farther than shirts too often. He knew how to get whatever he wanted from women, and it wasn't usually difficult.

Those thoughts and memories were uncomfortable; he wanted to be better and stronger and noble. Was he attempting to seduce Lady Sabrina without even knowing that was what he was doing? What if all his years of manipulating women to do what he wanted had made it impossible for him to have an honest relationship? Maybe it was ingrained in him, an evil flaw he had let take such hold that he could not free himself now.

His chewing slowed, and he swallowed hard, staring at his plate. He couldn't treat Lady Sabrina the way he'd treated other women. For one thing, he knew she would not stand for it— blushing and breath-catching aside. For the other part, women were another vice, another thing that helped him hide from himself. The distraction was dangerous for him and vastly unfair to them.

Lady Sabrina was also a *lady*. She held herself with confidence and decorum. Her good opinion of him meant everything, and he wanted to be the kind of man a woman like her might one day see as worth spending her life with. That idea startled him, and he put down his knife.

Was that really what he wanted?

Had he changed so much that he wanted marriage and security?

The thought came with a release of tension that felt like settling into a warm bath or stepping off a horse after too many hours in the saddle.

If marriage meant feeling the comfort of friendship and flame of passion together, he could not think what he would not do to have it. That must be part of what Uncle Elliott had meant when he talked about the good of marriage.

But could he be faithful? It was not an expectation for men, but when Lady Sabrina had ranted about the injustice of infidelity, he'd remembered the insecurity he'd felt as a child when his father had flirted with a maid or stood too close to one of his mother's friends at a party.

Mother would drink too much wine on those occasions, and later there would be yelling and crying, and the next day his mother's eyes would be swollen from crying. Sometimes her lip would be swollen from his father silencing her when he could take no more.

If his father had been faithful, then his mother would have trusted him, and they could have spoken civilly to one another. Loved one another. Lived as partners and companions instead of antagonists. So much could have been different.

Could it be different for Harry if he remedied the hurt he'd seen in his mother by keeping his own marital vows? He thought that it could.

But he was getting ahead of himself. He had been off the bottle for only a week.

He went back to his meal, trying to sort his surprising and unexpected thoughts. When Joshua returned for the tray, Harry still had not found balance.

Too soon—or not soon enough, based on how happy he was to see her—Lady Sabrina returned for their game of chess.

He watched her cross the floor of the bedchamber to him, regal and self-possessed, and he felt that same something move through him that he'd felt earlier in her company. If he'd lived his life differently, could he have already become the type of man she would want to spend a life with? She didn't trust men, and she certainly didn't trust the type of man Harry had been.

"Mr. Stillman?"

The questioning tone in her voice told him that she'd been speaking, and he felt a flush creep up his neck. He wondered how long he'd been staring. "I'm sorry, what was that?"

She furrowed her eyebrows. "Are you all right? You are looking at me as though I am a ghost."

"More a phantom, I think," he said softly, then looked away as his earlier questions buzzed inside his head again. Was he flirting with her? Did he know the difference between talking to a woman and flirting with her?

"A phantom, am I?"

He looked back in time to see her rosy full lips pull into a wide smile. Did he want to kiss those lips or did he just not know any other goal to set with a beautiful woman?

Before he lost his nerve, he dove straight to the heart of his quandary. "Are you certain you will never marry again, Lady Sabrina?"

She sobered instantly, then busied herself with setting up the chess pieces. He watched her long fingers position the pieces and wondered what the difference was between admiration and attraction. He admired many people. Had he ever admired a woman, though, without there being attraction involved?

"I believe we have exhausted that topic, Mr. Stillman."

"I just want to make sure of it."

She looked up at him, guarded. "Why?"

He swallowed and threw whatever remaining caution he had to the wind. "I have never had a female . . . friend." Goodness, what was he doing? He bumbled forward, however, speaking fast to get all the words out. This new man he was becoming would be forthright and ask for help when he needed it. "The more time we spend together, the more confusing it becomes for me, and I know this is terribly indelicate of me to bring up, yet I feel I have to. I need you to convince me that whatever connection is between us is nothing more than friendship so that I do not get the wrong idea."

His face was on fire when he stopped for a breath. "I have never been *friends* with a woman before," he repeated. "Therefore I don't have anything to compare this to." He clamped his mouth shut to keep from saying anything else.

She blinked and swallowed and then smiled. Not sweetly, but not necessarily patronizing either—somewhere in the middle of those two positions.

"Mr. Stillman," she said in an even and controlled voice. "I have male friends; we discuss politics and our families and what travels we might have in the future. Having friends of the opposite sex is invigorating and, I believe, helps me to be a more complete person with a wider understanding of the world beyond what I gain through my female friends. I can assure you that whatever it is you feel between us is, and will only ever be, friendship.

"It will not feel like your connection with Mr. Ward or other men as there are topics you and I will never discuss and things that will never happen. For instance, I might walk through a park with a woman friend, but I would never walk with you because of the impression it would give.

"We are friends, and it is all we will ever be."

He felt he should be relieved by her explanation, but he wasn't and didn't understand why. "You are certain you would never change your mind and want . . . more than friendship from me?"

She finished setting up the chess pieces. "Yes, Mr. Stillman, I am certain. Not only have I no interest in marrying, but I am five years your senior, and, if I might be so bold, I am your superior in class, wealth, and life experience. Even if I were open to a relationship in general, it would never work for *us*; the balance is off." She smiled patronizingly now. "But we get on well and seem to understand one another enough to be friends, which is quite nice, is it not?"

Harry let out a breath he didn't realize he'd been holding. "That is such a relief to hear."

Her expression turned skeptical. "Some men would feel insulted."

"Well, yes, I mean you *have* just told me I am stupid and low-class and immature, but . . ." He paused to consider what he could appropriately say, but then realized he'd already broken all bonds of good manners and might as well say all that he felt. They were friends, after all, and could therefore be honest with each other.

"I enjoy your company very much, Lady Sabrina, but I have so much to learn about this new kind of life I want to live. Thank you for helping me to learn those things I should already know, such as how to be friends with a woman. I fear the years I have spent in such filthy dissipation have kept me from learning what a young man should have learned during those years. I want . . ."

He took a breath and held her gaze. "I want to be the kind of man that a woman like yourself might want to be with someday, and I feel overwhelmed by all I have to change about myself to become that sort of man."

"Does this mean you are reconsidering marriage? Two nights ago, you seemed as set against it as I am."

"I am reconsidering everything. If I am to be a responsible man who is not ruled by vices, then perhaps I can be a husband and a father and—"

He stopped as he saw her catch her breath, the way she did when he winked at her or complimented her. Yet he'd said nothing of the sort. She quickly repaired the expression, and he decided to continue.

"I see a very different life ahead of me, and I am eager to make up for lost time in learning how to live it. But I am in no hurry. There are a great many things I need to prove, to myself most of all, before I can be confident of offering myself up as a partner to someone else. I suppose I am beginning to think ahead, that is all."

She smiled, masking anything he thought he might have seen in her expression. "I have no doubt you will triumph in that life, Mr. Stillman. You are a man of intellect and growing insight that will guide you on this journey now that your goals are set and your mind is clear."

"I cannot tell you how much it means to me to hear you say that, Lady Sabrina. I respect your opinion very much, and that you could have a good opinion of me after all I have put you through is priceless to me."

She nodded and looked away. The air had changed, certainly because of the raw honesty of his thoughts. The old Harry would never have done such a thing, and she likely was not used to such openness either, though she had handled herself with grace and elegance.

"You won our last chess match, though it was under less than virtuous circumstances, so you have the first move," she said, turning the subject completely, which he appreciated as he had no idea how to do so himself. He would remember the technique, however, for later days when he would need to restore comfort to an awkward conversation.

"I am a rule-following man these days, so I shall accept my position." He leaned forward and looked over the board, then glanced up at her.

She was also leaning forward, which left only two feet of distance between them as she surveyed the board, surely mapping out a dozen moves and countermoves before the game even began. This close, he could see the fine lines around her eyes and the texture of her skin, which was not as smooth as most of the debutants come to London for the Season. He had heard many women lament their fading youth as they got older, but he hoped that she did not share that feeling. There was a depth to Lady Sabrina that youth could never claim, and though he wished she would tell him more about her marriage and her younger years, he did not need to know the details to understand that they had shaped and formed her into the woman she was.

She met his eye, and he grinned to hide his inspection she would likely find offensive. "If I win this game," he said, "you will call me Harry."

She narrowed her eyes. "And if I win?"

"You continue to call me Mr. Stillman."

"That is hardly a prize," she said.

"Then, please—name your prize."

Two spots of color appeared on her cheeks, but she coughed

as though that was the cause. Then she looked back at him and cocked her head—goodness, she was beautiful. It was all right to think that about a friend, right?

"If I win," she finally said, "you will write me a poem."

"Ah, then I cannot lose tonight regardless of who is victor," he said, sitting back and moving his center pawn forward. "Let the battle begin."

Chapter Twenty-Seven

They spoke of politics again—Mr. Stillman was terribly ignorant of the topics of discussion from this last Parliamentary session—and Sabrina tried to keep her focus on that conversation and the game before them. The conversation they'd had when she'd first entered, however, kept circling in her mind. He felt something for her—something he couldn't make sense of—and though she felt she'd done a good job of convincing him it was friendship, she knew that wasn't what *she* was feeling.

How could she have let this happen?

When he'd asked her what she would like her prize to be if she won, the thought that had popped into her head was a kiss. If she was not so skilled at keeping secrets she might have said it out loud. And then what? She had just finished convincing him that she would never want more than friendship from him—*couldn't* want more than that—yet she wanted to kiss him?

She glanced up from the board to his mouth. Right now, this moment, if there was a way she could kiss him and have him forget it happened, she'd do it. When his attention was directed her way or even when he was listening to her express her thoughts about one topic or another, she felt . . . wanted. Sabrina had never felt wanted before.

Her feelings were obviously a result of the situation; she was his caretaker, and he was handsome and charming, and, goodness, he was knitting her a lap blanket. She felt drawn to help him as Lord Damion and oddly responsible for the beating he'd suffered. All that complexity had her emotions tangled up like silks thrown haphazardly in a basket.

"You support the Tory agenda, then?" Harry asked.

"Anyone with an ounce of sense supports the Tory agenda. It is the only agenda that has room for the growth that is happening in our country, whether we want it to or not. The Whigs, well, they think they can keep things as they've been, but they can't. The past two decades have shown that. There is no stopping the progress that will continue throughout this century, but if we act wisely, we can improve our society while also preserving the strength of our country, which is the most powerful government in the world."

"What long-term consequences do you see from this rise in industry? Textiles, for example? We've been so dependent on imports for some of the things we can now create ourselves—what will that do to our foreign trade?"

He moved his rook, inadvertently putting himself in check. That meant she was two moves away from winning the game . . . and earning a poem from him as her prize. Since she could not ask for a kiss.

But she couldn't risk a poem either. It would be too intimate, and after the realizations she'd made regarding her feelings for Mr. Stillman, she couldn't risk words he wrote just for her. It might lead her to pondering too much on his better qualities, thinking more about his fine face and body and . . .

She moved her knight on the opposite side of the board. Calling him by his given name seemed the wiser choice.

She began explaining her thoughts on the impact of England producing more of their own goods, but she kept her eyes on the board.

He moved a pawn—not resolving the issue with his rook— which left him in check for a second turn! Sabrina's competitive spirit screamed in protest, but she stuffed it down and made another insubstantial move, talking the whole time. His sincere desire to learn from her seemed to have led him to listening so hard that he did not see his own folly.

He moved his rook on his next turn, thank goodness, but now he'd left himself open on the other side. Gracious. She moved another pawn and saw straightaway that she'd left her own hole on the board.

Harry's lips turned up in a slow, tremor-inducing grin as he moved his knight into the space she had opened. "Check," he said, triumphant.

Sabrina pretended to be frustrated and made a move that looked like she was trying to get out of the mess she was in, but she didn't try very hard.

Three moves later, Harry had captured her king. He picked up the piece and balanced it on his open palm. "I won this game fair and square, Lady Sabrina, you know that, right?"

Breathe. Let it out. She nodded in surrender.

"So, then, from here forward you will call me Harry."

She attempted a weak protest. "I do not think that is a good idea."

"You agreed to the terms," he reminded her. "And it is not

such a hard thing for friends to address one another more comfortably."

Sabrina stood, knowing she needed to leave. Everything was too much tonight. She smiled, though she could feel the tightness of it. He was watching her with an eager grin. She finally nodded, taking heart in the fact that it wasn't a poem that might compare her to a sunset or a flower.

"All right," she conceded. "You won. Now I shall bid you good night."

"You must call me by my name before you leave," Harry teased, still grinning as though this was just another game. Which it was . . . to him. "I want to hear my name on your fine lips."

Fine lips? She swallowed and met his gaze. "Good night . . . Harry."

He kept smiling, and she felt every particle of it. Then it softened like a light being dimmed, and she felt his eyes taking her in, moving over her like physical touch. She could not breathe by the time he met her eyes again.

"Good night, Sabrina."

Chapter Twenty-Eight

Sabrina was lingering over breakfast and yesterday's papers the next morning when she received a letter from Mr. Gordon asking that she come to his office as soon as possible. They were scheduled to meet for her monthly meeting on Friday; his summoning her two days early was cause for concern. She was tempted to look in on Mr. Stillman—Harry—before she left, but could not come up with a reasonable excuse. After last night, she needed to be more cautious than ever. She needed distance from . . . Harry. Perhaps a trip to London was exactly in order.

Were she a stronger woman, she would stay in London until Harry was no longer in Wimbledon, but she did not have such fortitude, and the plans for when he would be ready to travel had not been confirmed. She *would* stay in London tonight, however, regather her defenses, and then proceed with more caution during the next week and a half he would be at Rose Haven. She had suffered through greater discomfort than this before; she just needed to keep her wits about her.

She arrived at Mr. Gordon's office at one o'clock in the afternoon, having taken Molly to her mother's workhouse on the way because Molly had received a message two days earlier that her mother was failing quickly.

Mr. Gordon was standing behind his desk when Sabrina entered, and he sat as soon as she took her place across from him.

"What has gone wrong?" she asked immediately.

"Malcolm will still not accept the payoff. I have tried every possible way to change his mind—even offered an additional fifty pounds to the fifty you suggested. He insists that either Mr. Stillman or Lord Damion must pay the full amount in person."

Sabrina startled. "Lord Damion?"

Mr. Gordon nodded slowly. "He offered that option yesterday, which is why I asked that you and I meet today. Obviously Lord Damion cannot meet him, which means Mr. Stillman must meet with him in person and pay off the debt himself so we might be done with this."

Sabrina slumped in her chair and stared at the tips of her shoes poking out beneath the hem of her lavender walking dress. It was difficult to think of Mr. Stillman as just another one of their foxes, and the idea of him meeting with Malcolm was impossible to consider. Yet she must find a way to be objective.

When she didn't say anything, Mr. Gordon continued. "Will Mr. Stillman be recovered enough by Wednesday next to pay off the debt in person? It will have been nearly a month since the attack."

Sabrina was still focused on a different aspect. "Do you think Malcolm is attempting to uncover Lord Damion's true identity?"

"Yes, I think so. Did you find the letter you gave to Mr. Stillman at the conclusion of that first meeting?"

Sabrina shook her head slowly. The staff had looked

everywhere, and the letter had not materialized. Which meant Malcolm's men must have taken it. Which meant they must have known that was where Mr. Stillman had been going. Had they followed Mr. Stillman but then lost him before Jack had brought him to the pub? What would have happened if they'd found her that day?

Sabrina was sick to her stomach at the possibilities. She looked up and met Mr. Gordon's compassionate eyes. He had been Richard's solicitor and not hesitated when she asked him to continue to work for her after Richard's death.

Creating the persona of Lord Damion had been his idea. Buyers and sellers and partners continually questioned Sabrina's ability to make decisions because she was a woman, but no one questioned Lord Damion, even though they all knew the name hid his true identity.

The irony of some people's willingness to work with an un-identified man over a respectable woman was irritating, and yet the Lord Damion persona had allowed her to become wealthier than most of the men she did business with. She thought back to when she'd told Harry that there were no good men—how had she not thought of Mr. Gordon? Or Joshua? Or Jack?

"If Malcolm's intention is to flush Lord Damion out, how far will he go to do it?"

"I don't know," Mr. Gordon said. "But we must take it se-riously and use every caution as we move forward. If Malcolm's intention in meeting with Mr. Stillman is to extract information about Lord Damion, then we are safe. There is nothing Mr. Stillman can tell him that will lead to you—at least not directly. And I do not believe there is any reason for Malcolm to connect Lord Damion with Lady Sabrina."

"Mr. Stillman could tell him about The Lost Tartan," she said. "And Jack."

"Mr. Stillman is our only option," Mr. Gordon said after a moment. "I can impress upon him how important it is to protect Lord Damion's information."

Sabrina nodded, but she felt sick. Sending Harry back to the man who'd had him beaten was wrong. But there was no Lord Damion to go in his place.

"I don't see any other choice. I will ask Joshua to travel with him in the unmarked carriage, though I can offer only what help Harry asks of me. The only thing 'Lady Sabrina' knows is that he owed money to unsavory people but a trustworthy lender has helped him settle his debts."

"Harry?"

She blinked and pulled her eyebrows together. Was that a question?

"You address him as Harry, now?" Mr. Gordon clarified.

She felt herself flush, but Mr. Gordon spared her an explanation. "I shall craft a careful letter encouraging Mr. Stillman to take you into his confidence and to request your help with the meeting. I'm sure I can persuade him that you're the only person who can help him." He paused, watching her for a few moments. "And perhaps if he is well enough to travel to London it will serve as a natural transition into his removal from your care."

Sabrina was brought up short. "What?"

"Mr. Stillman has remained under your roof because he has not been well enough to travel, correct? If he can manage the trip to London, however, then he can settle into his uncle's house in Town."

The idea of Harry leaving her so soon left her feeling flat, which was all the more reason for her to hurry him on his way. Whatever connection she felt between them was not sustainable and would fade as soon as they no longer shared company.

"I shall be prepared to offer whatever assistance he needs for the meeting and leave the coordinating with his uncle up to him, unless he asks me for help," she said, standing. She avoided Mr. Gordon's eye for fear of what he would see in hers. "Please keep me informed of the correspondence between you and Ha—Mr. Stillman, and between you and Malcolm. Joshua can go along to ensure that Malcolm does not hurt Mr. Stillman further in an attempt to extract information."

She turned to the door and heard Mr. Gordon hurry around his desk in order to let her out. "Are you all right, Lady Sabrina?" he asked.

She nodded quickly, still avoiding his eyes. "Yes, thank you."

But she suspected they both knew it was a lie.

Sabrina didn't return to Wimbledon Thursday morning. Or Friday or Saturday or Sunday either. Each morning she woke up with the intention to return but found reasons not to.

On Friday, she sought out her friend Elizabeth Roundy, who lived in London year-round. On Saturday, she shopped for items she needed for her trip, rewrote her lists, and wrote out instructions for Mr. Gordon on every topic she could think of so that he could reference her advice should something come up regarding her investments while she was gone.

Mr. Gordon informed her that he had made arrangements with Lord Howardsford to receive Harry at the Mayfield house in London as soon as possible.

She also wrote back and forth with Therese, coordinating her responsibilities by pen and paper rather than simply talking it over with her.

Sabrina walked Hyde Park every morning and rested her head against the glass of her bedroom window, looking for her fox every night. She knew very well where her fox was: at her home in Wimbledon, likely wondering what was keeping her.

The draw to see Harry was so strong, she didn't trust herself to act on it. She'd never been in love before and had expected to live out her life without it. Was this love? Or something else? How was anyone to know?

On Monday, she received word from Molly that her mother had passed. Sabrina pushed herself into the situation in order to ensure Molly's mother was properly and respectfully interred without it being a financial burden on Molly. That night, Sabrina's nerves were on edge, and she did not sleep well.

On Tuesday, she finally ordered the carriage. Tomorrow, Harry would go to his meeting with Mr. Gordon. She could not abandon him on his last night. Also, she would be leaving for Brighton in a week, and there was a great deal of work to be done at Rose Haven before then.

The carriage rumbled toward home, and her stomach got tighter with every mile. It was beyond ridiculous for her to feel this way. They'd shared a handful of evenings together, and he knew only the parts of her she'd been willing to show, which were not the most important ones.

She was acting like a silly girl who thought infatuation meant something when she knew very well that it didn't. Her father had been infatuated with her mother, but in the end, their relationship had been a business transaction. Infatuation made women a commodity.

She leaned against the cushions and took a deep breath, drawing on her strength and fortitude. One more night in his company, a final chess match, and then she would have months to forget all about him. It would not be so hard once he was gone.

Chapter Twenty-Nine

*H*arry's palms started sweating when he heard the wheels coming up the drive. He used the armrests of the chair Joshua had brought into the foyer to push himself up, then settled the crutches beneath his arms. He'd made a great deal of progress in both his stamina and his balance these last few days. The only benefit of Lady Sabrina having stayed in London so long is that he'd had time to work on regaining his independence, wanting to impress her when she returned.

He wished he had a third hand so he might adjust his cravat. It had been so long since he had worn evening clothes that the tightness around his neck felt quite confining. He marveled that he had once worn a cravat each and every day; they were terribly uncomfortable. Were comfort his only consideration, he might wear a nightshirt every day for the rest of his life.

He heard the carriage stop, and he swung himself toward the door, keeping his right leg bent at the knee. Goodness, but he'd missed Sabrina.

Therese had first told him the travel was for a meeting with her solicitor regarding arrangements for her trip to Naples. The next day, however, when she'd handed him a letter from Mr. Gordon, she'd had no explanation for why Lady Sabrina had extended her trip.

So much had happened while she'd been gone—learning he'd have to meet with Malcolm and having Uncle Elliott move up his plans to come to London so that Harry might go there afterward—it had been heady to be so busy after a month of doing so little. He would leave tomorrow and never come back to Rose Haven. The sorrow he felt was raw and heavy, but at least he would have one more evening with Sabrina. He would not allow himself to wish for more than that.

He positioned himself in the foyer and nodded at Joshua, who opened the door and stepped aside as Lady Sabrina came up the last few steps.

"Good evening, Lady Sabrina," Joshua said.

"Good evening, Joshua," she said by rote.

She stepped over the threshold, removing her gloves, and then stopped when she saw Harry. She smiled, and that smile allowed him to put a cap on his lingering sadness about leaving.

"Mr. Stillman," she said, moving toward him with bright lips and bright eyes. "How nice you look. What is . . ." She looked at the crutches and frowned. "What are you doing out of your room?" Her eyes traveled the length of the stairs and back. "And down here—on the main level? Joshua, help Mr. Stillman back to his room and—"

"Joshua and Steven from the stables brought me down; I did not navigate the stairs. And Steven has made me this pair of excellent crutches." He leaned on the left crutch so he could hold out the right one. The top braces were wrapped in thick linen which was more comfortable beneath Harry's arms. "I am improving my use of them by the day."

He demonstrated by walking to the base of the stairs and back, his right leg bent so it did not touch the floor at all. Therese had hemmed his black trousers at the knee so the fabric didn't interfere with the splinted portion of his leg, wrapped in fresh linen this afternoon. It was a sacrifice, cutting up one of the few pairs of pants he owned, but Sabrina's smile had already made it worthwhile.

"You are not putting any weight on that leg?" she asked, sounding doubtful.

"Not a bit," Harry said, then nodded his chin toward Joshua, who was looking quite invested in the scene taking place in front of him. "Joshua can confirm it."

"Yes, ma'am," he said to Sabrina. "Therese made him promise, and I have stayed on hand as he practiced in case he needed assistance."

"I have been practicing in the mornings," Harry added. "And then Therese makes me rest all afternoon, though she's allowed me to use the Bath chair. I can manage it almost as well as a phaeton, I daresay."

"And you are not in pain from so much time upright?" Sabrina asked.

"My leg aches afterward, but I sleep with it propped upon pillows. I will be extra cautious tomorrow to make up for *this*." He waved his hand toward the dining room and watched her eyes follow the direction.

After hesitating longer than he thought polite, she finally undid the tie at the neck of her cloak, handing it off to Joshua. "And what, might I ask, is *this*?"

"Dinner."

"Dinner?" she repeated. "That is cause for so much effort on your part?"

"Yes," Harry said, lifting his chin. "Dinner in the dining room, with me."

She finally smiled her authentic smile. "You have planned a dinner for me in my own dining room of my own house?"

"When was the last time you ate dinner in your own dining room of your own house . . . with company?"

He saw the flash of embarrassment reflected in her eyes. She did not want him to know that she was lonely in this wonderful life she had built for herself. Three weeks ago, he would not have had the insight to see such a thing, but so much had changed since then. He hurried to fill the silence before she felt obligated to do so.

"Therese helped plan the menu with some of your favorites, including lemon custard for pudding. Before that, though, we have turtle soup, fresh cucumbers in sherry, turnips with braised greens, and pork loin in bourbon sauce."

"It sounds delectable," she said. "I do not often have coursed meals at home."

Harry winked and watched her catch her breath before using his crutches to propel himself across the floor to her. He turned so they were side by side. "It is not quite the same as taking a man's arm to be led into dinner, but you might manage to take hold of my elbow all the same and pretend it is less awkward than it is."

She laughed and put her hand on his elbow as he'd suggested. He "walked" her into the dining room, where Joshua waited with her chair pulled out. Once she was seated, Joshua helped Harry take his seat, which was much more difficult than assisting Sabrina had been.

Then Joshua left to fetch the soup course.

"What is behind all this?" she said, looping her hand through the air.

"A show of gratitude," Harry said. "It was exactly twenty-nine days ago that you saved me from the streets of London and . . . myself." He smiled sheepishly, then hurried to continue his explanation. "I thought it fitting for us to have a dinner party of our own on my last night at Rose Haven." He spread his arms wide. "At your expense in your dining room in your house, yes, but let us not forget that it was *my* idea."

She laughed. "Ideas are what change the world."

"Precisely."

Joshua entered with a soup dish in each hand. He set Sabrina's in front of her and then set Harry's in front of him.

Harry lifted his spoon. "There is one more reason for the dinner. Therese told you my uncle will be ready for me after my appointment tomorrow? She said she would write to you in London about it."

She stared into the soup, stirring her spoon through the broth as she nodded. "She did," she said. Was it his imagination, or did she sound disappointed? After a moment, she looked up with a smile. "I'm very glad you will be able to go to your uncle. I know you are eager to repair that relationship."

"I am," Harry said with a nod. "Did Therese tell you of my need for a carriage and possibly to have Joshua attend me to London?"

"Yes. And whatever you need is at your disposal."

He put his hand on hers and gave it a squeeze. "Thank you." He paused and looked around the lovely dining room. "I shall miss being here at Rose Haven." He almost said, "I shall miss you the most," but stopped himself in time. He'd promised himself he would not say or do anything that might be misinterpreted.

She turned back to her soup. "Rose Haven will miss you too," she said. "Have you decided what to do about your estate?"

"Yes!" He grinned. "I had a letter from Lord—Well, the lender who has made my recovery possible, and he has said that if all goes well with Malcolm, we shall renegotiate the contract. He is willing to give me an actual mortgage on the estate, which might spare me from having to sell it."

Her expression was rather neutral, he thought, for such remarkable news. "That sounds like a perfect solution."

"I don't know what I did to deserve two such saviors as I have had in you and this lender, but I shall not let either of you down. Now, what did you do in London?"

She told him of seeing friends and doing some shopping and preparing for her trip. He asked when she would go to Brighton, how long she would be there, how long the voyage to Naples would be. The more she talked, the more comfortable she became, and the more he had to keep himself from thinking that they would not have this chance again. Tomorrow, everything would change, and though he was eager to move forward on all that he needed to do, there was a growing hope that she might miss him as much as he would miss her.

How would she react if he showed up on her doorstep a year from now? He could as easily imagine her pulling her brows together and shutting the door in his face as he could imagine her clasping her hands together and smiling at him adoringly. Actually, he could not picture the adoring smile.

The custard dishes were empty, and he could tell she was tired from her journey. Harry signaled for Joshua, who brought the crutches and helped Harry to his feet. Joshua then pulled out Sabrina's chair, Harry put out his arm, and Sabrina took it without him asking her to.

"And what else have you planned for the evening?" she asked.

Harry frowned in embarrassment. "I'm afraid all I planned

was dinner. Therese made me promise to return to my room as soon as we were finished."

Sabrina straightened. "Good heavens, if I'd known that, I would not have let the dinner draw into two hours."

"She did not set a time, only the end of dinner, so we have complied with her instruction perfectly."

Sabrina shook her head and looked at his leg. "How are you feeling?"

He paused but then told the truth. "I will be all right, though I am looking forward to lying in my bed again. I need to improve my mobility now that I shall not have Therese and Joshua at my beck and call."

They reached the bottom of the stairs, and she turned to face him. "I worry that your leaving is premature, Harry. I shouldn't want your recovery to be compromised."

"I wish it were an option to keep things exactly as they are, but it is not to be."

He would meet with Malcolm in the morning and settle the last of his debts, then go to Uncle Elliott's London house for one week before removing to Howard House for another month at least. He would be only fifteen miles from Falconridge at that point and could better manage the changes that needed to be started there.

By October he hoped to be settled into the house he had not lived in since childhood and working on the improvements more directly. He was looking forward to proving himself and building a respectable life. Lady Sabrina had risen above her birth and marriage; he could rise too.

At some point, he would revisit his uncle's offer of inheritance upon marriage. If the idea crossed his mind that no other woman would have the conversation and intellect he admired so much in

Sabrina, he pushed it aside. He needed to get used to a different life than he'd known before he could truly consider sharing that life with someone else.

"You have saved my life," Harry said, leaning on one crutch so he could reach out and run his thumb down her cheek. He had not realized the intimacy of the touch until she shivered slightly. He held her eyes and dared not try to interpret what he saw in them. Longing? A wish that things were different? He was quite sure that was what she was seeing in his.

Harry became aware of Joshua hovering in the hallway behind him and removed his hand. "Thank you, again, for everything, Lady Sabrina. The impact you have made on my life will not be soon forgotten. And thank you for the use of Joshua and the carriage tomorrow."

Joshua took his cue and stepped forward, followed by Steven, who had apparently been waiting around the corner. Harry had forgotten it would take both of them to return him to the upper floor.

Sabrina stepped back from him as the men approached. "Might I come and read a chapter once you are ready for bed?"

"That would be a perfect ending to a perfect evening," Harry said with a grin that settled the energy between them back to that of friends. "I may even finish that lap rug if I can talk you into two chapters instead of one."

It was nearly an hour later when Sabrina knocked on his door. She'd changed into a fresh dress—light yellow with blue accents at the hem and sleeves. Her raven hair was down and plaited to hang over her shoulder. Harry had a momentary vision of a bride entering her new husband's chamber on their wedding night. He set down his knitting.

"I hope it is all right that I undid myself from the day," she said nervously, flicking a hand at her hair. "My head was beginning to ache, and I find releasing my hair from the pins is often the best way to stave off the worst of the discomfort." She gave him a sheepish smile, and Harry could not bring to mind the memory of even one of the many women he had pursued in all the years of his life. Lady Sabrina had rendered all of them inconsequential.

The wanting he felt, however, filled him with shame and regret. Shame for letting his thoughts about her venture into such baseness, and guilt for the realization that having acted out on all those other moments of wanting had put a woman like Sabrina out of his reach. She did not know the details of how far-reaching his debauchery truly was, and, if she did, she would certainly not laugh over the dinner table or present herself so casually.

"It is f-fine, of course," he said and pasted a smile on his face that he hoped hid the direction of his thoughts. "I have been in a nightshirt every time we've met, except for the first time in that alley and dinner tonight. On what grounds could I possibly object?" When she smiled in return, he forced his eyes away from her and picked up his knitting. "I must say I had no idea you had so much hair. It must weigh ten pounds at least."

Sabrina laughed as she crossed the room and pulled the chair close to his bed. "My mother's hair was the same, thick and long and, yes, heavy. I appreciate you having no objection to the lack of formality."

"Of course," he said, shrugging as though he were completely unaffected.

She seemed nervous, too, and though he wondered why, he dared not let the thought linger. "Chapter seven tonight, I believe," he said brightly to cover all that he was feeling. "And eight, if you've time."

She nodded toward the lap blanket. "Assuming your fingers don't cramp before then."

"Cramp?" he said, offended. "Cramping is for amateurs, and I have been knitting for nigh on ten days now."

She smiled, then opened the book and turned several pages. "All right then, chapter seven."

By the time she closed the book some time later, Harry had managed to recover from the desire he'd felt when she'd entered the room. The lap rug was not as long as he would have liked, but, in fact, his hands *had* begun to cramp halfway through chapter nine. Of course, he couldn't say as much.

"You did not finish," she said, nodding toward the pile of yarn in his lap.

"I shall have time in the carriage tomorrow, fear not."

She placed the book on the nightstand. Then she moved the chair back to its place, crossed to the fireplace, and pulled the cord that would bring up his glass of warm milk. She looked at the rise of his covers over his right leg.

"Is it feeling better?"

"Not yet," Harry said, setting his knitting on the unoccupied side of the bed meant for two. "But it will."

She furrowed her lovely black brows. "You overdid it today."

"Perhaps," he said. "I shall be careful tomorrow once I am at my uncle's house. You must trust that I have no desire to run faster than I have strength in this, Sabrina. I never want to be this dependent ever again, and I will mind myself accordingly so that I do not go backward in my progress."

"You have become a much better patient over time."

He cringed to think of that first week when his need for drink had been all-encompassing. "I like to think that the separation from the vices that landed me here has allowed me to become the man I should have been all along."

She looked up at him, a thoughtful expression in those eyes the color of strong coffee. Oh, how he would miss the way she inspired him to be a better man. She had told him that what he felt for her was friendship, but after the days when he had missed her and the evening they had just shared, he no longer believed it. What he felt for her was much more. He longed to hear her thoughts with the same yearning he felt to touch her shoulder, kiss her throat. He wanted to know more about her childhood, her marriage, her friends. There was such a wholeness about her, a deep and rich draw that contributed to dangerous sensations inside him.

Mind yourself, he commanded. *Be the man you should have been.*

"I think you are rather hard on yourself, Harry."

Harry shook his head, but he could not take his eyes away from hers. "You say that only because you do not fully understand the man I have been."

She pursed her lips slightly, disarmingly so. "Maybe I know more than you think."

Her words surprised him, but the intent behind them captured him as surely as a net. She was suggesting that she didn't care about his past—could that be true? Against all the commitments he'd made to himself, he moved his hand to reach for hers.

What is one more conquest? a voice said in his head. A familiar voice. One he had listened to far too often in the past, and one he could not afford to entertain now. He lifted her hand to his lips and pressed a kiss upon it. The gesture could be interpreted any number of ways.

She caught her breath. He felt his own heartbeat in his ears.

"Thank you for a perfectly perfect evening," he said.

Their hands remained joined, and she stared at them for a few seconds. Then she looked into his eyes and stepped toward the head of the bed, leaning down until their faces were mere inches from one another.

Dear Heavens, had she any idea what she was doing to him? He breathed her in, feeling the fog moving into his mind, the longing and yearning as strong as his need for drink ever was. The intoxicating scent of roses did him no favors.

"Might I request one thing that would truly perfect it for me?" she asked in a throaty whisper.

He swallowed. "W-what would that be?"

The glint in her eye ignited him, and before he could remind himself of his changed ways, his hand was behind her neck, though she needed no guidance to bring her lips to his.

Chapter Thirty

Sabrina did not have a great deal of kissing experience, but even in her ignorance, she knew Harry was accomplished in the art. His lips against hers were soft, the kiss sweet and slow to start. When she pressed for more, however, he did not hesitate to answer. The intensity of the moment enveloped her, cutting off all thoughts of the past and the future and keeping all of her senses acutely focused on the taste of his mouth. The smell of his skin. The sound of a low moan from deep in his throat that made her shudder in response.

Her hand went to his scruffy cheek, while his arm went around her back and pulled her closer. He led and she followed, kissing him as she had never kissed a man before and feeling the sensation of it pulling her under.

Warning bells went off somewhere in her mind: she was alone with Harry, in his bedchamber. This was ruination and immorality and . . . so help her, she wanted to be wanted. To be the sole focus of his attention.

He pushed his hands into her hair, and she ran her hands

down his back, under the neckline of his nightshirt. Oh good gracious, he wore only a nightshirt!

And then his face pulled back from hers. She met his eye, smiled, and leaned in for more, but he took hold of her arms and held her away from him. She tried to catch her breath, still gripping the collar of his nightshirt in her hand.

"Sabrina," he said, breathless—breathless because of *her*. A sense of power moved through her that had nothing to do with commanding a dinner party or leading an auxiliary discussion. Had her name ever sounded so sensual?

"Harry," she said in an equally telling tone and leaned toward him again. There was something so right about this, something she'd been looking for and never found. He moved toward her and met her lips—again—and everything began to fade—again—and then he pulled away. Again.

"I can't," he said, and the regret in his voice pricked her heart. "We can't do this, Sabrina. It isn't right."

The reprimand, no matter how kindly stated, made her feel instantly foolish, and she let go of his nightshirt and stood up straight. The smell of him still surrounded her like mist.

"I could not stand to be the subject of your regret in the morning."

Humiliation rose up like a volcano, flushing her face as she stared at him. The embarrassment cracked enough to let in something even more unwelcome.

What is wrong with me? Why am I so undesirable?

She turned away from him, blinking back the childish tears that had come on suddenly.

"Sabrina," he said, "you deserve better than a man like me."

She walked toward the door, mortified and aching. How could she have forgotten who he was? Who *she* was?

"Stay," he called after her. "Let's talk about this. Let me ex-plain why—"

There was a knock at the door, freezing Sabrina halfway be-tween the bed and the door.

The door opened, and Therese entered with a tray holding Harry's glass of warm milk. When she saw Sabrina, she startled, then looked concerned in a way that made Sabrina feel even more the fool. Her mussed hair likely told too much.

"I shall take care of this, Therese, thank you."

"I was going to check Mr. Stillman's leg. It was swollen after dinner."

"It is much improved," Sabrina lied, her smile growing brittle on her face. Anger at herself buried the other emotions threaten-ing to break her apart, and she invited the fury. "That will be all, Therese. You can assess Mr. Stillman's leg in the morning."

Therese glanced past Sabrina's shoulder to Harry. He must have nodded or something because the woman's face relaxed slightly before she gave Sabrina a quick nod. "Very well. Good night."

"Good night," Sabrina and Harry said in unison.

The door closed, and Sabrina turned back to the bed, or, rather, to the nightstand, where she placed the tray. She could feel Harry's eyes on her but did not meet them.

"I do not need you to explain anything to me, Mr. Stillman. You have made yourself quite clear."

He reached out to touch her arm, and she stepped quickly away, keeping her eyes on the floor. How could she have let down her guard? And with him of all people? She knew better. She *was* better. She needed to get out of this room before she lost all dig-nity.

Her hand was on the knob when she heard his voice from behind her.

"Good night, Sabrina. I am sorry that such a wonderful evening ended poorly. I pray you will forgive me."

He would go to London in the morning and not come back. He would be out of her house. Out of her life. And then she would do everything she possibly could to help herself forget how he had looked when he waited for her at the bottom of the stairs tonight.

What it had felt like to talk with him over dinner at a table she'd sat alone at for so many dinners over the years.

How it had felt to be touched.

What she would not allow herself to forget, however, was how it had felt to be rejected. *That* feeling was one she would hold close—one more brick in the wall she would keep around her heart that obviously could not be trusted to act in wisdom or prudence.

Chapter Thirty-One

Therese was in her office going over the daily book when Sabrina found her the next morning. "What time is Mr. Stillman removing to London?" she asked, trying not to let her words sound clipped.

Therese looked so closely at her that Sabrina feared there were signs of her late-night tears, even though she'd inspected her reflection in her looking glass and deemed it acceptable. The woman would not ask, however, and Sabrina would not explain.

"Steven will have the carriage ready at eleven thirty. Mr. Stillman's appointment is at two o'clock."

Sabrina gave a sharp nod. "Very good. I shall be calling on Mrs. Clemson this morning and will likely not return before he leaves. It is a pleasant enough walk so I will not need the carriage." She lifted the letter she'd written to Harry and slid it across the desk toward Therese. "I've included my farewell here. If you would be so kind as to give it to him when he is prepared to leave."

"Would you not rather give it to him yourself?"

"No," she said coolly. "This is mostly well-wishes toward a

full recovery and acknowledgment of his dedication toward improvement."

It had occurred to her that morning that his rejection could have been because of his commitment to pursue a more noble life. Allowing him honorable motivations brought small comfort to her jagged humiliation. She wondered why she was not yet used to rejection after so many years of it. She had not been enough as a daughter, a wife, or a mother either.

Yet Harry had done her a favor; she would have woken up today with unfathomable regret had he not pushed her away. Her shame now served as the very blade she'd needed to cut through the draw she'd felt toward him.

She was finished with Harry Stillman.

Therese watched her closely, but Sabrina pretended not to notice. She pushed the letter closer to Therese, who finally picked it up.

Sabrina forced a smile. "Well then, I shall be off. After my return, I shall be finalizing my schedule and hope to have a written version for you by this evening." Sabrina put on her gloves—pink to match the pelisse she had chosen, hoping the cheery color would invite a brighter mood than she felt.

"Very good, ma'am," Therese said, rising to her feet. She glanced at the letter in her hands. "Are you sure you would not like to give this to Mr. Stillman yourself?" she asked again. "He looks forward to your time together like a child awaiting sweets. I believe he will be very disappointed not to say goodbye. You remember he will be going on to his uncle's house upon the completion of his appointment?"

"I am well aware of his arrangements," she said with enough ice in her tone to make her teeth hurt. "It is time for all of us to move on with our lives—Mr. Stillman most of all. Good day, Therese. I shall see you this evening, if not before."

"Oh, Sabrina," Therese said, dropping the pretense of formality as sympathy filled her eyes. "What happened between the two of you last night?"

Sabrina took a step back, half turning toward the door as she shored up her resolve to put last night and Mr. Stillman behind her.

"I understand the staff's curiosity about Mr. Stillman and myself," she said pointedly. "The situation is highly unusual and certainly fodder for speculation belowstairs, but I have done only what any other Christian woman would do for a man in need. I will be grateful to have equanimity restored to this household for the short time before I leave. I would ask that you help me in setting to rest any inappropriate speculation that has taken place. Thank you."

She turned on her heel and took the back entrance off the kitchen rather than the front door for fear she might cross paths with Harry. She passed both Maria and Constance en route and ignored their curious gazes. She could only imagine the conversations that had taken place with the staff after her late-night chess games and that silly dinner last night. Did they know she'd gone to see him last night with her hair—and her moral compass—free of constraints? Her throat burned.

She walked along the carriage lane that wound to the front of the house, down the short drive, and, when she reached the street, turned toward the village. There was a walking path that ran parallel to the road, and she tried to manage her pace so it would not appear she was fleeing the scene, even though that was exactly what she was doing.

As Rose Haven disappeared behind her, she hoped Therese

would take her words to heart and never speak of last night, or Harry Stillman, ever again. Would that she'd kept better boundaries so as not to give the staff so much fantasy to indulge in. Would that she'd kept her own fantasy from distracting her from reality.

She was an independent woman. She did not need a man, and she should not have let herself want Harry for *any* reason. She would learn from this and strengthen her character so she would not look beyond the mark again.

She took a deep breath of the country air and let it out, slowing the pace that had become almost a march as it kept time with her angry and racing thoughts. When she returned to Rose Haven, Harry would be gone. Healing would begin.

One day soon, she would set sail for Naples and not return until spring.

One day, last night's poor judgment would be the smallest hitch in an otherwise straight path.

One day, the memory of his rejection would not hurt her the way it did now.

Chapter Thirty-Two

Dear Mr. Stillman,

I send my encouragement and well-wishes as you leave for your uncle's home to begin your fresh start. You have realized remarkable insights about yourself these last weeks, and I hope that you see your potential and will make the most of the opportunities ahead of you. It has been a pleasure to be a part of this journey, and I hope that you continue to recover well.

In support of the changes ahead, I hope you will accept the enclosed fifty pounds as a foundation you can build upon for the future. In regard to repayment, I hope that one day you will see someone who needs a helping hand and repay this gift in kind. Improvement in this life depends upon the individual, and I wish you the very best as you begin anew as a better man, capable and worthy of your place in the world.

Sincerely,
Lady Sabrina

Harry held the fifty-pound note, wishing his circumstances allowed him to leave it behind. Lady Sabrina was a remarkable woman, a point she proved over and over again. He did not deserve her, let alone her money. However, fifty pounds would make a substantial difference in this transition, and he had nothing else. He refolded the letter and slid it, with the money, into the inside pocket of his coat.

Obviously, she was not coming to say goodbye, and he wished for the hundredth time that he could replay last night differently. If he'd claimed himself too tired after just one chapter, or if he'd stopped her before she'd kissed him . . .

Yet if he'd done that, there would have been no kiss, and he could not wish that away. A kiss had never been more than pleasure until Sabrina's. He'd never felt the flush of being wanted the way she'd wanted him, been aware the way he'd been aware of her, or felt that the physical was an expression of the feelings he held inside.

He'd also never had the presence of mind to know better than to continue, and yet that had come with a cost. Though not as heavy as the price would have been if he hadn't stopped. It was perhaps the first time he understood that sacrifice was giving up something good and immediate for something better and long-term. Or that sacrifice could feel like such a pit in one's stomach.

He patted the letter in his pocket. Lady Sabrina had never written him before, but there was something familiar about this letter. Perhaps it was nothing more than the words in her letter sharing similar sentiments to those she had expressed over the weeks he had come to know her. Except he wasn't sure he'd come to know her all that much. Her character, surely, and her temper and passion and shrewd mind, but there were so many things she kept hidden from him. That he'd never earned her trust enough for her to show him the whole of her felt like a great loss on his part.

A knock sounded at the door, and Joshua entered the room. "Your trunk is loaded, sir."

Harry picked up his crutches from where they rested against the side of his chair and settled them beneath his arms. He swung forward with practiced motions and followed the footman to the stairs, where Joshua took hold of his right arm and Harry used the crutch on the left side to hobble his way down, careful to keep his right leg lifted enough to not catch on a stair.

Therese waited near the door, and when he reached her, she looked at him with tears in her eyes. She had cared for him these last weeks, yes, but she also cared *about* him. That he could earn that sort of consideration without manipulating it gave him hope he could build different relationships now that he was sober and aware of how important people could be to one another.

Therese stepped forward and put her hands on either side of his face. The intimacy surprised him.

"May I give you some advice upon our parting company, Mr. Stillman?"

"Prop my foot for the drive and take things easy?"

She smiled, the skin around her eyes crinkling. She held his gaze, then whispered, "Do not give up."

Therese did not know where he had come from and where he wanted to be, but he took her advice to heart as though she did. He would not give up his sobriety. He would not give up on rising to his potential. That he had this chance at all was because of Lady Sabrina and the people she had chosen to surround herself with. He would follow her example and make a life as close to this one as he could.

"I won't."

Therese continued, "On Sabrina."

Her name washed through him, and he felt a lump in his throat at the thought that he would not see her again. Therese saw something between them? She knew what he felt for the woman who had saved him in so many ways?

If only those things were enough.

He replied in a whisper. "It is not like that, Therese."

She lowered her hands. "It could be."

He shook his head. "She deserves much more than I could give her."

"She deserves a man to love her."

If that were all she needed, perhaps there would be a chance. But she needed a man who was her equal or at least not so far below her place. She needed someone she could trust, and though Harry was determined to be better, he had only a dishonorable past to show as evidence, which was no evidence at all.

"Then she should find a man who has earned the boon of a woman such as herself."

"I think you are that man."

He took a breath and let it out with a sigh. "I wish that were true, Therese, but it is not. She saved me, and I shall never forget that." He kissed Therese on the cheek. "Thank you so much for your ministrations to me. I shall always remember the kindness I received in this house."

Five minutes later, the carriage rumbled down the drive. Harry closed his eyes and tried to focus on the overwhelming gratitude he felt for this second chance and the fact that his mind was clear enough to understand the full scope of the gift. London was full of young men on paths as dissolute as his had been. Few would ever be offered the opportunity he'd been given, through first Lord Damon's mercy and then Lady Sabrina's.

When he felt capable of controlling his emotions, Harry leaned forward and removed the nearly finished lap blanket from the basket he held between his feet. He traced the stitches and hoped that after all that had happened between them, Sabrina would still want his gift. He would add whatever rows he could on the journey to London and then send the blanket back with Joshua. He wished he had time to write a letter to accompany the gift; he wished he had any idea what he would say if he had.

Harry knitted while Joshua looked at the countryside sliding by the window. His wide eyes and exuberant expression gave the impression of a young boy afraid he would miss something if he blinked too often.

"Have you ever been to London, Joshua?"

"Not since I was a boy, sir." He turned from the window to Harry. "I have been to Hayes many times, however. My aunt lives there—she's married to a cleric." He grinned proudly, but then his smile fell. "Hayes is very much like Wimbledon, though."

Harry knitted a few more stitches, but something niggled at him. "Weren't you with Lady Sabrina the day she found me in London?"

"Oh, no, sir, that was Adam. He is her driver in Town, but he came all the way out to Wimbledon that day. I only helped him bring you up to the room once you arrived. You were in very poor shape, if you don't mind my saying so, sir."

"Yes, I was in rather poor shape," Harry said, thinking over the bursts of memory he had of that day—something he tried *not* to think about most of the time. Even now, he could feel the panic beginning to bubble, a residue of what he'd felt when Malcolm's men had attacked him in the alley.

But something pulled at him, and so he walked through the barricades his mind had erected. He was about to face Malcolm again, and it would be wise to go into that meeting with as full an awareness as possible.

"Adam and Lady Sabrina brought me back from London by themselves?" Hadn't there had been another man helping to put him into the carriage? Or was he confusing that memory with the two men who had beaten him?

"Yes, sir. Adam drove, and she attended to you in the carriage."

He could feel Lady Sabrina's hand brushing back hair from his face and whispering that everything would be all right before he drifted back to unconsciousness. He could not picture Lady Sabrina helping to carry him to the carriage, however. He'd been unable to walk, since both legs had been beyond use, but he hadn't been dragged either.

The memory became a bit crisper.

There had been someone holding him under the shoulders, and another man holding his legs—the broken one hurting so much he kept crying out. Harry could remember the back of that man's head. Dark hair, with gray shot through. Lady Sabrina would not have been able to hold the weight of his torso, which meant it had to have been another man.

She'd been calling out instructions: "Watch his head . . . Hurry now . . . You must hold his right leg above the knee, Jack."

Harry startled at the memory of the name. Jack?

The memory moved back to before he'd been carried out of the alley, when he and Lady Sabrina had been alone amid the crates and barrels. He was lying on the ground, nearly unconscious with pain, crying while someone—Lady Sabrina—kissed the back of his hand.

I need to fetch my man and my driver. They can help you to my carriage.

Her man.

Jack?

Jack was the name of the man who had led Harry to The Lost Tartan to meet with Lord Damion on that fateful morning.

Was that right?

He thought hard. Yes, the man who had met him at the bridge had been named Jack; Mr. Gordon had said so in the letter he'd sent regarding the appointment. Jack had been slight . . . with dark hair shot through with gray. So, the man carrying his legs had been the same man who'd led him to his appointment with Lord Damion.

"Joshua," Harry asked.

He reluctantly turned his attention away from the window. "Yes, sir?"

"Do you know a man named Jack?"

"I know several Jacks, sir."

"This one is thin, bearded, and would know his way around London."

Jack had led Harry around the streets on their way to the appointment like a man who had lived there all his life. He closed his mouth to stop from asking too many questions—Lady Sabrina's staff was careful of their mistress. But if he asked in a way that didn't seem to be about her . . . "I think he might have helped get me into the carriage that day in London. He had a chipped tooth."

"Oh, do you mean Jack Corbans?"

Chapter Thirty-Three

*H*arry nodded, forcing himself not to react to Joshua's confirmation of this connection.

Jack worked for Lord Damion.

Jack had helped Harry as Lady Sabrina's "man."

Lady Sabrina's footman knew Jack.

Harry's mind became very still and quiet, like when he'd been a boy and come across a fox or some other animal in the woods around Falconridge. Within that stillness was focus, and with the right focus, he would not miss a single movement of the creature that would run if it knew he was watching.

"He seemed like a good man," Harry said evenly.

"Yes, Jack is an excellent fellow. He was a groom at Wimbledon House when I was a boy. There was some trouble with his son that Lady Sabrina's brother helped him with, and they set up Jack in London after that. I haven't seen him in ages."

"What does he do in London?" Harry asked.

Joshua shrugged. "Don't know. I haven't seen him since he left here. I think I was fifteen when he went up to London. Must have found work up there, then. Handy that he was there to help."

The first night Lady Sabrina had come into Harry's room to introduce herself, he'd been tense and suspicious. Waking up in an unfamiliar place with fractured memory of what had happened left him at a disadvantage in every way. His entire body had hurt, and he'd needed a drink so badly he'd been too sick to care about manners.

But he remembered asking Lady Sabrina why she had been in that part of London at that time of day because it had struck him as strange. His meeting with Lord Damion had been so early, but her explanation of having a special appointment with a cobbler had seemed reasonable enough at the time.

But Jack had been Lady Sabrina's groom here in Wimbledon years earlier. That could not be a coincidence.

Did Lady Sabrina *know* Lord Damion? Was she in league with him somehow, and did they share Jack's services?

That didn't sit right. There was something both too simple and too complex about that possibility. But there *was* a connection.

Both Lady Sabrina and Lord Damion were noble.

Both wealthy.

Both in the same part of London at an unusual time of day.

The only part of Lord Damion Harry had seen was his red gloves. He'd told Ward that Lord Damion was a slight man . . . because he had never considered for a moment that Lord Damion was actually a woman.

Both generous.

Both mysterious.

Both saw a potential in him that no one else did.

Things Lady Sabrina had told him filtered through his mind:

"If there were a guarantee that only good men were in positions of power, it might be different."

"I believe that as I seek to create a world I would wish to live in, that world becomes more of a possibility."

From her letter just this morning, she'd said, "I wish you the very best as you begin anew as a better man, capable and worthy of your place in the world."

And from Lord Damion's letter: "The world needs good men. I hope you will choose to become one of them."

Last night, when he'd said she didn't know the kind of man he'd been, she'd said, "Maybe I know more than you think."

A dozen conversations played through his mind. Her asking about his sisters but not his parents, as if she'd already known they were gone. The determination she'd had to dry him out, which was also one of the requirements Lord Damion had set as part of his reformation.

"Joshua," Harry asked, his breathing quickening, though he hoped it wasn't obvious. "Do you know a man by the name of Mr. Gordon?"

"No, sir," Joshua said.

Harry was relieved. Perhaps he was chasing windmills, then. Mr. Gordon worked so closely with Lord Damion that—

"But he seems a nice enough man."

Harry's eyes jumped from the blanket in his lap to Joshua's face. "You *do* know him, then?"

"I don't *know* him. He's only come to the house that one time, and he was in a hurry so I didn't get a good sense of him, but, like I said, he seems nice enough."

"W-when did he come to the house?" Harry held his breath.

"Uh . . ." Joshua scrunched up his face as he thought about

the question. "A few days after you came, I think." He paused. "Early on, though; you were still sleeping most of the time."

"And he came to meet with Lady Sabrina?"

Saying her name shut down Joshua's willingness like a gate, as though making him aware that he was discussing his mistress's personal business. His face closed, and he nodded. He turned back to the window but glanced sideways at Harry, who had the presence of mind to go back to his knitting so it would look as though that was what held his attention now.

His whole body began to tingle, and he fumbled through his stitches, stopping to unpick a solid dozen.

Lord Damion was Lady Sabrina.

Lady Sabrina was Lord Damion.

She had been the person on the other side of the slide that day at The Lost Tartan.

She was the "nobleman" who wanted to hide her philanthropy toward dissolute men from the *ton*.

How had he not made the connection before? But he knew why—because it had seemed impossible. One did not wonder if perhaps there were fields of pink grass somewhere in the world, because grass being green was an irrefutable fact. One did not verify each morning that foxes ran along the ground and falcons flew on the wind, rather than the other way around. Harry had not woken up expecting his leg to be healed because he knew it wouldn't be. Just like he knew that Lord Damion was a man and Lady Sabrina was a woman and they were two separate parts of his life that did not touch.

It wasn't just details of her former marriage that Lady Sabrina had hidden from him—it was Lord Damion. Which meant everything Lord Damion knew about Harry, she also knew. Which meant that last night when he'd pushed her away because she didn't know just how horrible a man he'd been, she *had* known.

He had still done the right thing in refusing the advances, and he was sure she agreed with him in the light of morning, but she'd made those advances with a full understanding of the man he'd been. Because she believed that men could change, and she saw the changes he had made. It was not a stretch of his imagination to think that she'd held herself against the building tension between them, that she'd tried to tell him it was normal for men and women not attracted to one another to still be friends.

The bubble of hope he felt amid this remarkable discovery displaced any anger or hurt he might otherwise have felt at discovering her lies. During their conversations, she'd all but told him why a woman would pose as a man in this world. Lord Damion's motivation was to change the world, one man at a time, but only another man could do such a thing. The young men she rescued would not respect or trust a female benefactor. Yet in that one thing, Harry believed she had been wrong.

Lord Damion had saved Harry by paying off his debts and giving him another chance to make a life worth living, no doubt about it, but *Lady Sabrina* had been the stronger influence encouraging him to make personal changes in the weeks since. It was Lady Sabrina who'd helped him see his course ahead. Lady Sabrina who had given him confidence that he could rise above the pain of his childhood. Lady Sabrina had been the standard he had set for his improvement: to be as good a man as Lady Sabrina was a woman, to be the sort of man a woman like Lady Sabrina would one day trust enough to share a life with.

Oh, if not for this meeting with Malcolm he would turn this carriage around immediately and kiss her breathless. If she could be persuaded to tell him everything she hadn't told him already—about her marriage and Lord Damion and whatever other secrets she'd kept careful and safe—they would both know each other better than anyone in the world knew them. That was a connection that would surpass status and money and past mistakes.

This meeting with Malcolm.

The rising tingle was replaced with a flush of fear.

Malcolm.

Mr. Gordon had made this meeting sound simple. Malcolm was insisting Harry pay off his debt in person. Harry would go to Mr. Gordon's office and collect the payoff amount he and Joshua would then take directly to the appointment. Harry's goal in the meeting was to complete the payoff and receive an official receipt.

Harry had been anxious about returning to London and seeing Malcolm again, but leaving Rose Haven had been the bigger regret and therefore deadened the reasonable dread for the upcoming confrontation.

If Lady Sabrina happening upon Harry in that alley hadn't been a coincidence, could he count it as a coincidence that Malcolm's men had been there too? They *had* asked him about Lord Damion before they'd broken him into pieces. He'd avoided those memories so strongly for weeks that he hadn't given that detail enough thought. The letter he'd received from Lord Damion at the conclusion of their meeting had never been found.

A dozen questions piled up in his mind. He considered asking Joshua, but Joshua was his security, and Harry didn't want to transfer his anxieties to the large footman.

Harry had been sitting still, needles poised but silent as all these bits of information had snapped together in his mind. Now, he began to slowly go back to his knitting, planning how he would approach Mr. Gordon with what he now knew. It would not be the meeting Mr. Gordon was expecting.

Knit.

Purl.

Knit.

Purl.

Click.

Clack.

Click.

Chapter Thirty-Four

*H*arry was forty minutes late for the appointment with Malcolm but didn't feel nervous until he recognized the man who stood outside of the currently closed club where the meeting was to take place. The man was one of the men from the alley that morning almost a month ago. Harry caught his breath and felt sweat gathering at his hairline.

He reminded himself that Joshua would be there and that he and Mr. Gordon had gone over every detail—or, well, as many details as they could once Mr. Gordon realized that Harry wasn't angry and that he wanted to do this to help protect Sabrina.

This will work, he told himself, sitting up straight and taking a deep breath. *It has to.*

As the carriage came to a stop, Harry thanked the heavens he was no longer a drinking man. If he were, he'd have gone to a pub instead of Mr. Gordon's office as soon as he'd figured things out and drunk himself silly rather than confront this situation. But he wouldn't be the kind of man to run away like that anymore. If he could play this out the way he and Mr. Gordon had planned it, then in an hour's time, he could put this entire experience behind him. Only then could he figure out how to approach Sabrina with what he knew.

"Remember my instructions, Joshua," Harry said when the man put his hand on the door pull. "Stay close, don't show fear, and if I tell you to go or bang on the door or the wall or whatever four times, you run for the nearest constable no matter what else is happening."

"Yes, sir."

Joshua's enthusiasm for London had ebbed once Harry had returned from his meeting with Mr. Gordon, serious and intense. He'd given Joshua instructions while they wound deeper into the side streets and alleyways that were Malcolm's hunting grounds.

Joshua opened the carriage door to let himself out first, removed Harry's crutches, and then helped Harry descend from the carriage. Harry kept his chin lifted and his attention on everything around him. Malcolm's man stepped toward them, but Harry kept his eyes on the opening of the street some yards away while purposely taking his time in finding the right position on his crutches.

When Jack walked across the alley as though strolling down that street, Harry felt himself relax. Sabrina's man had gotten Mr. Gordon's message and come without question. Jack nodded in greeting, and Harry lifted his chin a touch in acknowledgment. Two other men followed a few steps behind Jack—his boys were taller and broader than their father. Harry's confidence increased.

Malcolm's man pushed open the door, allowing Joshua and Harry to enter the club. Harry was tempted to use his crutch to sweep the man's legs out from under him, but he only had to remember the black club the man likely had hidden beneath his coat to think better of it. He would not win a physical confrontation with this man, but he had to believe he could best Malcolm at this meeting of minds now that Harry's mind was clear.

His gut churned as he stepped into the club, flooded with memories of how clubs just like this one had chipped away at his character one chink at a time. He did not place all the blame on these establishments—he'd been a willing participant—but they certainly played their part. Not only on the wasting of his life but on the wasting of so many other lives just like his.

Early on during his time in London he'd remarked to a friend how generous it was that the clubs gave free drinks to the patrons. Now he could see that was part of the trap. The women the club kept on hand were another portion, and another set of victims. The clubs were appealing to the worst part of young men, completely capturing their senses and their will in the process.

Once Harry's eyes adjusted to the dim room, he recognized another man standing next to a door on the far side of the room. As Harry had told Mr. Gordon, he'd only ever seen three individual men with Malcolm and suspected that was all the security Malcolm kept on hand. Certainly not an army, and one fewer man than the four Harry had on his side—though Jack would not come into the club unless they remained inside for fifteen full minutes. Poor Joshua had no idea what was truly happening, but he was sturdy, and Harry felt sure he would be an asset if things went poorly.

Harry nudged Joshua toward the door the second man guarded. Malcolm would be behind that door, sitting at a desk, most likely, and grinning like a king upon his rotten throne.

When they reached the door, the guard put his arm out, blocking Joshua. "Only Mr. Stillman goes in."

"Mr. Stillman isn't going in there without me," Joshua said

with impressive fortitude for a man who, though built like an ox, spent most of his time opening doors and hanging up coats.

"It's all right, Joshua. You know what to do if anything goes wrong. They'll be here before these blokes know what's hit them."

Malcolm's man looked confused, and Harry smiled. "Did you really think Lord Damion would send me to this den of thieves without precautions?"

Harry didn't wait for an answer and simply stepped ahead of Joshua, leaning on his left crutch so he could open the door by himself. He'd practiced the move three times at Mr. Gordon's office, wanting to make the right impression from the very start of this meeting.

Malcolm sat glowering at a desk placed in the center of a tiny room just as Harry had expected. Half a dozen lamps lit the windowless room almost to daylight levels, which Harry hadn't expected. He blinked quickly to help his eyes adjust to the brighter light and focused on keeping his breathing even so the cramping fear he felt in his gut would not show. The door snapped shut behind him, but Harry managed to hold back the flinching.

Joshua can take care of himself, he told himself, then prayed, *Oh, please, let Joshua be able to take care of himself.*

"You're nearly an hour late," Malcolm said, his eyes narrowed and his nostrils flaring.

"Am I?" Harry said, lifting his eyebrows and drawing on all the arrogance that had once sustained him. "My apologies. Though if time were your concern, then you should have accepted Mr. Gordon's payoff weeks ago. Having waited that long, one might think another half an hour would not be so difficult." He lifted his right crutch. "And, thanks to you, I no longer move as quickly as I might otherwise."

There was the slightest twitch of Malcolm's left eye, the one with the scar beneath it. Had the unsightly scar pushed Malcolm to do business in the underworld because he could not find more legitimate work? Or had the scar come after he'd sold his soul to the vipers who lived in the shadows and preyed upon the feeble and stupid?

"Where've you been all these weeks, Stillman?"

"In Wimbledon. It's a lovely place—have you ever been?" Harry took two more swinging steps to the chair set across from Malcolm and awkwardly lowered himself into it, resting the crutches across his lap to keep them on hand. If necessary, they would make decent weapons, but mostly he wanted to avoid the indignity of having to bend over and retrieve them when he was ready to leave.

Without wasting any more time, Harry reached into his jacket pocket and removed the thick stack of bank notes Mr. Gordon had given him. So much money! He tapped the stack on his knee to straighten them and then began counting them out into a fresh stack on the desk. He kept waiting for Malcolm to interrupt him with questions about Lord Damion, but he didn't.

When Harry had finished counting, he pushed the stack forward. In some ways, he considered it little more than blood money because it represented the price Harry had paid for those activities that had seemed like fun at the time but which had nearly killed him. He was determined to remember this feeling of handing over so much money to a slime of a man like Malcolm in case he was ever tempted to try his luck again.

"That's thirty-two hundred pounds; you saw me count it out. Lord Damion and I agreed that since you insisted on meeting with me in person, we were not responsible for the additional late fees, especially since my inability to come to London for the meeting was due to your incapacitation."

If Malcolm was surprised that Harry was the one to bring Lord Damion into the conversation, he did not show it.

"Who is he?"

Harry raised his eyebrows. "Who is who?"

"Lord Damion. Who is he?"

"Ah." Harry sat back in the chair as casually as possible. "He is the lender with whom I have made arrangements in order to escape your tyranny."

"Who—is—he?" Malcolm repeated in a tone that sounded like spitting. "What is his real name?"

Harry laughed, then answered in the same emphasized cadence, but without the spittle. "His—name—is—Lord—Damion."

"Who is he *really*?"

Harry sighed dramatically, then leaned forward and pushed the money closer to Malcolm. "I was told to obtain a receipt proving that my debt has been paid in full, so if you wouldn't mind." He motioned toward the pen in the stock on the side of Malcolm's desk.

Malcolm smiled an ugly grin, and Harry repressed a shudder. The man was worse to look at up close than from a distance. But he was also thin and his head hung forward like an old man. "You ain't leaving this room until you tell me everything you know about Lord Damion."

Harry leaned back again. "All right, but what I know isn't worth all this trouble. He is very rich and very powerful, and he helps stupid men like myself who get into tangles with repulsive men like yourself." He bowed slightly in Malcolm's direction.

Malcolm's eyes lit up. "You've met him, then?"

"Of course, I have met him. Do you think he would lend

thousands of pounds to a man he's never met?" He laughed. "Now, my receipt, please?"

"Who is the man behind the phantom?"

"Like I said, I know him only as Lord Damion."

"What does he look like?"

The image that came immediately to Harry's mind was how Sabrina had looked last night, her hair braided over her shoulder, the ruffles of her dress almost hiding her curves, but increasing his curiosity at the same time. He quickly realized he could not risk the distraction of *that* image, so he changed it to the memory of the night she'd yelled at him for hiding brandy in his bed. Oh, but she'd been frightening.

"Average height, dark hair, dark eyes. Handsome."

Malcolm pulled back. "Handsome?"

Harry smiled. "Oh, yes, *quite* handsome. Rosy lips. Slim, elegant fingers." He was pleased that so far he hadn't needed to lie. Sabrina *was* average height for a woman, and she had dark hair and eyes. And she was, in his opinion, a very handsome woman.

Malcolm made a disgusted sound in the back of his throat; Harry smiled wider.

"Lord Damion has interfered with my business," Malcolm said, his eyes fixed on Harry with a glare that no longer felt intimidating. This man lived in the shadows and worked in the dark, like rats and spiders. He was small and despicable, and he pulled men down to the depths of misery in order to feel better about himself.

Harry had taken a similar course, but he was a different man now. He was going to use his advantages to be an influence for good, the way Sabrina did.

Malcolm continued, a slight hiss in his voice that Harry felt was overdramatic. "I intend to put an end to his interference."

"See, that's the part we couldn't quite figure out," Harry said in a light tone, cocking his head to one side. "Mr. Gordon and I suspect that you hoped I would continue believing I could earn back the principle, and therefore, you would make a mint in interest until I was out of funds. But I *was* out of funds when Lord Damion came in to pay my debt. Then you were so put out about the debt being paid, which was strange. I would think you'd be eager for the money since I couldn't make the interest payments anymore. Why is that?" He waited two beats and then answered his own question. "Actually, I think we have it figured. Let me know if I've got it wrong."

He cleared his throat as Malcolm narrowed his eyes even more. It was a wonder he could even see out of the slits.

"In reviewing the four clients that Lord Damion has helped by paying off their debts to you over the last few years, each one of them had a wealthy relative of some kind. I can't remember all the names, but the most recent one—before me, that is—was Mr. Bartholomew Hopkins. His father owns a successful plantation in America, though you know that, of course. Now, Hopkins does not get on with his father, but he has enough of an inheritance of his own to make him capable of gambling to excess, and, on at least a few occasions, his father has paid off substantial debt for his son, despite their strained relationship. Sad, really, how many of us dissolute young men run off the people who could help us most."

Harry didn't have any way to keep track of the time, since he'd traded his grandfather's watch in order to pay his back rent, but he thought he had a few more minutes to make his point before Jack would make his presence known.

"As I'm sure you know, my uncle is the Viscount of Howardsford and returned from India a few years ago rich as Croesus.

He's also paid off my debts a time or two in the past, and I am guilty of having mentioned his name as a credential when seeking admission into some of the more elite clubs. Targeting young men with rich relatives is a rather brilliant—if not evil and debasing—business model on your part. By taking on clients who you know have family to pay off their debts means that when a man continually falls into debt, you continually make more money. More than you would off a man who learns his lesson the first time—am I right?"

Malcolm's face was turning red, which Harry took as confirmation that he was right. Thank goodness. Mr. Gordon had already worked that part out before Harry had shown up at his office demanding answers. That Mr. Gordon and Sabrina were going to let Harry go into this meeting without any of this information had been madness on their part. And sheer desperation. What if Harry had known more about Lord Damion than he had? What if Malcolm's men had tortured from him information he hadn't known he knew?

There was no time to think on that right now.

"Here's what you did not know," Harry continued quickly. "Lord Damion works only with men whose families have verified that they are cut off, hence they will no longer be rescued. As far as we can figure, the first time Lord Damion took on one of your clients, you wouldn't have known that your former client would leave London as soon as the debt was paid. Lenders take on new debtors all the time to pay off the old crook, now don't they? You expected that client to go back to the tables and start all over again, necessitating that he come back to you for additional lending. But he didn't, which must have been rather vexing.

"When Lord Damion brought an end to what should have been a long-term client for a second time, you must have been very frustrated. Then when Hopkins *also* changed his habits so completely, you'd have known that Lord Damion posed a threat to your plan for repeat customers. It was just unlucky—or lucky, depending on one's view—that I was the next of your clients to make an arrangement with Lord Damion." He shook his head. "The one point I can't figure out is how you knew I was his client *before* Mr. Gordon contacted you about resolving the debt."

Malcolm looked fit to explode, and yet Harry felt sure he would take the bait—this was Malcolm's first chance to show himself the superior in this exchange. He tightened his jaw as though trying not to give in to the temptation. Harry decided to press a little further. He had not lost all his skill as a gambler. What did he have to lose?

"On the night you and your men confronted me in the alley, I wasn't yet working with Lord Damion. My debts were extreme, and you must have wanted to make sure I didn't disappear, but I got away that night. The next time I ran into your men, they were within a few blocks of the meeting place with Lord Damion, which means they had some idea of where I had been, but they did not know for sure. If they'd known, they wouldn't have needed to ask me during the beating." He paused when Malcolm pressed his lips together even tighter. Harry shrugged. "Not that it really matters." He nodded toward the stack of money. "The receipt, please?"

"You should choose your friends more carefully, Mr. Still-man."

Friends? What could his friends have to do with any of this?

Harry frowned at the satisfaction evident on Malcolm's face.

And then like a sudden, hard slap, he understood.

Ward was the only friend Harry had left—or so he'd thought.

Malcolm grinned as the power dynamic in the room abruptly shifted.

Harry had waited for nearly an hour at Cumberland Gate after he and Ward had run in opposite directions from Malcolm's men in the alley that night. Ward had been winded and wide-eyed and claimed he'd had a devil of a time losing his pursuer when he finally arrived. Harry had commiserated; he, too, had heard footsteps dogging him all the way to George Street.

If he hadn't gotten completely smashed as soon as they arrived at Ward's parents' house, he might have spent more time wondering what had taken Ward so long to get there.

And *Ward* had been the one who had sought out Hopkins and gathered the contact information for Lord Damion.

Harry hadn't spoken to Ward about the details of his correspondence with Mr. Gordon, and he hadn't told Ward about where he was supposed to meet Jack on the morning of the meeting, but he'd left the letters in his room at Ward's London house.

The first time Ward had visited Harry at Rose Haven, he'd asked who Lord Damion was, and though it had seemed natural at the time, was it? Hadn't Sabrina accused Ward of being no friend at all? And once Sabrina had put Ward on notice of his behavior in her house, Ward had disappeared. Perhaps because he had never wanted to visit Harry in the first place and had only come on Malcolm's errand. Perhaps he'd been convinced that Harry hadn't known anything significant about Lord Damion. Just as Harry couldn't believe he hadn't put Lady Sabrina and Lord Damion together before today, he wondered how he hadn't seen this possibility.

Harry felt a lump in his throat, and yet he could not be certain that if the places had been reversed, he wouldn't have done the same thing to Ward if the price had been high enough or the threat severe enough.

"You can give Lord Damion a message for me," Malcolm said, leaning forward across the desk, still looking triumphant. "I will discover who he is and—"

"What?" Harry interrupted, pushing aside his hurt and responding sharply. "Blackmail him to keep the nobles from knowing that he's saving their sons from rubbish like you?" Harry flung one hand in the air for dramatic gesture. "Storm his castle with the half-wits you keep on hand?" Harry laughed, but without humor, letting his eyes bore into the other man. "He knows he can't stop you from your despicable work, Malcolm, but he can make good men out of the few of us who are finally, truly, ready to rise out of the gutter."

Malcolm jolted forward, causing Harry to startle. His thin lips pulled back from his teeth in a snarl. "You'll be back. Every one of you will be back, and Lord Damion won't be helping you again. Once I discover who he really is—"

"I will *not* be back," Harry said resolutely, savoring the truth of those words, the freedom they promised him, and the depth of his commitment. "You forget that the men he is saving are the sons of his friends. It would not ruin *him* to have it known. He hides his identity so that when we have finally become the men we are supposed to be, we don't walk into a room with him and feel beholden. He hides his identity so that men don't seek him out in the drawing rooms or try to use their connection to him as leverage for his helping a young man not yet broken enough to comply with his terms. He is attempting to preserve their dignity by allowing their past to truly be their past. So do your worst. He shall continue his legacy of mercy and redemption."

He leaned forward until he and Malcolm were mere inches

from one another. He could smell the smoke and the drink on his breath—had he ever smelled like that?

"My receipt. Please."

"I ain't done with you yet, Mr. Stillman. You know more than you're saying, and I'll be the one who decides when—"

Yelling and thumping from the other side of the door cut him off.

Malcolm stood in the same moment Harry swung his crutches to the floor. He pushed himself up with the left, while swinging the other toward Malcolm like a sword. The shaft of wood caught Malcolm's shoulder and sent him crashing into the bookshelf against the east wall.

Malcolm didn't fall to the ground as Harry had expected, so Harry hopped toward him on his good leg, swatting at him with the crutch as though he were a cook batting a cat out of the kitchen with a broom.

Malcolm ducked and tried to block the hits, but he couldn't help retreating from Harry's attack until he was literally backed into the corner with Harry's right crutch pushed against his throat.

Harry was breathing as though he'd just run across London, and he had to lean on his left foot and crutch to keep himself upright. "Give me the receipt"—he took a breath—"and we can bring this to an end."

Chapter Thirty-Five

Malcolm scrunched his face up like a rat, but Harry didn't realize why until a glob of spittle hit his cheek.

Harry yelped in disgust, yet he couldn't let go of the crutch at Malcolm's throat or the one holding him up. The ruckus in the other room continued as he glared at Malcolm and tried to ignore the slime sliding down his cheek. "That is absolutely disgusting, and if I were not trying to be a gentleman, I would spit right back."

"Smith!" Malcolm suddenly roared. "Now."

There was a grunt and a thump on the other side of the door, but no one answered Malcolm's call.

"I only needed that receipt, Malcolm. You have made this so much more difficult than it needed to be. I hope when you have time to reflect upon your actions, you will learn from your mistakes."

Malcolm suddenly grabbed Harry's crutch and threw it to the side, something Harry had expected him to do before now. Malcolm wasn't used to fighting his own battles, but Harry had been in more than his share of fights. He sat back on the desk and wielded the left crutch as Malcolm lunged toward the other side of the desk.

The crutch hit Malcolm behind the knees, sending him diving forward, arms wheeling for balance. Harry winced at the sound of the man's teeth cracking together as his chin hit the edge of the desk on his way down.

Malcolm tried to catch himself and instead sent the stack of bank notes skittering across the desktop, along with a variety of other papers and ledgers. Malcolm hit the floor, money and papers raining over him. He moaned but made no effort to rise.

Balanced on the desk, Harry pulled his handkerchief from the inside pocket of his coat and wiped the last of the spittle from his cheek. Absolutely revolting. He placed the left crutch back under his arm and pushed himself to his feet, wincing at the throbbing in his right leg. At some point in the altercation, he'd hit his leg against something. He had a feeling the pain was going to get worse by the minute now that the intensity of the confrontation had passed.

The door of the office few open and Jack stood there, eyes wild and chest heaving. There was blood dripping from his nose, but the scrapes on his knuckles, and the fact that it was him and not one of Malcolm's men, showed that Malcolm's men had gotten the worst of it.

"Ah, Jack," Harry said from beside the desk opposite of Malcolm's moaning form. "You are just in time. Could you retrieve my other crutch and get me the devil out of here? I've had quite enough of this place for one afternoon. The exertion has me fearing I might be sick all over my boots soon, and this is the only pair I have."

Jack sprang into action, retrieved the crutch, and then helped Harry center it beneath his arm.

"What about the money?" Jack asked as Harry took his first swinging step toward the door.

"Leave it," Harry said.

Jack made a sound somewhere between a whimper and a cough as he looked at the scattered notes.

"I know," Harry commiserated, but spoke loudly enough that Malcolm would hear. "But Lord Damion keeps his word."

Jack followed as Harry swung his way through the club. One man was unconscious on the floor, while another was braced against the wall, his hand covering his eye as he bent forward at the waist. The third man was gone, and Joshua, hurrying behind Harry, said the man had run off.

Harry felt dizzy and sick, but the men assisted him back into the carriage easily enough. Joshua arranged him on the back bench so he could put his bad leg out straight. The bravado was wearing off, and delayed panic was setting in, along with the pain. What if more of Malcolm's men were on their way? What if Malcolm reciprocated in a way that hurt Sabrina? Harry had downplayed the potential, but the truth was Lady Sabrina would suffer both socially and financially if her role as Lord Damion was made known. The portions of her work done under the name of that persona could also be affected if men realized they were partnered with a *mere* female.

Harry huffed at the thought of anyone attaching that description to Lady Sabrina. "Mere" *anything* did not fit her.

Joshua pulled the carriage door shut. His knuckles were bruised, but he smiled, and his eyes were bright.

"It worked!" Joshua said, then hit the roof so the driver would know to depart.

"Jack and his boys are away?"

Joshua nodded. "They were gone before you were even inside the carriage."

"Good." He shifted his leg and pain shot up his hip, causing him to inhale sharply.

"You're hurt?" Joshua said, leaning forward to look over Harry's leg. He'd assisted his mother with Harry's care but had never seemed particularly interested in the more skilled interventions.

Harry nodded, clenching his teeth together and trying not to think of how welcome a shot of brandy would be right now for both his nerves and his leg. "I'll be all right," he said, but his words came out clunky. He was supposed to meet Uncle Elliot at his house in Mayfair now that the meeting was over. How much would he explain about whatever new injury he had inflicted upon himself?

"It's too bad you can't come back to Rose Haven," Joshua said. "Mum could take a look at that leg and make sure everything's all right."

Therese.

Sabrina.

Harry stared out the side window of the carriage without really seeing through it, then he turned to Joshua. "I must ask your help in another respect, and I shall warn you that Lady Sabrina might not be happy with you at first for going along with it."

Joshua, who had just brawled with merciless thugs without hesitation, looked frightened at the prospect of upsetting his mistress.

"I do believe, however," Harry continued, "that, in time, she will thank you for doing as I ask."

"She's been very good to me, Mr. Stillman. I don't want to go against her orders."

"But did she actually *order* you not to return me to Rose Haven?"

He looked relieved. "That is all you want, to return to Wimbledon?"

"That is all."

His brow furrowed with concern once again. "But Lady Sabrina is not expecting you."

"Right, but circumstances have changed since she asked you to accompany me to this meeting." Bless him for going along with everything so far. Bless him even more if he would go along with this as well. Harry needed to see Sabrina. He needed her to know how much had changed for them in the course of only a few hours' time. "I *am* once again in need of medical treatment." He paused and made a face he hoped looked as though he were in excruciating pain, then let out a breath. "I believe she would want me taken to Therese, just as she had last time I was in need of care."

Chapter Thirty-Six

*S*abrina heard the carriage returning from London while she wrote out her final schedule for Therese. She had only five more days in Wimbledon, then she would travel to Brighton by carriage and sail to Naples a few days after that. If anything could save her from the confusing emotions of this last week, it would be an ocean voyage to a place she had never been. Right?

She prayed it would be the remedy, for she could not imagine continuing to feel as she felt now. Replaying last night. Worrying about Harry. Wishing things were different, even though they could never be anything other than exactly what they were.

The carriage wheels stopped in front of the house while she sanded the letter. Why had they not pulled around to the carriage house? She was folding the paper when she heard commotion from the first level of the house. Joshua calling orders. Therese asking questions, though Sabrina could not hear the words.

Sabrina left the letter and hurried from her study, then froze at the top of the stairs.

Harry?

"It will be best to get him to the bedchamber," Therese said, leading the way. Steven stood on one side of Harry with his shoulder under his arm while Joshua took the other as they carried Harry up the stairs.

Sabrina remained frozen. He was supposed to be gone. She was supposed to forget about him. Therese saw her and changed direction at the landing, coming to Sabrina's side while the men continued toward the east wing.

"Apparently there was some trouble at the appointment Mr. Stillman had in London, and his leg has been injured again. Joshua thought I should look at it." Therese did not wait for a response but quickly followed after the men.

Sabrina stood there, stunned and unsure what to do. When the spell broke, she hurried after them. Before she entered the room, she heard Therese yell from inside, "I must have those trousers off so I can see the injury."

Sabrina stepped away, then began to pace until Joshua came out of the room, Harry's trousers in hand.

"What happened?" Sabrina asked sharply.

"We jumped Malcolm and his men," Joshua said proudly.

Sabrina blinked. "'We'? You and Mr. Stillman? What on earth?"

"Ah, no, I mean Mr. Stillman had his part—wish I could have seen it—but mostly it was Jack and his boys and me." He puffed out his chest slightly. "Not until Malcolm's men made the first move, of course."

Sabrina blinked, her thoughts moving so quickly she could not make sense of anything until she landed on one particular element that felt like the tug on a ribbon that would unravel the knot. "Jack?"

"He might be small, but he knows how to fight, and I'm guessin' he's taught his boys 'cause they came in full charge."

"Why on earth would Jack be there?"

"Mr. Gordon sent for him."

"Mr. Gordon?" she said with just enough of an edge to close down Joshua's expression.

Joshua watched her a moment, confused, then nodded toward the stairs past Sabrina's shoulder. "Mum wants her bag," he said, then took the stairs two at a time back to the first level.

Sabrina stayed where she was, staring at the door. Steven came out and gave her a nervous nod as he hurried by. She nodded back at him a few seconds after he was already gone, distracted. Jack and Mr. Gordon working with Harry to jump Malcolm and his men?

Her heart thumped in her chest, pulled between a hundred thoughts, and she lost track of time waiting for Therese to emerge.

"Go on in, Sabrina. He's asking for you. Joshua's gone for my bag, but I need a few other things. I'll be a minute."

She did not know what to expect when she entered this room. Harry was in there. He was hurt. He had come back. And Jack had been at the appointment with Malcolm.

She finally gathered her courage and went into the room. Harry was lying above the covers on the bed, dressed in his shirtsleeves and with a blanket over his lap, covering him to the knee. The splint had been removed from his leg, which was propped up with a pillow. He did not *look* injured, which was a relief.

"Harry?" she asked hesitantly, emotions and questions buzzing like bees in her chest. She was used to taking charge, but she was at a complete disadvantage now.

"Would you please close the door, Sabrina? I would hate for us to be overheard."

He knew that Jack was connected to both her and Lord Damion.

Mr. Gordon was somehow involved.

There'd been an altercation.

She could not determine which thought should occupy her mind the most and therefore continued to race through all of them as she closed the door to his bedchamber.

What else did he know?

"Will you come here?" he asked after a few seconds passed during which she'd stood facing the door, trying to prepare herself.

She turned and did as he asked, but she stopped a few feet away. The last time she'd gotten any closer than this had been too close. Just last night. She'd planned to never see him again. His cheeks were bright, and his eyes were as captivating as ever.

He reached out his hand toward her, and though she hesitated, she took hold of it. How could she not? He tightened his grip as soon as her hand was in his and pulled her sharply toward him. She stumbled forward, catching herself on the bed as his other arm reached around her back and drew her toward him.

"Oh," she exclaimed, any further words of surprise cut off as his mouth pressed against hers, and she felt herself falling against him, half on the bed, half off. The same feelings that had overcome her the night before possessed her in an instant.

His arms held her tightly to him at first, but then relaxed as he lowered his head back to the pillow.

She was still bent over him. Still blinking. Still unable to make sense of any of this. He'd pushed her away last night, and yet now pulled her to him?

"I need some time to prove myself," he whispered, reaching up to run his finger over her lips.

"W-what?" she said against his thumb.

"You told me that it would be what I did once all the same choices were before me that would prove myself capable of change. I need that time so both of us know that what I have learned these last weeks—and what I have decided about the man I want to be—is a possibility."

"I don't understand."

He raised his mouth to hers again, and she lost all control. Again.

When he pulled back, they were both breathing heavily, though she felt light as a feather. "I want to marry you, Sabrina."

She stiffened, but he tightened his hold around her back.

"There is a process called separate estate—you know of it, yes?"

He stared at her until she answered. "A . . . a trustee is appointed as an executor of one's assets, which are then held outside of other agreements."

"Which, in the case of marriage, means that a woman can keep her husband from having jurisdiction over her wealth and property. It is not perfect, I know, but Mr. Gordon has surely proved himself trustworthy enough to be named trustee. It means you can marry without fear that you would lose your security."

"Harry." She tried to pull away, and though he resisted a moment, he let her go. She stood, straightened her skirts, and tried not to meet his eye. Where had he learned of separate estate? From Mr. Gordon? Were her employees conspiring with him against her?

"I know everything, Sabrina—well, not everything, I suppose—but I know you are Lord Damion. I know that you know everything about me and yet you still see the potential of who I can become. What's more, I believe you have fallen in love with me."

She stared at her shoes, not knowing what to do or what to think. Mr. Gordon had betrayed her. She wanted to cry.

"When did he tell you?"

"He?"

She looked up, lifting her chin. She was not going to turn into a submissive female just because he knew her secret. "Mr. Gordon told you everything."

Harry pulled his eyebrows together. "No. Once I confronted him with the puzzle I'd already put together, he told me of his suspicions for Malcolm's interest in exposing Lord Damion, but I figured out everything else on my own."

She didn't believe him and took another step away from the bed.

"You don't think I'm capable of figuring it out?" Harry said, sounding offended. "Well, perhaps all the talk you've given about my intelligence was only talk." He paused for a breath and then explained the connections he'd made in the carriage ride toward London. Things Lord Damion had said. Things she had said. Connecting Jack to both of them.

"I confronted Mr. Gordon about it. Naturally, he wanted to write to you and get your advice, but there was no time. We had to settle the debt with Malcolm and, we hoped, put an end to his speculation in the process. Asking Jack to help us was my idea, but Mr. Gordon orchestrated it. He was very uncomfortable with my plan, Sabrina, but time was of the essence. I was about to go into a meeting with a man who nearly killed me once. We had to think and act quickly."

It was a reasonable explanation, but she still felt defensive. "And the meeting?"

"It went well." He smiled, and she relaxed a little bit. "I think you'd have been rather impressed with how I managed it, even though I did not get a receipt." He slumped his shoulders but then straightened. "Malcolm was paid in full, however; both Jack and I were witness to that. Malcolm was trying to expose Lord Damion, who had poached some clients he had expected to be return customers for years to come." His expression turned serious.

"I want to prove to you that I am a trustworthy man, Sabrina. I do not want to take charge of you, I just want to *be* with you and know everything about you. I want to walk with you along riverbanks and sit across from you at dinner. The best part of today was when I realized that maybe such a future could happen for us now that you do not need to hide yourself from me. Maybe if I prove myself, you could love me without restraint—within the proper bonds of matrimony, mind you." He smiled again. "Maybe we can make each other happy, Sabrina. What do you think?"

Sabrina was an expert at orchestrating situations to achieve the result she wanted, usually without anyone noticing the skillful maneuvering. Now she felt exposed and vulnerable. She did not know how to manage this and could not begin to craft the right answer to his question. The vision he had crafted was powerful. A life with him? A respectable life of love and devotion *and* security? Was it possible?

Harry took hold of her skirt, the only part of her he could reach. He tugged her toward him, and even though she could have pulled away easily enough, she didn't. When she was close enough, he took her hand again. Easy. Confident. Comfortable.

She looked into his eyes and felt that familiar melting sensation that happened every time he smiled at her.

"I have nothing to hide from you, Sabrina. I am hopelessly in love with you, and I think you are in love with me, too, despite so many reasons not to be."

Gracious, Sabrina thought, feeling the tears rise into her eyes. She never cried—not in front of people at least—but her defenses had been tumbled by this man who was so very honest and real and . . .

Did he really love her? Wasn't he angry at her lies?

"You don't know what you are saying," she said in a stuttering whisper.

"I am saying that I love you. I am asking you to take my heart and keep it."

She shook her head as the first tear slid down her cheek. "I am five years your senior and—"

"And I need a woman of wisdom to guide me forward. When I marry, I will inherit a mine from my uncle, and I shall need your wisdom so I can do my best to manage the property. Neither your assistance nor the mine is my motivation in this marriage; it is only an additional benefit. Your age makes no difference to me, and you are quite truly the most beautiful woman I have ever met. Having you at my side, as my partner, makes marriage and family seem like a grand adventure."

Another tear fell. Pretty words or not, what he suggested was impossible. "I cannot have children, Harry."

He startled and pulled his eyebrows together. "What do you mean?"

She looked at the floor as her heart broke. She turned to leave, but he kept hold of her hand and wouldn't let her go. "Sabrina? You can tell me. You can trust me."

She told him about the years of her marriage where she'd been unable to conceive, about the baby she'd lost, and about the doctor's pronouncement that she would never have another.

"But you want children," he said.

"Wanting and having are very different things," she said, referring to more than her desire to be a mother.

"And there are children who want parents but don't have them yet. This has no bearing on my feelings."

She shook her head. "You can't know that. You have only just begun to consider marriage and family. A different woman can give you all of that—and more."

"I want *you*, Sabrina." His voice was butter and sugar and a summer's breeze. "To have and to hold and to love and to challenge all the days of my life."

She shook her head.

"Stop shaking your head at me!" He squeezed her hand and winked. "It is very rude."

"Harry," she said. "You—"

"You love me," he cut in. "Say it."

"Harry," she said with a whine.

"Say it, Sabrina. Unless you truly do not feel it, and if that is the case, then I will stop pressing you."

He released her hand, and she stared at his chest, not daring to meet his eyes. She felt the loss of his touch and comfort like a physical pain.

"Say it, Sabrina." His tone was even, careful. "Either you love me or you don't. Whichever way it is, you must say it so I can know what my future holds."

She wanted to run out of the room. She wanted to throw herself at him. She wanted to say the words she felt and let the future take care of itself. But how could she do that after all she'd been through? After all she had seen of the world and marriage and men's folly?

But she also remembered how lonely she had become. All the prayers she'd offered, hoping for joy in her life. She took a breath and with it came just enough courage.

"What if I do love you?" She looked at the coverlet, trying to maintain her balance both inside and out. "What then?"

She felt his smile without having to look at his face. He wound their fingers together and tugged her closer, kissing the back of her hand and then letting their joined hands fall to his chest. She looked into his perfect blue eyes.

"Then I stay here at Rose Haven until you leave for Brighton."

Brighton. She'd forgotten about Brighton again.

"We talk and learn everything we can about each other during that time—properly chaperoned, of course, so you do not get any inappropriate ideas." He wagged his eyebrows suggestively, and she felt herself blush. "And then you will go on to Brighton, and I will go on to my uncle's care.

"While you are in Naples, I will take responsibility for the management of my land, learn my place, study the inheritance I shall have upon marriage—thanks to my uncle's ridiculous manipulations. I do not want to be dependent on your money any more than you want to be dependent on mine, and his gift makes that possible.

"I must also prove that I can manage the vices that have nearly destroyed me—that is the most important reason for the wait. You have taken excellent care of me, but I must show myself capable of being the good man you've always seen in me even when no one but me will know."

He reached up and wiped at the tear trailing down her cheek; she could not hold them in.

"When you return from Naples, we shall see if I have hit the markers we both need me to hit. We will evaluate whether or not our hearts and minds are still equally devoted to this course. If they are, which I believe they will be, we marry by special license procured by your brother as quickly as possible, and you make me the happiest and luckiest of men."

She covered her mouth to hide the trembling of her chin.

"If you want to live in London," Harry continued, making her wonder when he'd had the time to think all of this through, "I promise to apply myself to learn how to best move in the world here and be an asset to you. If you want to live in the country, I shall bring my work boots and learn to tend roses. Wimbledon or Falconridge or Brussels or Naples—should you fall in love with it—wherever you want to be, just let me be there with you. Should we decide we want a family, we have the means to do so. Should we enjoy only each other instead, we shall enjoy it to the fullest. I want *you*, Sabrina, forever."

She stared at him through watery eyes, his image blurring before her. How had he known how to resolve her every concern? How could he make it seem so easy and so . . . possible?

"But none of that can happen if you can't tell me how you feel, Sabrina. I need to hear you say it."

She took a breath, wiped at her eyes, and then let go of his hand. His eyes went wide with fear, but she walked around the bed and climbed up on the other side. Instead of kissing him, as she so very much wanted to do, she nestled herself against him, and he put his arm around her shoulders, pulling her close.

"I love you, Harry," she whispered, reaching across his body to take his hand, threading their fingers together.

"Are you willing to share your life with me—not your money, mind you—but your body and soul and time and future?"

She laughed against his chest. "Just those things?"

"It is all I ask," he said.

"Well, then, I think you have made me an offer I can't refuse."

"Then we have a deal?"

She nodded against him.

"I need your verbal agreement," he pressed.

She raised up on one arm, then used her other hand to brush the hair from his forehead. "I love you, Harry, and upon our marriage, I will give to you my body, soul, time, and future in exchange for yours."

He smiled widely and pulled her toward him to seal such a promise. "'Cease we to praise, now pray we for a kiss.'"

Epilogue

Five Months Later

*M*en yelled and seabirds shrieked amid the creaking ropes and lapping water against the bows of the ships moored up and down the Brighton pier. A winter wind cut through the air, taking Sabrina's breath in the middle of her explaining to the dockworker what her second trunk looked like. They'd only off-loaded the one, and she'd been trying to locate the second one for fifteen minutes.

"There is no monogram, just the name 'Sabrina,'" she said. "The trunk is yellow." Harry's lap blanket was in that trunk. Every other item could sink to the bottom of the sea for all she cared, but that lap blanket was precious, and if it were lost she would never forgive herself.

"Yes, ma'am. I'll see what I can do."

He scurried away, and she held her hat to her head as another bracing gust of wind whipped past her. The weather had been mild in Naples, and yet she had been ready to be home, winter and all. Through the months she'd spent with Meg, she'd received only a handful of letters from England—three from friends, one from Nathan, and two from Harry.

The most recent letter from Harry had been sent in October, and she had no idea when, or even if, her response had been received. She was eager to see him, but there was much to be done before that could happen.

She would stay at Mrs. Ambrose's apartment in Brighton for a few days and write to Harry so he would know she had returned. After her time with Mrs. Ambrose, she would go on to Rose Haven to reestablish housekeeping there. Then there would be Nathan's wedding and the Season to prepare for, and somewhere in there she would see Harry, and they would . . . talk, as they'd discussed.

What that meeting would be like was an impossible thing for her to properly anticipate because she had no idea what to expect. Had he stayed away from the bottle? Were his feelings still what they had been when they'd left Rose Haven in separate carriages five months ago?

She stepped back from the bustle of the pier, pressing herself against a building to try to avoid the sting of rain coming in sideways. She felt a tug at her arm and turned to the dirty wharf boy she'd sent a message with upon disembarking from the passenger ship she'd been glad to quit. Mrs. Ambrose had promised her carriage to Sabrina when she arrived; the boy had put that action into play.

"The lady's carriage will come for you at the booth," the boy said, then put out his grubby palm.

"Thank you, sir," she said as she put a sixpence in his hand.

"Blimey," the boy said breathlessly before clenching his fist around the money. He looked up at her with wide eyes. "Thank you kindly, ma'am." He grinned and scampered away.

Sabrina had thought a great deal about Harry's quick acceptance of her situation—their situation, perhaps—regarding children. She'd fallen in love with Meg's children, so could she not fall in love with others? It was a question she had discussed at length with Meg during their time together.

When she looked back at the boat, two sailors were bringing her yellow trunk down the gangplank. She let out a sigh of relief and stepped forward to direct them toward the booth where Mrs. Ambrose's carriage would soon be.

The carriage arrived only minutes after she'd paid the porters, and the driver jumped down to load the trunks beneath the box. She reached for the door handle, but it turned from the inside before she touched it. Had Mrs. Ambrose come to meet her?

She looked from the drawn curtains to the open door of the carriage and her mouth fell open at the face framed there.

Harry grinned at her and hopped down from the carriage, easy as you please, on two strong legs healed and hale.

"Your carriage, m'lady," he said.

She reached out to touch his face, but he took her hand and looked around them before leaning in slightly. "We are in public, my dear. We wouldn't want to give rise to gossip." He winked, then helped her into the carriage.

She settled herself on one bench, watching his every move as he gave instructions to the driver, then stepped inside the carriage and snapped the door closed. He sat across from her, and they stared at one another until some invisible barrier broke, and they were suddenly in a tangle of skirts and coat and lips and touches.

In Sabrina's mind, she'd envisioned their first meeting to be formal, perhaps including a list of questions they would answer in turn to see if their expectations aligned regarding their possible future together. The reality was raw and honest and made all those well-planned questions unimportant.

Finally, she pulled back, her hands on either side of his face as she looked him over. "You are here," she said breathlessly.

"More importantly, *you* are here," he said, running his hands down her back and creating serious difficulty in her ability to maintain her focus. He traced his thumb against her rose-colored lips. She kissed it. He stared at her mouth, but kept talking. "I came a week ago. Took a room at the Grande Hotel and asked Mrs. Ambrose to alert me when you arrived. She thought it a wonderful game." As though he couldn't help himself, he moved in to kiss her again, then met her eyes. "I am well, Sabrina, clear and ready for your inspection. You've surely planned a long list of questions, and I shall submit to the inquiry."

She laughed, as though the idea of a list of questions was ridiculous. Never mind that such a list was in her bag at this very moment. "I did not think I would see you so soon."

"But it is a good surprise, is it not?"

"The best surprise," she whispered.

"You are still madly in love with me then?" he asked, raising an eyebrow.

"I believe you were the one madly in love with me," she corrected.

"Aye, so I am, so I am." His smile softened. "Has your heart changed in these months away?" he asked, a thread of insecurity woven between the words.

She nodded, and when his face fell, she explained. "My feelings have only grown," she whispered, emboldened by his increasing smile as she confessed. "I was so frightened that yours had lessened."

"Never," he said, shaking his head. He kissed her again.

There is so much to do, she thought as she kissed him back. So many details . . . to . . . arrange . . . and . . . secure . . . and . . .

Winter.
Sunshine.
Hope.
Joy.
Love.
Him.

Acknowledgments

This is the first time I have written a "playboy," and it's a character type I find difficult to like as a reader. Harry, therefore, was a challenge for me, but a good one, I think. Exploring why we make the choices we make and how many "bad" choices are a form of running away from painful things gives me a bit more grace in real life, both for myself and for others.

I am very grateful for those friends who helped me brainstorm how to make this story work: Jennifer Moore (*Solving Sophronia*, Covenant, 2020), Nancy Campbell Allen (*Brass Carriages and Glass Hearts*, Shadow Mountain, 2020), Brittney Larsen, (*The Matchmaker's Match*, Covenant, 2020), Becca Wilhite (*Check Me Out*, Shadow Mountain, 2018).

Thank you to Jenny Proctor for beta reading the final draft and to my editor, Lisa Mangum, for helping me find just the right romantic tension. Thank you to Heidi Taylor for overseeing the production, Breanna Anderl for typesetting, and Heather Ward and Richard Erickson for the beautiful cover.

Thank you, Lane Heymont, for your business savvy and advice.

ACKNOWLEDGMENTS

Thank you to all the readers who keep reading and, in the process, give me a job that I learn from and grow with year after year.

Thank you to my family for your love and support, and to my Father in Heaven for continually picking me up, brushing me off, and telling me I'm not done yet. I am blessed. I know it. I am trying very hard to live up to my privileges.

Discussion Questions

1. How do you feel the romantic tension of *Rakes and Roses* compares to other romances by this author?

2. This story represents a gender swap in regard to Sabrina having the power and control in the relationship. How do you feel about that aspect of the story?

3. Harry's vices are represented as the way he hides from childhood pain and trauma. Have you seen similar reactions play out in your life or in the lives of others?

4. It isn't until the end that Harry realizes he was betrayed by a friend. Had you already made that connection, or was it as much a surprise to you as it was to Harry?

5. Do you find Harry and Sabrina likable characters? Why or why not?

6. Do you have a favorite quote from the book?

7. If you've read other books in the Mayfield series, how does *Rakes and Roses* compare?

About the Author

Josi S. Kilpack is the author of several novels and one cookbook and a participant in several coauthored projects and anthologies. She is a four-time Whitney Award winner—including *Lord Fenton's Folly* (2015) for Best Romance and Best Novel of the Year—and a Utah Best in State winner for fiction. She is the mother of four children and lives in northern Utah.

You can find more information about Josi and her writing at josiskilpack.com.

A MAYFIELD FAMILY ROMANCE

Promises and Primroses, Book 1

Hearts and history collide as two couples
risk it all for a second chance at love.

"Kilpack smoothly introduces the Mayfield clan and sets
the stage for the series while making plenty of room for
developing this volume's central characters. The narrative
flows smoothly. Regency fans will be eager for more
Mayfield romances." —PUBLISHERS WEEKLY

"Kilpack [adds] refreshing twists to her latest sweetly
charming romance, the enticing launch of the Mayfield
Family series. Teen fans of Austen-era romances will
adore this novel's spunky heroine." —BOOKLIST

A MAYFIELD FAMILY ROMANCE
Daisies and Devotion, Book 2

★ "Protocol and posturing are skillfully revealed as both protagonists seek marital matches for themselves at gatherings filled with societal gossip and judgment. . . . This amusing adventure in misunderstandings will delight readers who appreciate rich settings and strong characters." —PUBLISHERS WEEKLY, STARRED REVIEW

"Kilpack expertly and delightfully gives fans of traditional Regency romances everything—engaging characters, dry wit, and a sweet love story—that they could ever desire." —BOOKLIST

"A sweet, original romance." —KIRKUS REVIEWS